PALM'S PROGRESS

BY INGE BORG

Published by New Generation Publishing in 2014

First Edition

www.newgeneration-publishing.com

New Generation Publishing

Delicta majoram immeritus lues
Undeservedly you will atone for the sins of your fathers

THE '**THIRTY YEARS WAR**' SPREAD DEVASTATION OVER MOST OF EUROPE. THIS BITTER CONFLICT BETWEEN CATHOLICS AND LUTHERANS BROUGHT MISERY, DEPRIVATION AND DEATH TO COUNTLESS PEOPLE IN THE SEVENTEENTH CENTURY.

BY 1630 THE SWEDISH ARMY HAD INVADED AND SETTLED IN GERMAN LANDS WHICH INCLUDED THE TOWN OF **STRALSUND**. FORMERLY A GERMAN FISHING VILLAGE ON THE BALTIC COAST, STRALSUND WAS GROWING INTO AN IMPRESSIVE TOWN WITH AN IMPORTANT HARBOUR AND SPLENDID BUILDINGS AND CHURCHES. IT HAD BECOME A MAJOR SWEDISH STRONGHOLD WITH A FORT AND A GARRISON.

DURING AND AFTER THESE TROUBLED TIMES GERMAN CITIZENS WERE REQUIRED TO PROVIDE SHELTER AND DISCIPLINED TRAINING FOR HOME-LESS CHILDREN.

VOLUNTEERS FROM MANY COMMUNITIES ACTED AS SURROGATE FATHERS AND MOTHERS...

PART ONE
REVELATIONS

One
Near Stralsund. 1664.

It was still dark but it did feel like early morning. A sleepy youngster, his eyes barely open, listened to the breathing of his mother and his brother, and to occasional raucous snorts from his father. The boy was also becoming aware of dangling thatch just out of reach by his head, held fast by cobwebs. There were large spiders attached.

'Sleep, I beg you, come back,' he whispered, head under the blanket, 'sleep, sleep..sleeeeeeeee'------and for some moments he slept.

But then, with a jolt he remembered: 'my big day, it has begun!'

Now his eyes were wide open. He recalled last night's owls: 'they bring certain death; is that not what people say? When their beaks knock on the window the end is near.' He'd blocked his ears. Although he felt safe in his father's cottage, some way outside the city wall, he now trembled, twisted, and turned, troubled, enough to slide under his threadbare blanket once again. How could the others sleep remembering those woebegone calls? Light, where was the light? Could he get up at last? Other, 'nicer' birds than owls had begun chirping, as if they'd never seen that red-gold fireball before. He listened to their cheery chatter... re-assured by such joyous approval as the sun rose at last, pushing all darkness away.

And then he remembered: Mother had told him to clean his shoes. 'For tomorrow', she'd stressed, 'for your big day! Place them by the door, son, put them on before you go!' She was unwell, dear Mother, but always thought of everything... like stuffing that apple into his pocket. He remembered her worn hands, he thought of her kindness.

'So, yes, this Big Day, it has begun. I must wake no-one', he told himself as he dressed, hating the shoes, now clean but very tight. He pulled a face as he pushed, forced his naked feet into them.

Soon he was stumbling through fields, past the swamp, through forest, on twisted uneven paths and then out to the sandy road along the coast, on and on and on, for longer, much longer than an hour, but at last, into Stralsund, slowing down by the nearest of the town gates.

A drowsy armed guard yawned, stretched and waved the boy on.

At last! On his left the Commander's House, across the market the Town Hall. He was covered in dust. He felt barely alive. He dragged his ache-ing feet through the market, his throat was dry. Saturday traders were setting up their stalls.

'Thanks be to God,' he muttered, breathless and fearful: 'the Town Hall, am I late, that clock... I forgot to count, did it strike eight?'

Another armed guard was pacing up and down by steep stone stairs. He nodded, demanding to know if he was 'Palm'. The boy nodded. His heart was still pounding. Could the stranger hear it? It seemed not.

Pointing, muttering: 'up, up those stairs, lad,' the guard pushed the youngster roughly and spat on the cobbles, right by the entrance.

'Not so friendly, that one,' thought the boy whose toes, also his heels, were aching mightily. There seemed to be swarms of bees, no, insects, buzzing upstairs,...no, not insects: quiet voices, muttering, mumbling, ever more clearly, as he, toes chafing, climbed painfully, up each rugged, hard, coarsely hewn, grey step. He groaned, quietly.

But then, all around him, bright light, fine things, walls of carved wood, glittering chandeliers...a man in flowing black robes now guiding, pushing him to stand on a wondrous rug. Oh, such colours, such patterns! 'On this rug,' whispered Palm doubtfully, his eyes wide open, 'here?' Now stood before an ornately carved table, not daring to move, facing seven sombre, solemn worthies all in black, the boy looked at each man in turn, in terror, but also with due respect.

'How they stare! I am being appraised. Like a beast in the market. Mother did remind me: do not forget, Palm, remove your cap, it is polite, indoors. Had anyone noticed? I have removed it from my head. Three pastors on either side of the old burgomaster, yes, I have seen such men before. All six of them: they think, speak and live only for God, except the ancient one in the middle who frowns, studies his papers and turns his head... just like owls do.'

Palm pictured the feared, feathered creatures with their rotating heads.

'Which one of these seven had sent that message I should come on the last market day of the eighth month? Why do they want me here? I, a mere farm-boy who knows nothing, and these owl-pastors who gape at me, at my sweaty hands, my caked, dusty shoes! I need water. My toes are surely bleeding. My throat is dry. Why! am I here?'

Palm stood before a row of staring eyes in confused fear.

Stony looks, long grey beards, black gowns, silence and flickering candles, then suddenly, in resounding tones: 'eel-feld, üle-feld'.

'What does this mean? Hard to tell, they speak with strange tongues. I must keep my head, the old one with rheumy eyes and matted beard, surely befuddled...he stares and raves on. What is this I hear? I have no mother? That I did have a mother but she died? No? Surely not:

Your real mother left you behind because she was in trouble with her King! This is what the mad one has just made known.'

Ulfeld, yet again Palm heard this word echoing below the high ceiling.

'Not understanding their raving it is best I remain stumm,' he decided.

'Speak, boy! Do you read? No? Do you care to see this name on paper? No? You shake your head. Do you have a tongue, Palm?'

'Yes, Sire.' Palm sighed, nodded and then spoke, slowly, clearly: 'Yes, I do, but I cannot read.' The questioner's head turned from side to side, lips tightly clamped. Then, slowly rising to his feet, waving both black-robed arms before him like a monstrous winged bat he declaimed in a raised voice:

'We, the Consistory, are struggling to inform you, Palm, those Űlefelds, Eelfelds, Ylfelds, they abandoned you, their miserable, yes, miserable babe, born months too early, barely alive. Abandoned!' Then, even more loudly, looking left and right, frowning ferociously he proclaimed:

'You, Palm, yes, you'...stabbing the air, pointing, 'you were that new born child. Your parents left you here in Stralsund, with us.' Still frowning, holding up both his hands like a beggar he implored: 'Now do you understand, boy?'

Palm, frightened, had recoiled slightly. He shook his head slowly: he did not understand, but he had to prove he had been listening. Morosely the men buzzed left and right, then turned to study him with deeply furrowed brows, yet again.

The boy glanced at each man, frowned at his feet, while having a mind to run from this place. The old man, seated again, both elbows on piles of documents, was supporting his chin with two thumbs, stroking his nose. Nodding earnestly, he began to speak more quietly: how he hoped Palm would believe every word: 'there must be some woman in Stralsund with breasts full enough to feed this poor scrap'...Ulefeld had said that, allegedly. His true father's words, according to the ancient burgomaster! Also: 'take this bag of gold ducats, seek out such a woman, plead with her... reveal nothing about us...she must treat this babe as her own. We leave by boat at dawn tomorrow'.

'Those were your father's words, Master Palm.'

'He called me Master Palm! Can they support this tale, all seven learnèd men?' Palm heard them speak, breathe and sigh, each of them staring at him, the scruffy boy from the farm. He did try to say something, but his voice broke, his face was burning. The whole hall would hear this. With much hesitation he whispered:

'Pray Sire, Mother and Father, do they know about this?'

The burgomaster leaned forward, bushy grey eyebrows up like two birds in flight: 'speak up boy, which mother and father might you be speaking of,' while the scribe and the ministers at the long table shuffled, looked at each other, clasped their hands as if in prayer. One of them stroked his beard, seemingly in thought. A further silence: clearly they too were not informed about this.

'I know only one mother and father...and I will always love them.' Bravely, taking a deep breath, feeling his shoulders twitch, the boy raised his hands, pressed them together and looking straight at the Old One he said: 'pray Sire, truly, why is it I am called before you?'

'Truly!' And then one tone higher: 'Truly? Insolence! Understand this, boy: head up, take note: this is a matter of consequence, a turning point!' The Old One had raised his voice. Once again on his feet...and irritable, looking left and right, he intoned sonorously:

'A vow was made to inform you, Palm, on the eve of your sixteenth birthday: your parents were persons of noble birth... do you hear, boy, what I say? You are nobly born, very near our city. Now that you have lived for fifteen years, we are obliged to fulfil our promise to your true parents. I am not at liberty to reveal more for the moment, but you were named 'Palm', a Swedish name. We, the Town and the Church, must help you reach the highest possible level in any skill you choose. First: to read and write: you will be taught here in Stralsund and you will be trained according to what is appropriate for someone with blue blood, and according to your abilities. Do you follow?'

Palm gazed at his feet. He remained silent. He felt foolish.

'Best thing to do is nod just a little. There must be a misunderstanding. Blue blood, what is this? I've seen mine and it is red. All I see are holes in my shoes, mud and dust on them and some of that mud now stuck to the precious carpet'. These were his thoughts. Trembling again he inclined his head and stared wordlessly at the patterned carpet.

The worthies turned left and right, sighed, eyebrows knotted together, signalling to one another other. After a long silence he, The Important One, got to his feet, and, fixing his eyes on Palm cleared his throat and enunciated slowly, sonorously, but with more measured care:

'You, Master Palm, will learn more about your true father in due course. We urge you to leave the farm at once and take up studies at the Dominican School in the former St. Katherine's where we appoint a tutor who will guide you to find a new life…yes, that's right, hear this again: your new life. In time you will understand and know many things. We congratulate you on your good fortune.' Now the Old One smiled, the first and only smile from anyone so far…then, benignly: 'and your foster-mother is ailing, we hear? Come to us when she has recovered her strength. Michael August Sack, your foster father, is to call here at noon of the next market day. We are instructed to hand him a reward. He ploughs, he sows and reaps, and above all he pays his taxes and takes care of his beasts. He is an honest man. Leave us now! Go home, Master Palm Ulefeld, and praise the Lord.' Still trembling, Palm bowed and staggered from the hall.

'Master Palm', he heard, his feet barely obeying him down the steep stone steps. His mind was a dizzying whirlwind: shreds, flecks of words and thoughts: 'foster father, another mother, noble lady, will she come, will she claim me', were flying about in his head. 'Ulefeld, my father? How can this be, someone is mistaken! No, no…I am the son of Lisebett and Michael, and my brother is called Christian.'

Stupefied by all he'd heard, and blinded by the morning sun, Palm staggered, stumbled, stormed, away from the Town Hall over rough cobbles on Stralsund's Old Market, now teeming with tradesmen and women. He was shivering. Still in shock his jaw trembled, tears welled up. But then suddenly angered, he pushed blindly through the crowd, bumped into vendors and stalls; apples, potatoes, mushrooms and eggs flew off the trestles...there, the grinning fortune teller, a scattering of cackling fluttering geese,...shoppers cursed, calling 'thief, thief, look out, clumsy fool, a robber,' and a startled horse reared, neighing loudly.

Stumbling on, avoiding tubs of wriggling eels and fresh oysters, herrings in pails, Palm was choking and sobbing: only one thing seemed to matter: to get away as fast as possible, away from town, away from these people, shouting, glowering, waving their arms...he had frightened a small flock of coarse wool sheep as he tore down Knieper Street to the unguarded town gate... out, out,...across the narrow strip of land, ' past the pond, two large vessels out there, far in the sea to the right, and left, ducks, gulls.'

'I must run, run, home, through the woods... only ducks by the wayside, some swooping, cawing seagulls, I could slow down now, through the allotments, graveyard further along, by the sea,...my heart pounds, my throat, my mouth is parched...I look back, see no-one, just the town wall, the gates and spires, and now the earth, the sky, and the sea, the most, the only important things.'

Behind a hedge, breathing heavily, the gasping boy sank to the ground, curled up and lay as dead for a few moments. Amongst the blades of grass and dandelions he spotted the curled-up zig-zag on the back of an adder, and gripped by new fear he moved away, slid, crept closer to the edge of the wood, into the shade, straining to remain alert, sweating...and only then, at last, a deep breath, his world receding, he went limp, whimpering like a small child. Gulls from the nearby Baltic screeched overhead. Healing nature was taking its course. On the horizon, near the dunes, soothing waves rolled over, approached, rolled over, approached, rolled over, glistened in the fresh sea-green morning air, while, deep, deeper down, even further-that mysterious stillness, under cool swoosh-ing waves, roll over, roll over, jade, emerald, soothe, soothe, in the distance many pillars, twelve if you counted the tumble-down ones, flowing seaweed beckoned, brushed against him-lightly slithered across his brow, shimmered, bubbled, shoals glistening playfully in and around his eyes, darting through his hair silver arrows of fish, distracting his viewing as he was borne effortlessly, weightlessly, through broken arches into a silent ruined city, deserted but for bubbles, mirrors, streaks of light- gleaming caressing, stroking-

-a fine lady, a queen, surely-her arms wide open, a sword in her raised right hand stood in welcome, eyes full of love, she smiled, yes, smiled but there was no sound, only feelings of love, waves of 'Palm, Palm, Palm, at last-you were lost but I have found you, here is your home, Vineta, I've waited so long for you-thousands of years have passed since the land moved, our kingdom submerged, in this tide-less sea, plunged into the depths. Come, my dearest son-'

Palm's dry eyelids opened. The restorative hallucination was fading. He blinked, saw the midday sun overhead, peering through patterns of rustling sun-specked leaves. A cormorant flew overhead, mocking him. Cackles of laughing gulls pierced his ears. He tried to moisten a finger to rub his eyes, but his tongue was so parched he could barely move his lips.

'Water, I need water, I must find my way back, half the day has passed. Home, yes, home...what will they be thinking at home?

Early blackberries, I know where the bank is, just a few mouthfuls for my lips, for my tongue to move, to soften my lips, my mouth inside, and further along that pond, brackish, not the best water, but I need it now, now, now'. He struggled, bent forward, almost on his knees, ancient instincts guiding him to find what he most needed... to recover, to linger in that refreshing, loving dream. 'How would it be to have such a mother,' crossed his mind and then, with a jolt: 'my mother, dear God, so ill only a few hours ago...and that apple, still in my pocket! I must get back home, they will be waiting, there is much to do!' A few bites, the sweet juice from the apple brought renewed strength.

Scrambling on, first through the darkness of tall pines, then marshy bog-land, sharing paradise with quails, cranes and wild geese he found berries, pressed them into his mouth, gulping, devouring their sweet, black wetness...he was still on the look-out for water. All the while there were his daily chores, already disrupted by the burgomaster's summons: the pig-shed, the roof repair, his mother's illness, so much to see to. What's more, he'd lost his cap!

'So, how do I make it seem like good news, that gathering of townsmen, their absurd, crack-pot story,...as for my brother: he loves a good joke, but when I tell him this he'll say I've gone too far. We are always together, how could I leave him behind? And Father, he must have known this might happen, if there were any truth in it. Truth? In such a tale? Never! But did father not look somewhat discomfited, hearing the burgomaster's request, when the messenger came?'

Apprehension, then hope, and now despair: 'Not in a month of Sundays can this be true, besides, I do not care for it, no, not at all.'

***

Palm's father, Michael August Sack, Pomeranian tiller of the soil, had, in his younger days been employed by a powerful landowner; later he inherited a small-holding from a distant family member. This allowed him the freedom to cultivate his own lands. From such good fortune had sprung solid plans for his ragamuffin sons, two boys most dear to him, their wholesome natures so in tune with each other.

A bit 'yonderly' perhaps, but a kind man, he involved them both, day after day, ploughing, planting and reaping, feeding and slaughtering pigs, sheep, hens and geese...the continuing cycle of life during each of the seasons on his beloved Pomeranian land. He constantly turned over in his mind, (an activity not unlike planting beets and potatoes) how to pass on to his sons all he had ever known and owned. It was not much.

'All this is surely the greatest measure of happiness the good Lord allows honest men: preparing ones youngsters to take charge....for the time of one's own eternal rest....that is what it is all about, and having enough to pay ones taxes,' he liked to remind himself.

'Just so long as there are no more wars, please God! Only then, you, my boys, will have all you need. Now, when I was a boy, events were unspeakable,' he liked to say...'for thirty years, such cruel times, that war, best forgotten! Good harvests, that's what is needed now, and friendship and trade with our friendly neighbours, Sweden and Denmark.' Wars and taxes remained Michael's greatest fear. He told his wide-eyed sons about the thirty long years when 'half the men in our lands were killed and robbed by cruel mercenaries just because Catholics and Protestants could not agree; and then the Swedes destroyed whole villages, towns and hundreds of castles: famine made people ready to fight to the end, to murder even. It was hard to understand. But now, after the 'Westphalian Peace', we've become used to the Swedes, they are honest enough, they protect us and they buy our beets'. Words such as these farmer Michael had gathered from all and sundry. His boys loved these tales; they had heard them many times.

'In olden days we had witches, even child witches and men witches', their father told them, peering into his sons' upturned, anxious faces: 'they had to be hunted and killed, for spoiling harvests and other evil deeds...and worst of all were those dangerous rumours, which blackened people, denounced by fearful neighbours'. Both young boys would cover their faces, frown and shudder while shaking their heads.

However, well hidden, and never revealed to his children, was another event, wilfully buried in old Michael's skull since a day some fifteen years earlier: On that day the burgomaster's wife had sent a naked bloodied babe to his Lisebett. Wrapped in finest cloth, small beyond belief, his wife had gazed at this boy child, barely breathing, shocked to see its pitiful, shivering smallness. With it came a message to the strong, healthy Lisebett, only just back on her feet from childbirth: 'Speaking woman to woman,' was the message, 'I implore you to care for this scrap, along with your own; I hear you have more than sufficient milk to feed two babes… for which I wish you well, and may God bless you.' Yes, old Michael never forgot that day. Without the slightest hesitation his beloved Lisebett had taken pity on the wretched bundle, cheerfully and generously agreed to do her best, asking no questions. 'It might, or perhaps might not, turn into a useful Pomeranian citizen,' were her words. Who was to say? Fate had bestowed a kindly smile on a very small boy-child.

***

There now! Palm's bearings recovered…the familiar knotted oak, he was almost home, conscious of the goodness of the spacious lake-land before him and of his family's love which had surrounded him for so long. Running off to start a new life in town no longer seemed an option, even though things had taken a turn he'd never have guessed in his wildest dreams. 'Life decides for you,' he muttered again and again, staggering through tall ferns, and gnarled old trees. There it was, the beloved half-timbered cottage under a vast drop of thatch, almost down to the ground, small windows, (they seem to be open?) smoke curling up gently from the chimney, a good sign. 'Mother has prepared our meal; they are waiting for my return', he knew. But then: 'strange, no-one about, where was the dog, where was everyone?'

Two distant windmills turned slowly, gently. Everything was still. It was hot. He saw the wheel-barrow, the pump, the barrel. Father would surely be resting after his morning's work. What was this eerie feeling?

Palm bent forward, pumped water from the well. The creaking mechanism disturbed a heavy, silent calm around the place. He took desperate gulps, again and again, from his cupped hand. Then he washed his face and his hands, wondering all the while at the quiet, immense, timeless silence. The only things moving were rabbit and field-mice furs, stretched into the shape of crucifixes and now suspended on sticks. They were drying out under the eaves. 'Mother will be stitching them together for something useful,' he thought as he bent low once again, this time to enter the dark one-roomed cottage. His eyes adjusted slowly to find Father and his brother, praying, or listening, seemingly turned to stone, huddled by the parental bed. The dog looked up, his tail rose...then whimpering, the tail dropped again. Silence.

In that instant Palm guessed: Mother was dead. He must have missed her parting by minutes. He stood frozen. A strange sound came from his throat, like a wounded beast in fear of further strikes, pleading, heart-rending. His brother turned round, tears streaming down his face, as he lumbered blindly towards Palm.

They embraced, they clung to each other.

'She asked after you,' he sobbed, 'her last words were: say yes to life, say yes to life... tell Palm, if I don't see him again, say yes... and then she stopped, and made a strange noise. I believe she's dead...I did open the window, so her soul could reach heaven without hindrance, and now you are here we must sing the Song of Dying and say the Prayer for Dying. Here, help father up, he is too wretched to think. Is it too late to call the pastor?'

The boys stared into each others' frightened eyes, looking for re-assurance.

'Too late? What are you saying? Perhaps she is asleep. No? Quick, come, we must try to call her back, shake her shoulders, shout into her ears...that's what people do.' Palm dragged his brother with him. The old man, still on his knees, slipped to one side, watching aghast, but with renewed hope, as his sons set about bringing their mother back. No amount of shaking and shouting seemed to wake her. With her sons' tears sprinkled over her face and hands like Holy Water, she lay, eyes shut, mouth slightly open, as if she still hoped to express a view, while this moment continued, became eternal.

In Pomerania it was customary to brace oneself against the fact of death; one did not allow fear to overtake one. Peasants liked to be prepared for the day when their inheritance passed to the next generation and to assist the dying person to enter the next life. A pastor was usually called in good time to administer the last rites.

But this was all too sudden, too unexpected, too soon.

For a while Lisebett's husband stood dazed. Then he paced about lost in thought. After that he remembered to cover the only mirror with a black cloth: the cloth would banish its demonic powers: mirrors were an unnecessary symbol of earthly vanity, he believed. Lisebett's cherished hand-mirror, a gift from her sea-faring father, brought all the way from a distant place he called Venezia, had hung as a lonely ornament on a wall for as long as her husband could recall. Family death had only happened once before, when Lisebett's father, the ancient sailor, had passed away years ago. Now in redoubled shock, old Michael tried to be mindful of the required mode of behaviour.

Despite his confused misery he managed to send one son to the pastor. There were rituals to be repeated: the tolling of death bells in three intervals... across flat Pomeranian fields, to make known the bereavement and to call the gravediggers. Their task was to dig a grave during a certain span of time: first tolling: lifting the meadow grasses, second ringing, to show the work was done halfway and then again, when the grave was ready, a third tolling. The intervals between bells were long for grownups, shorter for children, according to the size of the corpse. In this way neighbours far and wide would deduce the age of the departed.

Not long before neighbours assembled they would see to the practicalities: an oak coffin, stored in a nearby barn, was placed on trestles near the entrance, the foot-end facing the door. Someone reminded Michael of the importance of having the body carried out feet first so that no-one else could be drawn out by the spirit of the deceased. Poor man, all he could say was: 'wouldn't mind being dead myself. I am waiting for the Lord.'

The women washed, then clothed Lisebett's body in her tattered wedding gown, while the men found a book of songs to place by her hand, so she could intone a song of praise as soon as the Day of Reckoning began. She never had learned to read. No matter. Had she been a child she would have been given her favourite plaything, or if very old she would hold a candle, so that her soul could locate heaven more readily.

Across the land at sunset, over by the lakes, swarms of birds, thousands of them, came to rest, feet standing in the water, silent for once, heads turned downwards in deep, respectful repose.

That night Palm and Christian found it hard to sleep. Their father was holding a prolonged vigil by the coffin, muttering quietly, wrapped in his own thoughts. When he finally nodded off they guided him to his bed, gently. 'Come along', whispered Palm in his ear, 'she is with us, I can feel her presence, she is not complaining.'

'She never did', his father managed, 'she never, never did. I do so need her. There is little reason for me to live now.'

Is there anything more terrible than witnessing the tears of one's own father? Clinging to each other the boys stared at the old man. It was the first time they'd seen him weep. They were afraid.

On the next day the entire community gathered once more in the church to hear the Pastor's brief sermon. 'Her heart was tired', he said. 'She was a good mother and she helped her husband. May she rest in peace.'

When the burial was over, on the following day, contributions of food and drink were carried to the house of mourning, to comfort the bereft farmer and his boys. The neighbour's simple-minded daughter helped, after the feast, to wash and put away platters and goblets. In her placid and accommodating way she expected neither praise, nor thanks.

***

'Our mother, gone from us...we will never see her again,...the way she carried baskets of potatoes across the yard, that endless row of teetering ducks following her...never hear her sing again...never see her quickly moving hands wiping themselves clean on her apron before she extended them to greet a guest, or give us food, or put her arms around us when we made some foolish mistake.'

Overwhelmed by her absence, Palm tried to be comforted by the one object he truly associated with her, the mirror from 'Venezia', backed with mercury from 'Illyria'. How he loved these mysterious-sounding words, 'mercury, Illyria', the words should be sung!....'i-lyria, i-lyria'... and now, touching the reflective surface, staring into it, he pressed it to his forehead, his heart. He decided to rub it clean on his sleeve.

'If I stare at it long enough, perhaps, in some way, she has been captured under the mysterious lustrous surface.' But all Palm found were his own apprehensive mustard-coloured eyes, and, over the lower half of this face the first soft hairs of manhood. 'Strange, the mirror shows a grown-up.' He was startled: 'Perhaps Mother wanted me to understand something; like saying 'yes' to life?'

She was always saying it: 'yes, yes, yes.'

Should I go to the burgomaster, ask about things, learn, become clever? I could properly help my father and brother, more than by simply staying here. Christian and I often talk about kings and queens, have heard tales about Vineta: some old people say it re-appears to the shore when the moon is full, but it is the clever ones in town who know everything, they are the ones who will truly show me Vineta, and Venezia, where this mirror comes from...and how very strange that these names sound so similar; and that dream ...about my 'other' mother....yes, the learned teachers in town could help me discover this strange world.

All such things would have pleased my mother.

If only, oh, if only I could tell her!

He pressed the mirror to his chest.

'I must find Father. He will understand.'

Two

Back and forth, in the setting sun, swallows swing and swoop across the fields, over the lake. It is becoming dark. The world around is as it always was, but for the fate of three lonesome people.

Palm relived the moment when the clods of earth fell, remembering the consoling words spoken by the pastor...when he gradually could no longer see even the wood of his mother's coffin. He imagined her open eyes, now closed, and that dear face, and her hands now useless in that dark box. Then he blocked those thoughts. But they returned, they clung to him, they were painful. His eyes were wet.

The pastor's words echoed loud, hollow and unhelpful.

'Life decides for you', swirled about in the boy's head, aimlessly, without meaning. Just those words. Like falling autumn leaves, again and again...and yet again.

Huddled together outside on a log, bare feet on the still warm earth, the widower, his boys... also their pointy-nosed dog, worrying an ancient bone, rested near the place where Mother had been sitting only four evenings ago.

Her voice echoed in Palm's head: 'that sweet blue Forget-me-not, already in flower so prettily'...her pleasure still in his heart, and with it the tale she loved to tell: of the mediaeval knight in full armour, who, bending down to pick the flower for his lady, tumbled into the river. Overloaded by the weight of his metal coat he drowned, poor man, while throwing the posy to his beloved and calling to her, desperately:

'Vergiss-mein-nicht,'...'forget-me-not!'

Those little blue flowers lived, the story lived, but Mother was gone to rest beneath the Pomeranian field. He wiped away his tears, again.

***

Now there was stew, pork with carrots and swedes before them, carried over in a heavy iron pot by their neighbour's Ursel: the simple-minded daughter who could cope only with the simplest of tasks.

Ursel's vacant blue eyes were the same colour as those very flowers. She rarely spoke, she did not smile, simply turned back, when her duties were done.

The men-folk sat chewing listlessly and in silence, forgetting to thank her, still drowned in their inexplicable loss. Sighing, the widower glanced back at his cottage: 'It is haunted by death'...and the boys looked at each other, nodding warily...'but life must resume: the wooden plates need soaking in the bucket, to be scrubbed'. Michael frowned and retrieved a bone to throw to his dog. As he took the pipe from his mouth he surveyed the land, now stuffing tobacco with fingers moving in their familiar routine. 'Go Christian,' he mumbled, 'get me a light from the fire, and don't forget, bring mugs...and some cider.'

Alone with his father Palm seized the moment:

'It feels so strange to eat without her, father. Who will make our pickled cabbage? Who will stuff the sausages? Who will bake our bread?'

Grieving Michael grunted, sucked on his pipe, observed the birds, the sky, his worn, muddy foot-ware.

'It will rain in the morning: look at those swooping swallows'...then, after a pause, exhaling: 'I suppose we'll have to manage. The women in the village may help, perhaps find a maid, that Ursel perhaps... she could 'do' for us. We'll learn. This dying has happened so quickly, I cannot take it in. Our Father in heaven will show us. By the way', turning to his son, 'when you went to town, what happened there? You've said nothing.'

Palm, who had picked up a goose-feather by the log, drew a pattern in the sand, wondering if it was right to tell. Head down, eyes closed, then, scratching his head and after a long intake of breath, he replied: 'those towns-men, the men in black gowns, have suggested I come to Stralsund. I must learn to read and write.' He turned to look at his father's face. What would he have to say about all this?

The old man, still numbed by grief, seemed transfixed. He sat looking at his feet, turned to stone, drained.

Palm moved closer, bent forward, and tried to look him in the eye: 'They say I am not truly your son, father. Can this be so?'

Now there was pain on the old man's face, lips tight, shaggy eyebrows drawn together so they formed a straight line. Palm noted this expression: it was the same one his father made when the moment came to cut a pig's throat.

Old Michael opened his lips but seemed unable to speak. Elbows propped on painful, creaky knees, he rested his head in both hands and stared silently at the dry earth. After a deep sigh, he found his voice:

'I cannot lie to you, dear, most dear Palm...' raising his head, 'and this is not easy, believe me, my boy:

You, a small bundle, barely breathing, were brought to us, by order of the Swedish Commander in town. My Lisebett truly gave you life: with patient care, she succeeded where many others would have failed: at first she trickled small droplets from her breasts into your shrivelled mouth. Later she nursed you and Christian, one babe at each breast... and soon neither she nor I thought of you as anyone but our very own.

In truth, you are not our son, you stem from some strangers from another country who were in great difficulty and had no time for you. Your birth-mother was unwell. We never heard another word from her, nor from your father.'

The old man scratched his head, looked puzzled and now also peeved:

'Don't tell me they come to claim you now?'

'No, no, father, no-one has claimed me! It seems there had been some mysterious promise that I should learn to read and write, and other things. I will be told all. It also seems these people were of noble blood.' Old Michael had begun rocking back and forth on his hard bench, his head supported in cupped hands. He was deep in thought.

'What should I say, father? If I did go I could always return and help you and Christian, when I have learnt all there is to understand.

Father, should I go…will you let me go? And I did forget: there was a message: you too must go to the Rathaus! They said to come at noon, next Market day.'

Now old Michael shook his head, closed his glistening eyes and, as if to ward off a severe blow, leaned forward and raised his arms.

But it was only to embrace Palm.

Lisebett had warned him this would happen one day. She told him, many times: 'Mein lieber Michael, believe me, you too must learn to say 'yes' to life'! Now he tried to show neither shock nor fear. Still under her influence he knew that Palm must take his chance, but he also believed the boy would return one day, take care of everything, a learned, important person, not just a peasant.

Why, yes, of course, the answer was clear:

'You do what is right for you, son. Yes,' he nodded, 'I will always call you 'son'! Only one thing I beg: you explain all this to your brother!'

Old Michael's voice faltered, tears were streaming down his furrowed cheeks. He had only just lost a wife and now also a son. It was too much.

Palm could not bear to look. He rose, then knelt before his father and put both arms around the old man.

The pointy-nosed Pomeranian's tail beat a contented gentle rhythm into the dry dusty earth as he watched the two men.

THREE

Palm had moved into a small room upstairs in the school house of the Dominican School in Stralsund. It is part of the orphanage.

Seated, or standing day-in and day-out before his mentor, the boy was first taught about daily ablutions, cleaning his nails, combing his hair and how to stow away newly tailored clothes, how to wear them and on which occasions, how to carry himself, how to bow and how to address others.

The learnèd tutor, a stranger come especially from Amsterdam, was leading his charge 'from the dark'. The only ray of light was a daily morning visit to the Lutheran Church adjacent to the school. The boy had already become pale from the bitter lessons of over-coming permanent homesickness, cooped up as he was.

Soon, from early hours until sunset, Palm received patient instruction to make marks on slate. First with lead, when, rough peasant hands, clutching a slate pen which appeared to have wishes he could neither predict nor control, finally, painfully began to obey. Squeals of the slate, under excess zeal and pressure, reminded Palm of many a frightened pig about to be slaughtered; still, the task of controlling a perfectly shaped *A* on a defined spot was even more taxing. Biting his lower lip and drawing deep breaths he sighed and tried again and again.

His garments were like those of any other young townsman in Stralsund; hose, breeches, buckled shoes or fine soft suede ankle boots, a long jacket with seven pleats down the back and a high stand-up collar, to wear over white blouses of fine linen, even a felt cap in a fetching orange shade, and gloves, and, ...when he stood, for the first time before a full length mirror, he bowed to the figure before him, (which was bowing back) and did not recognize himself. Despite all evidence Palm was, in his own mind, still an out-of-place yokel, good-natured, raw, and clumsy.

The tailor laughed for a long time, told other customers about the lanky, awkward boy, who talked as peasants do, brought along by the imposing newly arrived bearded teacher from the orphanage of the former Dominican Convent School which was now preaching the Lutheran cause.

Palm's daily lessons sounded somewhat like this:

'Large letters', announced the teacher with enthusiasm, 'and the very first one is ***A***, as in 'aaah,'...you *do* understand Master Palm, what I mean, this shape represents *this* sound: A...aaah....say it, now, write it, while you practise, Palm, you shall give me examples of things you know, names, or places, which have *that* sound, I want you to enjoy learning with me; you must ask any questions you please. I do believe learning the 'aaa'l-phabet will be an eye-opener in more ways than one. You are soon a man, I will not teach you as if you were a small child.'

'Aaa...dam' smiled Palm, then, bolder, 'Amber, Abbott, Ab..salon'.... the new scholar found himself on the right path, enjoying each encouraging nod from his tutor,' and 'Aaa-braham's Bosom,' yes, this was pleasing, a game, even with a voice that was breaking, croaking as best it could.

Encouraged, already sensing Palm's enquiring mind, the tutor asked: 'where have you heard the name 'Absalon', Palm, did you not perhaps mean 'Absalo*m*'?

'No, no,' came the eager reply, 'the Pastor spoke of him in church, Sire, and also called him 'Axel'...Absalo*n* drove away pirates, those nearby, on the island of Rügen; then he became a bishop. The pirates were called Wends. They wended their way to the other end of the world. But this was four hundred years ago, when there was much trade between the Swedes and the Danes, and us Pomeranians. No-one cared for those terrible Wends.'

'You surprise me, young man,' said the mentor.

'Now please explain what you mean by 'Abraham's Bosom'; it sounds to me you have knowledge of the Scriptures as well as of history.'

‘No Sire, not really. When my mother died the pastor said she was now in the abode of the departed, in ‘Abraham’s Bosom’. I remember it because it sounded so, well, warm and comforting...’

‘God bless you, Palm. It is an adventure, a great pleasure and honour to be your mentor. Tomorrow we try the next letter *B*, for Bosom, Besom or Beelzebub.

***

In Palm’s room there was a small window of thick circular panes through which he could see, spy on, other boys, numbers of them, both small and older. ‘All orphans’, he was told. They moved about in a leafy enclosed yard, from time to time during the day.

His own narrow bed against a panelled wall served as a place to sit; there was a carved oak chair with arm-rests and a small table bearing a pewter holder for a candle. He was to spend time with other boys only when he had learned to write, read and do things with numbers. Until then he must adjust to his new life, spending hours each day in the company of a man who, steeped in knowledge, was kindness personified.

Palm proved to be an eager learner. Within four weeks he constructed simple words, short phrases, with a quill pen, while absorbing daily doses of history, religious studies, simple mathematics and his favourite, geography. As soon as his reading became adequate young master Palm Ulefeld, who now, understanding the construction of his true name, was promised access to a dark room filled with books: the well-stocked Library.

After such a very long summer of mental and spiritual force-feeding the farmer’s boy had become pale, his mind overloaded: he was drowning in topics and ideas. The mentor, in loco parentis, urged him to go to town for exploratory walks, not too far nor too long...not to spend any time in idle talk with strangers, just to return refreshed. ‘You are not a prisoner, Palm’ he smiled, ‘only come back safely for the next dose of knowledge with which I hope to feed your mind and soul.'

Palm now knew about the 'Consistory,' a governing body of the local congregation, similar to the one which had so frightened him on that market day in the summer, now an eternity away. He realised reports passed to and fro between them and his mentor. They had allowed him a modest number of jingling coins in his pocket, to spend as he pleased; a new experience to be feared and enjoyed.

Just a few streets to Stralsund's harbour, one of the best natural harbours on the Baltic, that's where he was drawn: to sunlight, sea breezes, gulls, anchored ships and sailors. Wearing a fine woollen cloak, autumn now well on its way, he sauntered through the narrow streets, across the Old Market, down towards the liveliest area of Stralsund, already seeing, over the town wall, tall masts stirring the sky. There was something about this young man, perhaps just the way he carried himself...a fine head of long brown, slightly curly hair, fresh complexion and amber-coloured eyes, which made people stare. Palm looked away, wondered self-consciously what he was doing wrong.

'Breathe, deep breaths, sea air inside me. This must be the way, but bitterly cold. Seaweed, smells....I long to be close to the water, close to Vineta, and my beautiful dream, my best secret...just to gaze, watch the boats, if there *are* any, and stare across to the island, Rügen, the land of Absalon, he who was made a bishop by a Danish king,.did *he* have to learn to read,' crossed Palm's mind, and, 'what will become of me, when I can? Not a bishop I think. No, I would not care to become a bishop. If only someone, anyone, would tell me about the man who was my father, my supposed true mother? When I last made enquiries my mentor stared out of the window, then sighed: *'Palm, be patient, I am not allowed to talk about this with you....it is for the best, be patient!'*

'I am, most of the time. It is becoming harder. I'm not sure why.'

Waves beat, crashed against the jetties, rocks, a stiff breeze, grey-green white crested waves, gulls with unnerving pained cries swooped low. A number of boats were anchored, sails rolled up; there was much to see. Inhaling smells of tar and fish Palm noticed two sailors, distantly, on shore...unsteady, laughing, stumbling and holding each other, so as not to fall over, the wind very strong further along, why else would they be falling over, picking each other up, shouting; a fight, perhaps? 'They must be my age, shrieking and shaking with laughter'. Palm stared, envious of the high jinks, the tomfoolery. They approached, giggling and pretended to bow.

'Huzzah!' called one: 'Hail, you should find the inn, they serve good beer and victuals in this cold climate, or don't you mix with commoners?'

They reeled about, frolicking, taunting him, then ran on, leaving Palm alone, an outcast. He missed his brother, his parents. He missed real life, laughter, warmth, and belonging.

Rejected, dejected he turned back, then stumbled clumsily up Langenstrasse: there was the towering spire of St.Jakobi and in the distance St.Nicholai church, still visible, although early darkness of autumn afternoon had fallen.

'Now for the way back...the school is close enough'.

Just a short detour to the left of the New Market he heard unexpected sounds, both disturbing and ravishing, from the door of the Marienkirche. His senses warned him, his insensibility blocked all reason...he faltered, stopped, then allowed himself drawn into the dark gloom, where he stood, rooted to the stone floor, instantly overwhelmed by an incubus, a wraith... the immensity of a never-before experienced macabre catastrophe, surging sounds of piercing intensity vibrated in his chest. 'My heart has stopped', he thought. Overpowered, dizzy and faint, he took shelter in one of those wooden boxes to keep steady, to hide. His eyes were watering, his chest constricted, trembling, his teeth had begun to chatter, he was cold and terrified. There was no-one about. He had never felt more alone. The only human he could talk with was probably waiting for him at this very moment.

'I must tell him about this!' Palm stumbled out and noticed a paper posted to the Church entrance.

He read: **BUX.. TE.. HUDE.. AB END.. KON.. ZERT,**

...then hurrying back through the dark unlit cobbled pathways, he repeated to himself: 'kon zert..bux te hu de kon zert bux.'... an incantation, warding off unknown demons, to consult his mentor.

FOUR

Permanently concerned, eyebrows drawn together by two strong folds above his elegant nose, questioning eyes, anxious to penetrate impenetrable knowledge, such was the appearance of Professor Martin von Ruetz, a tall, fine-boned pedagogue in his early thirties. Now in the employ of St. Katherine's school, this imposing man, his long pale face partly concealed by a dark curly beard and moustache, had studied the Law: his skills were acquired first in Berlin, then Heidelberg, and finally in the Low Countries. Improving his Latin, conversing with clever men in a society filled with open minds, all this was part of his life.

To all appearances a Lutheran, also an adherent of the highest cultural and scientific ideas prevalent in intellectual circles of the 17th century, he remained, nevertheless, a free and rebellious spirit. He lived in the time of Rembrandt, of first performances of Hamlet and King Lear, in a time when great thinkers like Bacon, Spinoza and Cervantes, Galileo and Descartes were opening the world's eyes to bewildering human behaviour and to the puzzlement of life and death. He liked to believe he was one of the rebels in many countries who questioned established facts and who advanced knowledge in the sciences, medicine and the arts.

'Ah, in *my* younger days' he'd say, 'in the fifties, and early sixties, I spent much time in the Kunst-Winkel in Amsterdam (the art gallery where youths and students liked to meet to exchange ideas).It was in these circles a man called Spinoza truly made sparks fly!'

Such stimulation, surrounded by open-minded men, the evaluation of ideas current in those days became a formative experience. Discussions on politics and history, his studies of Latin, also the approach to sciences and to philosophy were finely honed, morality and law were discussed, advocated, or found wanting. For him this was a time of breaking through shackles, his time of personal change.

There were debates on free love and even scandal.

Such matters appeared to be of particular interest to Martin von Ruetz, this notable son of minor Pomeranian landed gentry.

Then, out of the blue came an unexpected summons from Stralsund, a good six days' coach ride from Amsterdam. He was to be questioned by authorities dealing with Palm's unusual circumstances: Might the Professor care to focus all his abilities on just this one, singular boy; on a post with a huge responsibility and unusually high remuneration?

There were stipulations: the boy must not be told his origins; as a Lutheran, with an all-encompassing knowledge he should learn to move in the best society; and remain motivated to learn as quickly as possible. The time taken should not be more than three, possibly four years. The tutor must take full responsibility for this boy.

Would he be free and able to sign such a contract?

It was a tall order.

Professor Ruetz accepted. He needed money for obscure, unrevealed matters. Only marginally guilty about having walked away from his own family obligations, he now fully accepted responsibility for an apparently malleable young man who was no relation whatsoever.

The challenge so far had proved surprisingly rewarding. The boy received guidance with grateful and gracious behaviour, and with unfailing keenness. From one week to the next young Master Palm resembled a twinkling gemstone being cut and polished.

***

Today was different. The gleaming gem had cracked, Professor Ruetz felt an obligation. His usually questioning high brow now crumpled with deep concern, he put an arm around the trembling pupil, guided him to the only chair, put a rug over the forlorn shape. 'There now, stay still for a while' he stood back, 'I will return with a drink and we can talk. Close your eyes, Master Palm, order your mind.' The boy tried; eyes tightly shut he put his head back and took a deep breath.

'Calmer now, teeth stopped chattering? Poor fellow! Something has conjured up old fears, memories, re-opened old wounds... here, pull this rug around your shoulders. You are old enough to share some wine with me, it will strengthen you, help you tell me what has so shocked you. I will ask for your evening meal, Cook can feed us both at the same time...There now, sit back. The wine will warm you. Tell me everything. Take time, Master Palm, we can work on this difficulty together. First of all: where have you been?'

Palm closed his eyes, obeyed. His strangely croaking voice faltered, then:

'... in the church, Professor, I heard sounds, sounds that attacked me with such power, like angry beasts, and then fooled me into acceptance by sucking my body into mists and clouds and lifting me up, but dashing me down again, and I saw myself in the sea, sinking and crushed, where my mother was, in Vineta, still holding a sword, as before...I could barely walk, so strong was that music, and then I saw the words BUX TE HUDE ABEND MUSIK and returned here, to you.'

He looked up at his tutor, a trusting child.

Martin Ruetz felt a surge of huge responsibility.

'Come now, Master Palm, Vineta is but a legend, and what is this tale about your 'mother' in the sea with a sword...are you remembering a dream, what *are* you talking about? You surely know the difference between dreams, legends and truth? Truth, which can also be called reality? If it is a dream we must try to understand it. We must learn to distinguish between Possibility and Impossibility, Certainty and Uncertainty. Some people are born fools and some are born sages. Which do you choose to be?'

Palm stared numbly in front of him, muttered, even more confused: 'the words I read on that door, Professor, what was their meaning?'

'No meaning, but a name, boy, a reality: Dietrich Buxtehude is a well-known organist. He lives in Denmark and has probably come to the Marienkirche to try the new organ, a masterwork over 20 meters high, to play to our townspeople who enjoy such things. The sound he draws from this immense organ is nothing evil, not to be feared, but to be marvelled at: he is famous for his inventions. He calls the events Abend Musik, because they happen in the evenings of the five Sundays before Christmas. What you heard was probably only a try-out of the instrument, as he has never played here before. Are you fond of music, Palm? Have you ever touched an instrument?'

Palm's cheeks were flushed from the wine, his eyes now fully open.

'Oh no, Master, but once my father did: he dug very deep in our field years ago, before I was born, I think. His spade hit a gleaming muddied object in the earth. It appeared undamaged, made of bronze and when he had cleaned it he took it to the Swedish Governor's House. It was a horn, as big as a man with a winding decoration which could be made to emit a strange cry, eerie and frightening. The Governor rewarded my father and praised him for finding such an ancient instrument.'

'Upon my soul, was it truly a horn? I would like to see it,' Professor Ruetz exclaimed with great enthusiasm. 'We must ask what has become of it... and the organ you heard is made of similar pipes, which is why it sounds so powerful. Old horns have been found in many places in Pomerania and Denmark and are said to be as old as the time of Jesus Christ, our Lord. Have you heard of Joshua who blew down the walls of Jericho with seven trumpets, just think, what power! And then there were Olympic Games which included contests just for such instruments, the players were judged on the volume of sound they could produce.'

Palm seemed puzzled. 'Games'? 'Olympic?' No-one, not even his father, had ever mentioned such words. But the teacher became unstoppable:

'There was one trumpeter who played so loud that many in the audience were stunned as if with blows to the head... he was a giant who slept on a bearskin, but I doubt it was *that* which made him so powerful. Ancient trumpets were used for magical rites at sunrise and sunsets. Who knows, Palm, what your father's trumpet was used for. Where can it be now, we must find it!'

After this the boy, not surprisingly, had no further problems hearing the ardent sounds of organ pipes. With such a mentor each event opened up a cornucopia of new topics to stimulate and thrill. Teacher and pupil went to hear Buxtehude and shook the great man's hand. He was neither old, nor bearded, in fact no older than Professor Ruetz.

In Palm's mind the impassioned organist had turned into a giant, but when they spoke after the performance the boy learned a new wisdom: skills can be learned and passed on, step by step and if one takes trouble they can be remembered and stored with the help of noble teachers.

'Do you sing in the Church Choir, Master Uhlfeld?'

With this question the famous organist set in motion a train of events, although Palm barely dared look the man in the eye, let alone respond.

***

When pupil and teacher returned to their lessons Professor Ruetz opened the door of his cupboard, lifted out a small skull, and held it up for Palm's inspection. Palm recoiled, began to shiver. It reminded him of his life in the country.

'This is a treasured possession, Palm, from Italy, where I was given it. It belonged to a boy with a wondrous voice, who was famous in his cathedral for the exquisite pleasure he provided listeners. His father had consented to have the child's testicles removed when only eleven years old, to preserve the exquisite sounds he could sing. This turned the boy into a 'castrato'. But he died, still only little older than you. The father, already richly paid for allowing this operation, eventually sold his own son's skull...and it was handed to me as a farewell gift.'

Palm's eyes opened wide. He had turned pale. His farm life flashed before him: 'slaughtering' days, when hens had their heads chopped off, or binding the legs of struggling pigs before the fatal blow to their heads...how could this be-to cut heads and testicles off boys?

The teacher placed the skull on the windowsill. Together they sat looking at it. Pained, Palm turned away. What father would do such a thing? Was it for the money, or was it for the love of beautiful sound?

On the following morning the Professor promised early instruction in note reading. After a few months Palm might like to join the school choir, when his voice had settled?

They would listen to some rehearsals first, contemplate this matter; later they might decide together.

PART TWO
GENESIS

FIVE

Blustery, sharp, almost wintery weather....Palm's cap trundled along the waterfront and no amount of chasing, lunging, swooping, scooping, was swift enough to recapture it despite additional serious attempts, leaping and shouting assistance from a young sailor crossing his path. They cursed, they laughed; with feet and garments soaked Palm was reminded of similar romps with his brother, trying to catch hens or ducks, near a lake, now an eternity ago.

This sailor, not very different in age, strong and cheerful, grinned while they exchanged hearty handshakes and decided to fight their way back, facing capricious gusts, squawking gulls, back to the harbour, to the inn nearby. A warming drink was needed. On the way in they stopped, stared at words engraved on a stone post: It was the sailor who read the words out loud:

PLEASING EVERYONE
IS IMPOSSIBLE

Puzzled, with raised eyebrows, conspiratorial smiles and shaking heads they squeezed inside the inn filled with sailors, fishermen and assorted layabouts.

Two wenches were serving ale, 'lobscouse', herrings, also baked fish, freshly caught in the early hours. The young men winked at each other, eyeing rumbustious guests, and finally exchanged names: 'Palm, Palm Uhlfeld' (savouring his own) with a slight incline of the head ...and in reply, self-assured...'Jan De Groot...from Cap Diavolo...'

They glanced at each other, grinning, clumsy and awkward.

'Cap Diavolo, is that far from here?' asked Palm, 'a strange name, I have never heard of it.'

Jan, who spoke German, but like a Dutchman, explained his Dutch father had recently returned from the other end of the world, had assisted a Commander called Jan van

Riebeeck: they'd set up a station at the foot of a strangely shaped mountain, 'like a table set close by the sea.' This mountain, allegedly two miles at the top from end to end was to become a replenishment Station for Dutch fleets going to the East Indies, for the Dutch East India Company...

'So, you are, he is, a Dutchman?' Palm, wide-eyed, was impressed by such unimpeachable authority....'and Dia*v*olo, Dia*b*olo, which is it? Your mother must be a Dutch woman and did she too travel to Cap Dia...bolo?'

'I have heard it both ways, what does it matter, it is a new place and no-one knows,' was the sailor's curt reply, 'as to my mother, she speaks German and has waited three years to see my father safely home. He returned with strange tales, how it seemed the most distant corner to the south of Africa, rough and mountainous viewed from the sea, but on arrival such immense fruitfulness of the land and a shame there were no Christians living there, with such good fresh water and fruits and herbs, also roots, and many hares and bucks, oxen and sheep...' the sailor looked about hoping for something to drink......'but *real* people well, almost none, only wild-looking figures, with dark skins who live as animals, soulless and damned without religion'. The sailor faltered: a vision of golden, youthful womanhood stood before them, bearing mugs of foaming ale.

'Lobscouse is off', she recited, 'so is redcurrant jelly, but will you enjoy baked fish, chunks of brown rye-bread? It is the same as at the Mariners House on Franken Street, but less costly, and there is still pike soup'....her windswept curls tumbled prettily from her inclined head, eyes half-closed, trying not to look too directly at the young customers.

Palm beamed up at her. He was having a good time and could hardly believe such a lovely creature was standing close by him. Of course, she resembled the underwater Queen of Vineta, his 'dream mother'....still haunting him whenever he lay awake at night. Here she was, flesh and blood, pocketing his coins, forcing them one by one into a jingling leather purse dangling from her belt, blushing and biting her lips.

After a curt reply she darted away.

With quickened pulse his eyes followed her curves, curls, and curtsies.

Jan, impatient to spin *his* yarns, resumed where he left off: the overpowering table-like rock, another rock like a resting lion, his rump by the sea, and then most strikingly the 'wild ones,' the inhabitants who called themselves 'Khoi Khoi', who made strange clicking noises when they spoke.

'Their women feed naked babes, tied to their backs, by throwing long breasts over their shoulders to connect with hungry mouths; I could show you a picture of them, fashioned in England after a long journey by an Englishman, thirty years ago. I keep it in my bunk on board.'

Who ever heard of such things! Sailors must be ever vigilant, sharp-eyed beings. Palm's spirits were aroused; he was agog, carried away.

'It is also called the Cape of Storms,' Jan was enjoying his powers of description: 'when my father took me there we arrived in spring-time during the most untamed frightening winds and waves I have ever seen and indeed, we were nearly drowned. It was my first visit. But ashore, after the winds died down, it seemed like paradise: a lost Garden of Eden. Even in autumn the Cap Diavolo-Diabolo is more lovely than anywhere else on earth. There the seasons are the opposite of ours in Holland and Germany....why not come, join the crew, my captain is on the lookout for new sailors...we could be friends on the long journey, we are needed while we are there for building and planting. The fort was completed some years ago. You would see and instruct the 'Hottentotts', or the Khoi; they are the wild ones, but great hunters and fighters, brown all over: they do not harm us especially if we give and teach them useful things.'

Palm, already befuddled, smiled dreamily: 'how tempting, to run off, to disappear to see such marvels, but of course, it will never happen, just contemplating it...what a pleasurable sensation, also this lovely serving maid, with golden curls and ample bosom', her wide red skirt brushed against his arm, as she reached forward to collect her money.

'I wonder what *her* name is.' He grinned contentedly: a beery man, much older, had just called her over: she is 'Minna'. She had smiled boldly at him, yes, she *had* noticed him, before she moved on.

Palm was certain.

Candles on the heavy long tables flickered among the shadows of diners, bottles and dirty plates, as lively, hungry men filled their bellies. Later, when they stepped out into the dark harbour front, winds chilling, gulls screeching, they exchanged hearty farewells.

'I leave you, Jan de Groote. Do we meet again, tomorrow, same time?'

'Why, of course, with pleasure. I have more to tell you. I will bring two pictures...you will be astonished, you can be sure.'

***

Palm knocked and found his teacher seated, studying by candle-light. There was an uncomfortable silence: he barely looked up, then, somewhat irritably: 'It is one of my rules to sleep before the clock strikes twelve... anything to report after your rather long *exeat,* Palm?'

'Indeed, Sir. I need your help. I have been invited to travel with a new friend, a sailor. I need to see your globe again, because it does sound like a very long journey. Could I leave for a while and continue our studies later? My new friend Jan, a sailor from Holland, tells me there is work to be done...in Cap Diabolo; his captain is looking for young people like myself. Will you show me Africa on your globe? I think I must go to the very end of it.'

The professor, his elbows on the table, folded his hands as if in prayer and frowned at the book before him. Plainly at a loss, neither of them moved. Experience had taught the older man to remain calm, enter into the mind of any pupil, before making a reply. He began by stroking his beard, for a considerable time.

'Very well,' turning his head slightly he noted the eager expression and flushed face of his charge. 'Do bring that globe! But in the morning... We can discuss this *tomorrow.'*

Palm, realising he had crossed some as yet unknown boundary, sloped off to his room, stretched out on the bed, where he drowned in the deep sleep of one not accustomed to ale brewed for sailors.

On the following day, sharing their breakfast, teacher and pupil sat face to face. Hesitantly, cautiously, Palm worked his way to sailor Jan's proposal. He had studied the globe, such a trip would take about half a year, and that was just *one* way.

'There is no guarantee of safe return or even of arrival,' countered the professor...'a fleet of five ships left Holland in 1652, I was a young man when I heard about this: two ships arrived after a terrible journey: there had been hundreds of burials at sea. Dangers are legendary. Often, too often, ships don't arrive at all, the coast of West Africa is littered with skeletons and shipwrecks...'but then the tutor offered to accompany Palm, to meet Jan de Groote, for a 'serious' discussion. With wisdom, realising Palm had experienced a call to 'adventure' and 'manhood' the teacher held one ace in reserve, a determining factor. It would surely shift Palm's restive mind.

***

That very afternoon teacher and pupil stood outside the Inn, waiting for the sailor. There was time for discussion. What was the meaning of the inscription on the stone: PLEASING EVERYONE IS IMPOSSIBLE? Could it be the cook... not always fully minding his tasks? Perhaps the supply of ale was running out?

'Well, yes and no,' smiled Professor Ruetz, 'think on: expecting to please everyone, at *all* times could be a delusion which works against one's best interests, *per exemplo*, think of this motto with regard to our Hanseatic League, who travel far and wide, pleasing everyone in every country, bringing 'contentment' and 'wealth'? How often do ventures at sea fail: boats wrecked, sailors drowned, goods lost?'

With satisfaction he noted a perplexed youth, out of his depth, who still needed to learn about risk, dashed hopes and delusions. This most excellent teacher collected in his mind all deficiencies as they arose, stored them up for future opportunities to open up his pupil's mind.

There! Stumbling along the pebbly waterside Jan de Groote appeared, waving his cap. On arrival he bowed stylishly to Palm's ...'good evening', while wondering about the impressive and much older 'companion'. He bowed a second time, just to make sure.

'My new friend', Palm smiled anxiously at his nodding tutor, then, reassuringly, at the sailor, extending one arm to open the entrance. All three customers proceeded to a quiet corner of the inn; busy late afternoon diners had not yet arrived.

Palm cast about unobtrusively for Minna. Jan, with a flourish, drew three rolled–up papers from inside his jacket, tied with red tape. He placed them on the table. 'One is an old map, at least one hundred years old, drawn by a cartographer from Antwerp, but it will do. I will show it later, but now, as promised, these are the pictures from Cap Diavolo, although I obtained them in London, another place I must tell you about.'

Jan untied three sets of ribbons, held down the curled edges of the first one and explained with enthusiastic pride:

'Here, witness a man and a woman as drawn in 1638 by the fine Sir Thomas,(not that I know the man)! When you see these inhabitants you feel they must be tamed, like wild beasts. But in my view it is not quite so. I have known them to be helpful, friendly and good with their hands. Especially if they are rewarded...Their skins are as dark as this oak table, no doubt burnished by the sun which is mostly very hot there.' Palm, his hand covering his mouth, and the tutor stared at the picture, weighing up troublesome notions of frightening nudity.

'And now this', announced the sailor, 'see the second picture: somewhat unpleasing: on the shore are gallows and a torture wheel for breaking limbs much in use in this distant place. Threatening rocks seemingly piled high, a castle and a walled garden, but this is not well-observed, these rocks are quite unlike the real mountain. This artist has no eye to speak of: a Frenchman, who calls it 'Le Cap de Bonne Esperance' which I believe to be a name which has caught on: 'the Cape of Good hope'....I much prefer it to 'Cap Diavolo'; I do feel this Dutch East India Company town could become just the place for persons from Europe, even England, away from wars and troublesome religious reforms...to make a new settlement. Judge for yourselves how many boats have arrived safely, large and small, the bay both tranquil and lovely, alas also sometimes with foul weather, this cannot be denied.....'

'There are many wild, but now also tamed men and beasts. But what is truly needed: young men to work and develop this wondrous place. I speak as ambassador, I help to find new recruits with skills, such as planting vines for Jan van Riebeeck, the Commander who brought vines from Holland twelve years ago and again the following year...they have all rooted and he has gardens on the eastern slopes of the mountain'. The sailor nodded at Palm, '*you* know about planting, your skills would be rewarded. Slaves from West Africa have already arrived on our ships and lodge in their slave quarters. And now teachers are needed to set up a school for slave children in the expanding settlement.'

The boy-sailor looked up at his audience expecting, hoping for response. 'Ag man,' lapsing for a moment into his father's tongue, 'dis mooi, ek sê vir U, mynheer'....(it's beautiful Sir, I'm telling you) you should try it for a while. You too, Mynheer, together with Palm...you could see for yourselves. Now here is this old map: it is a fine attempt showing the entire globe flattened out.' He unrolled some parchment and pointed at an unlikely flattened, bulging mustard-coloured blot: 'the Dutch East India Company has been exploring this coast for years, since 1595...although a Portuguese, Da Gama, was the first to reach India and another one called De Saldanha climbed up the mountain over one hundred years earlier. All these men have traded with Khoi tribes, but also fought battles with them. The Khoi are very fierce. They roam inland, live in reed huts and are fond of tobacco. We want to teach them our language and our ways. Their name means 'men of men...'

By now Jan de Groote's audience was no longer limited to Palm and his tutor: three or four other guests, skippers and sailors had been eyeing the pictures with exclamations of dismay or enthusiasm, leaning over shoulders, pointing, laughing. Some shook their heads in disbelief imagining the months and months on board. Only when pike soup was brought steaming...some, then all, dispersed to their own tables.

Palm's teacher, as intrigued as the others, was sufficiently in control of his duties to ask further questions revealing risks and dangers ahead. There was discussion of scurvy. 'No, no, red wine prevents scurvy,' so the sailor; also the eternity at sea and the dangers of each and every day, the time one would have to stay to satisfy the Dutch East India Company and illnesses and dangers of the equally long return journey.

Even back in Europe there might be lurking dangers, as witnessed just a few months earlier in London docks. Jan's boat had been engulfed:

'....we woke at three in the night to loud calls from the shore', he told the listening men, 'a huge fire had burned three hundred houses and was by dawn burning all the way to the great bridge....this fire running from one place to the other... we could see it from the water and people throwing their goods into small boats or even into the water...such screams and the poor people trying to get on boats and everywhere terrified pigeons, not knowing about fires, getting their wings burned and falling down before our eyes....

....It was the East wind; it blew for several days, thirteen hundred houses were destroyed, almost one hundred churches, but very few people died, only twenty, it was extraordinary. I like Englishmen, although I cannot speak their language. Quite bold they are and much suited to explore the world. I saw, to give you an example of their ways, a military man condemned to death in London town, why I am not sure, but he was taken to be hanged, drawn and quartered, looking calm and cheerful. I had a day off and followed the crowd. They were shouting approval when he was cut down, when they saw his head and his heart. One needs to be strong for such events. Even in the Cape of Good Hope, there is much need for displays of just such fortitude and discipline. You will have noted on the picture the place where evil-doers are despatched, quite near the waterfront. The Cape needs strong henchmen at all times, such discipline is found to be the most effective.'

After this sales-pitch Jan de Groote's Pike soup was cold. Most of the other listeners had withdrawn. Some had lost their appetite. The boy shivered. His teacher, smiling, turned to Palm's friend: 'You have made yourself very clear, De Groote, we thank you for your astonishing account. No doubt you will find interested parties here in Stralsund. Palm and I will discuss your proposal. Allow me to be your host today, to pay for our meal.' He studied his student's face: 'Will you call the girl to receive our monies?'

Palm had suppressed all thoughts about Minna, and indeed, today's serving wench was a different one. Just thinking about Minna made his heart race, his face burn. But the tutor had gained valuable insight into many things, including the heightened emotions of his pupil. 'What is my teacher thinking? He said not one word, after the rowdy folk at the eating place...and now this disturbing silence, sea wind pushing from behind; we are through one of the town-gates, I feel the cobbles underfoot, always not enough light, just the odd candle near windows as we pass, the streets confusing, but the professor has chosen our route according to the available lighting, knowing the way, first Semlower Street, left...after the Rathaus, then right at Boettcher-street and we will be safely 'home'. It seems a longer way in the dark, why did we not bring a lantern? Darkness is blindness....not knowing ones thoughts, not knowing what to do. How I wish I were like Jan de Groote, bold and confident and travelled. I've not even sat in a coach, let alone a ship, I've seen nothing, been nowhere. Just the farm and now this dark, cobbled, windy harbour town! However: I really think I begin to know what I want.

SIX

'Tomorrow: a truly big day! My tutor appeared as interested in Jan de Groote's proposal as I was....I saw him observing, listening to Jan who wishes us to set sail for the magic mountain. Instead of Latin grammar, algebra and the history of ancient Greece we looked at the globe, and discussed practical matters. We must go to the docks to see the ship. What else? Jan will tell us. And should I tell father, *step*-father... and my brother? They must be told. What if we never return, for one reason or another? I can't sleep, it must be already tomorrow, but still dark, early. Crackling, scratching under the eaves, just pigeons and gulls, waking up, no owls in towns, thanks be to God. These dark months, this cold time, sun rising late. Oh, to sail away on a ship, unbelievable, my puny arms pulling up sails, ropes, doing real things, in warm sun,... my tutor could teach me on the ship if he had books with him. Yes, we will take books. And then those dark-skinned warriors when we get there! The church-bell, still only four strokes.'
Palm's eyes are now closed...he has nodded off at last.

***

In and out of sleep...but now dressed, young Palm feels strangely excited. The bell strikes nine.

'I wait and wait. In *his* room! But Professor Ruetz chooses to be late. When I am so anxious to discuss yesterday! What can he be doing, where is he?'

Early sunshine streams through the high curved window of the tutor's chamber, casts small circles of light from rounded panes onto the thick curved alcove wall. Palm's eyes wander around the room: 'handsome, his carved table...a small crucifix, and this wooden book-stand, candle burned right down and wax all over the base....wooden bench along the wall, supported by carved brackets; my tutor has left thick tomes and cushions strewn carelessly and also, that curious skull, which now usually rests on the windowsill, his slippers tossed casually under the ledge. Not like him....where is he? And why does he keep that skull? Perhaps he once cared for that singer boy...Here, his folder, on the table. Am I to open it, for today's study perhaps? I might as well prepare myself.

Palm looks at an engraving: a winged woman seated, glowering, angry, a smaller winged creature, an infant, beneath a set of scales, also a starved, unhappy beast on the ground.

And yes, it is a long-nosed bony hound not unlike that of his father's.

Above it all, over a peaceful ocean, is a rising sun. Palm frowns, looks at it more closely: 'Or might it be a comet? Not that I know comets. Here, letters on a banner, no, perhaps on the wings of a bat, *melencolia*...this makes no sense. Bats are symbols of the devil, I've heard. I had better find an explanation, my teacher is testing me, I think. It may be Latin. We've only just started that. Let me see. A ladder, going up to some heights not shown; I see a timer, sand running down and a bell over a board of numbers. By the woman's feet are scattered nails, a broken inkwell, a saw, a circular object. All of this disorder. What is the meaning of this riddle?'

'My teacher's comes, I hear his steps.' Palm rises to his feet.

'Palm! Forgive me, I was trapped in the library by the school's history master. He has helped me with some historical research. Ah yes, I see you have found the picture...can you make sense of it? It is by a man from Nuremburg, by the name of Dürer, dead more than one hundred years. His fame has spread all over our country because of the printing press. I treasure this picture. Do be seated. What does it say to you?'

'I must humour him,' thought Palm, 'show an interest, although my thoughts are with the proposed journey.'

The tutor was now leaning over him, also studying the picture.

'It says, Sir, ahem...we could get on such a boat and set out to sea and, well,' now also leaning forward to peer at it more closely, 'this strange word: I hope you will tell me its meaning! The dog must be dead from starvation and the angry woman has more difficulties to bear than I know of. How unhappy she looks, even though her child is already able to write on a small board...and the objects scattered around, nails, hammer and a saw, well, they imply she is worn out from too much hard work. There are numerous keys attached to her belt, but whatever they may unlock has brought her no happiness... her only hope is the sea, the sky, as her husband, who may be a stonemason, has left her with such an intelligent child.

They both have wings, they must already be angels.

Or is the clue in the mysterious word above, '*me len colia*'? What is it?' The boy, disarmingly perplexed, looked up at his mentor.

'Of course, Palm. It is Latin. And your observations are satisfactory.'

'But Sir, what is the meaning?' Professor Ruetz had closed his eyes.

'It is an affliction' he sighed, 'men, but also women suffer it: It brings a black mind-set similar to homesickness, of groaning and longing, moping and knowing no remedy. 'Melancholy' describes a fearful misery of reason overthrown. We call it 'Weltschmerz', 'pain of the world', it happens to old and young, can be due to overburdening deep thoughts and efforts of many kinds. You recall Aristotle? I spoke of him when we discussed Greek philosophers; well, it was his conceit that men *who excel in great art are melancholics*, as if they had been left to suffer pain from the pangs of giving birth to their endeavours. I myself am not sure about this. But for now, after last night, let us change the topic. The time has come, Palm: you and I must evaluate the future, *your* future. Pondering this picture may help us reach the correct decision.'

He stood by the boy, looking over his shoulder. Mingled with hope and possible belief in salvation and good in all men, there was substance but also scope for doubt in the tutor's knowledge. Classical learning, untiring study of philosophy and debate with men of science, religious knowledge and other refinements had well prepared him, for most but perhaps not all challenges.

He had made notes on Palm's family history, updated to the best of all available information. There was also that recent visit to the Swedish Commandant, for a secret interview, guarded by a military man.

'When one comes face to face with something unavoidable, Palm, it is a day one never forgets. Life is about challenges and change: today I have what seems to be an unexpected awakening for you, for us both.'

Palm's heart skipped a beat. Head raised, he waited to hear his teacher's words, as he looked into those admirable, inscrutable eyes.

'Are we about to sail to Africa with Jan de Groote, for a new life of danger and adventure?' passed through his mind....then, strangely, he felt threatened. Man and boy looked intently at each other, silent, waiting...Finally, after a profound sigh, Professor Ruetz declaimed in a strangely formal voice:

'I am instructed to inform you ...are you ready for this? It is not what you expect: *who* and *where* your true mother is.'

Palm was not ready. This was certainly not what he expected. There came over him a feeling of falling into a deep pit. All blood drained from his face, he said nothing. Frowning, aware a reply was expected, he asked:

'Should I see her? Where can I speak with her, where is she, please tell me, if we are about to leave for Cap Diavolo, for Africa?'

'Calm yourself, Palm. This is a complex situation. First of all: have you heard of Christian IV, King of Denmark? His first wife died. The second wife was a noblewoman, and her children were legitimate, but for some reason could not inherit the throne. One of these children was called Leonora Christina, and she was born in 1621.Today she is forty-six years old. She is your mother: one of the daughters of a Danish king.' The mentor's face remained inscrutable:

'Ergo: you are the grandson of a king, but a king who lives no more.'

Palm stared at the floor. This new beginning was taking an improbable turn.

Silently the mentor touched Palm's shoulder to show the boy he was not alone. For a while he studied the boy's face, giving him time…then: 'Strange and possibly not true, is that what you think? Have I ever, *would* I ever tell you anything other than the truth? Look at me Palm. No need to speak. First your face was white as a sheet, now you are flushed. I think you should take some water. Breathe deeply…'

Palm was silent. After a short while the tutor continued:

'You, Palm, were born on a storm-tossed boat, approaching the coast near Stralsund. But your arrival in this world was far too early …many weeks, even months too soon, you showed only the faintest signs of life. For a while, you appeared lifeless, so much so your father was about to bury you at sea. Your mother already had ten children, and then you, so small, not fit to live, appeared. Shivering and unsteady on deck, your father took one last look, pushed the shawl aside and saw your eyelids flicker…so, wracked with renewed doubt he bundled you in your mother's shawl, and once the boat had docked, staggered with you through stormy winds and squalls to the Commandant's House.

Saved by your father's conscience! Life was precious in these parts; during the Thirty Years War thousands of children lost their lives in the devastation, leaving half the population dead. Each new child was important. Instructions were left to find you a surrogate family, should you survive. Provisions were made. In a desperate hurry, apparently in difficulties, your father and mother travelled on. But you Palm, you lived! I suspect your mother believed you *had* been buried at sea.' I also suspect your father never told her the tiny bloodied body had shown a sign of life and that he had taken you to the Commandant; How could she have lived with that? Neither your drowning nor abandonment would offer any consolation, close to death herself as she was from shock and loss of blood. We must assume she did not know the truth. She may have believed you'd sunken to the bottom of the Baltic, entangled with seaweed, food for herring and eels and other healthy creatures.'

Their eyes met, the boy's face now drained, white as chalk.

'No need to speak Palm, just hear me through: instructions had been given, written down, I have seen them. No-one has ever made further inquiries and one assumes you are forgotten. Besides, Palm, I know for a fact your mother is now a prisoner in the Blue Tower in Copenhagen. Of her ten children some have died.

She must assume you are dead. Now your future is in our hands, in your own, in mine and in those of the governing body who looked you over on Palm Sunday. We must work as a team until you come of age. Will you trust me Palm? We have funds for less than three years.'

Professor Ruetz adopted a show of formality and politeness for Palm's sake. What he would have liked to do was to embrace the now deeply disturbed boy, show him warmth and provide courage.

He could not remember ever before harbouring such feelings.

'My mother in prison...and my father, why can't he help; what can she have done, has she done, to deserve such punishment?' Palm was in no position to stop tears streaming down his face, tears of stress, shock and surprise but also of huge disappointment.

'I have written it down for you, Palm, to the best of my ability. Her story is already becoming history. Your father died in 1652. We will not say too much about him for now. First I must talk about her, then later, about you, *Master* Palm, and *your* future.' The teacher peered out through the small panes on the window...'Here, make use of my kerchief, dry those tears; they are not manly and serve no purpose. Do you ride, Palm? I could arrange horses for us, so we can get out on fine days as we have today. Do you prefer, white, perhaps grey? For now, let us take a walk, away from the town, into the countryside. When you are quite ready I will tell the story of Leonora Christina, your mother. It is windy. Leave your cap, just cloak and gloves for today. Let us meet downstairs by the entrance in a few minutes.

Palm moved as in a dream. Suitably attired they strode, first a reluctant pace, then increasingly brisk, towards the town-gate. They had been given safe passage from town into the rough road near the graveyard and the seafront. They marched by the allotments, trees, autumnal colours against a sunny sky, just a few scudding fluffy clouds, a fresh feeling and release from the dizzying turn of events. Palm turned to his tutor, suddenly keen to hear more.

'Please tell me again Sir, I would like to know more about her, that 'Leona Christa...'

'Leon*ora* Christ*ina*, Palm, and yes, I long to tell you. But bear in mind what I was told may not be the whole truth. It was information from the Swedish Governor. His knowledge came from the Swedish king's ambassador. News that has travelled far often arrives in a distorted way. So, for now, this must be *our* truth: She was born in 1621, in July I think....and grew up in Copenhagen, in the Royal Palace. The King's first wife had passed away. He already had a great many children. The second time he did not marry in church. Again, I have no knowledge why; still, the relatives, courtiers, and nobles of course, were no fools: once Leonora Christina was born they made sure she was ennobled with a title, since she could not be a princess.

The King's, that is, *your* grandfather's happiness, did not last: he accused his wife of infidelity with another man. One does not betray a king. So he also divorced his second wife, your grandmother, and humiliated her by sleeping with her servant, Vibeke. Not just once, but for many years. Vibeke too brought into the royal household a brood of children. I was informed the jealous rivalry amongst the numerous children of Christian IV was a bitter struggle, but little Leonora Christina was firmly established in the King's benevolence. He wanted only the best for her. She grew up in the Royal Palace, along with three of her elder half-brothers. Imagine this girl looking from the windows of her home, and how she could see, across the courtyard a tower, the very one where she is now imprisoned. How strange this must seem to her now, don't you think?'

Teacher and pupil, marching along the coast road by the Baltic Sea with earnest expressions, together pondered the curious fate of Leonora Christina. Professor Ruetz had remembered to fill a flagon with water from the school well, it felt warm from resting in his pocket, but with so much talking his throat had become dry. He slowed down, stopped briefly to wet his gullet, offered a drink to his charge, as he wiped his chin with the back of his hand. 'Are you ready for more, Palm?' The boy nodded eagerly, 'oh yes, I am, if it pleases you, Professor.'

'Well then, let me see: Your mother, aged only nine years old, had been promised to a man who was lord-in-waiting to the king. This man was the seventh of seventeen children, proud of being a descendant of Charlemagne; his birthday was also in July, like your mother's. He was fifteen years older than she.

Later, just a little before your age now, Master Palm, when *she* was fifteen years, she was given in marriage to this great favourite of the King, who had by then become well-known as the signatory of an important peace treaty with Holland. The King thought highly of him.

Palm stopped in his tracks: 'Who is this Charlemagne, Master? If my father is related to him... then so am I.'

'Indeed' the mentor nodded, clear thinking, Master Palm.'

He smiled robustly, but then fell silent for a while. He needed to think.

Then: 'I will be pleased to do a study with you on your famous ancestor, as preparation on the view you will take of your father. Suffice it to say he, Charlemagne, lived 900 years ago and that almost all royalty of lands from Italy to Sweden are in some way related to him...and indeed, he was a man of huge importance. There are such men, never forgotten. Another name you might like to remember along with Charlemagne is that of Confucious, a Chinese sage of immense wisdom. Let us put them both on our list! He was no relation of yours, but rest assured, we will deal with them both, in a few days.'

'An unusually interesting time', flashes through Palm's head, 'all my discoveries seem to lead to yet another irresistible chunk of my background. What luck I have *you* to tell me so many things'...he muttered engagingly, grinning submissively. 'My perfect student', thought the professor. Smiling benignly he was aware this would be a means to an end from which Palm would derive little pleasure.

'Today is the day we spoke, just a little, about Leonora Christina, although there is a limit to the information I can give as her life was so intimately linked to that of your father. I understand they were very close, that she adored him. For the time being it is all you need to know. The reason for her imprisonment must belong to a future discussion. No more on that, I cannot continue. But, we *did* promise to meet one more time with Jan de Groote...we must give him word of our current situation, so changed from yesterday. He is about to sail to Amsterdam. What do you say, Palm? Can you see your position now: you are not free to leave Stralsund, not until the promised education is complete. I am under oath to turn you into a gentleman. Such matters take time. And there is so much waiting for you. Do not misunderstand: this does not mean you can *never* go to Cap Diavolo...but there must be a postponement. Then, and only then we talk again, perhaps on de Groote's next round-trip from the Cape.

You are silent! Tell me your thoughts, Master Palm!'

Freedom curtailed, his chances pushed aside, Palm tried to hide his disappointment. Teacher and pupil had been resting on an embankment overlooking the vast rocky beach, the waves in the distance rolling over, swelling and vanishing, without a pause, under the patient orb of a radiant blue sky, an amiable breeze, languid circling and complaining gulls.

'I am vexed' thought Palm. 'Yet it would seem churlish to argue with my tutor who knows everything and everyone and appears to have a plan for my future. Why not allow this to happen, since he knows so much, means well, seems so fond? I must trust him. He is all I have.'

Together they stared at the Baltic and at the island across the water. An atavistic memory was unwinding in the boy's mind: 'here it may have been, near this spot, when I was almost thrust overboard by my father, and also where that dream of the crowned mother came to me, with her arms spread, when she called out 'my son' and I believed I had seen the remains of Vineta.'

The teacher studied his pupil. First Palm seemed to nod repeatedly, then he shook his head from side to side: 'Now I *do* have a mother but she sits imprisoned in a tower, and I have no idea what she has done. Which iniquitous crime allows men to lock up a noble woman? What shameless devilry had come over her? Do I truly wish to know?

If only I were a beast, even a pig; they know things, almost as people do, but they cannot feel shame.

I would wish to feel the same love for my true mother as I did for my stepmother, Lisebett.'

Then they fell silent.

'This *must* surely be *melancholia*'... passed through Palm's mind.

Seven

The Inn was overflowing. 'Huzza, huzza,' shouted guests in great numbers, raising tumblers, laughing, clatter, chattering, celebrating noisily; in one more, sober corner men were throwing dice.

Two sombre visitors found a way to the only quiet corner which afforded at least some chance of actually hearing what was to be discussed. They bore a lantern, now extinguished. Their sailor friend, already settled with a frothy tumbler of beer, beamed from ear to ear: 'Here I am, Jan de Groote, so honoured to welcome you both, my new and interesting friends in Stralsund.' He rose to his feet, inclined his head in greeting. They bowed and returned the courtesies.

Secretly de Groote congratulated himself on having achieved at least one potential catch: a gentleman, possibly two, who appeared to appreciate the news of an adventurous trip to the other end of the world, to that magic mountain. It was not simple, even in Amsterdam, where one hoped to be in one or two weeks. The task of rounding up possible emigrants was time-consuming and frustrating. Although the republic's merchant fleet had become the world's largest, it was full of rough sailors, yes, not such a difficult task with those, but fine gentlemen with constructive talents, with imagination and a will to help others, such were the ones needed in a new settlement. He had a strong hunch: Master Palm had been won over last night: just the right age, good with his hands, intelligent, unencumbered. The older, more serious one, well, he too might be quite a catch...we must converse for a while.'

'I had hoped you might come down to look over the ship today? It has two large and two smaller masts; we are part of a fleet belonging to the greatest trading nation in the world. To make the return to Amsterdam more profitable we are loading malt and timber to drop off on the way back to the low lands. I was looking out for you.....'

He lifted his mug. He looked at them expectantly.

'Alas, forgive us, de Groote. There will be serious talk tonight. Big decisions are required, life-changing events. Such things must be considered with caution. Let us begin by ordering our meal, and ale, and hearing more of *your* tales of distant lands. Palm has been nowhere as yet, but I have spent time in other towns at least, and in Amsterdam quite recently. A long journey, tiring, by coach and horses. I could not believe my eyes when I first saw Dam Square, brimming with traders and wealthy merchants; commodities from all corners of the earth being weighed at the Waag and one ship after the other sailing up the Damrak. Thanks to the money, the riches, which are pouring in, your city has a welfare system with regular alms being doled out to needy citizens. We will not say too much about the Oude Kerk, and the notorious women in that area, but the Nieuwe Kerk, such splendour, despite the fire. Now there is also your Royal Palace, still under construction...'

The professor nodded and smiled, remembering: 'Just being there was rewarding but also a necessary part of my studies for there are fine teachers, thinkers and speakers in your city. Such a flourishing place! I stayed in the Houtgracht for a while and also around the Voorburgwal. I found prosperity and stimulating thinkers and people in fine homes, and that Van den Enden's bookshop and his Kunst-Winkel, you must know these places?' De Groote's young face flushed with pleasure: 'A man who knows and appreciates my home city! What an honour to spend time with you, Mynheer. You even appear to have a few words of 'de taal.'

Palm, listening to all this, felt strangely threatened: things were not the same. The sailor, just a stranger, and his teacher enjoyed lively exchanges while he was left brooding, feeling unsettled, after those revelations this morning. He had no desire to smile, or even talk, and again they started up: 'De Drie Fleschjes' and the varieties of Gin you buy there, and now about Spinoza, a man of influence and wisdom. Well, I have never heard of him. What is he to me? My own professor, suddenly a complete stranger, speaks with fervour of the teeming life in Amsterdam, as if he were languishing in Stralsund for *my* sake...deprived of the real world, longing to be elsewhere.'

Palm, consumed, suspicious: his teacher preferred talking with this wretched sailor.

Dejected, his eyes roamed and there she was: his favourite Minna. She had seen him too. Their eyes met, they smiled. Palm instantly forgot his resentment and immersed himself in tender admiration of her special loveliness.

'She will surely come over to this table. And if she does it means she really cares... if she does not it means she has a lover already, or she is very shy. I would love to,.. try to, hold her hand, look closely at her face, look into her eyes.' His dreams were disturbed when his teacher turned to him: 'May I suggest, Master Palm: might you now be ready to speak to Jan about *our* proposal?'

Uncomfortable, too sudden, this return to reality!

Palm's pleasing reverie had flickered out of reach, harshly displaced by reality: his teacher still held the reigns and was gazing expectantly at him. But realising there would be nothing forthcoming the tutor re-directed his speech at the sailor:

'It seems I must speak for us both, de Groote. Palm and I are greatly stimulated by the thought of seeing the other side of the globe. But we need more time. Young Palm, who is perhaps not very much younger than you, is under a binding contract to become an educated man. He is to take up some as yet unspecified place of authority in society. I see him in Law perhaps, one day. We need another three winters and summers of intense labour before he becomes free to leave books, learning and immersion into wisdom and history of our world behind for a while. What you propose has a flavour and attraction which will, by then, prove a perfect counter-balance to all he has absorbed. I can imagine us both longing for the day when we embark on such a venture: to sail away from the Baltic to the North Sea and then to the Atlantic, perhaps for quite some time. The Dutch East India Company will surely take many years to establish this important refurbishment station, and the governor may by then be able to make use of two men from northern countries, both able-bodied, who can make a contribution to the best of their ability, as men of honour and integrity. Do I bore you?'

De Groote and Palm stared at Professor Ruetz. Such authority! Who would dream of arguing with his reasoning? They remained silent, drank their ale, stared at the grainy wood pattern of the table top, elbows on the table. Palm raised his head, rolled his shoulders and sighing, shook his light-brown locks from side to side (noting the tiny cricks in his neck) and muttered: 'So be it, so be it! It is as it is, life must run smoothly. I agree with my teacher's suggestions'....and then, mysteriously: 'One must roll ones head like this more often, the muscles in the neck become so tight...'**Kopparbeit is de schworst säd de Buer, dat seih ik an mienen Ossen*, ...that old saying of my father's, when he'd pat his yoked beast's muscular neck, smiling at his little jest; he only rented that ox you know: it is the best help for ploughing, making furrows in beet fields.

*('*Head work is the hardest' said the peasant,' I see that with my oxen'*...Old Pomeranian German).

Jan de Groote looked bemused. What was it with this Palm...was he Pomeranian peasant stock or was he a gentleman? Had he had too much to drink? In confusion the boy stared at his food, then tucked into diced herrings mixed lavishly with sliced potatoes. Glancing at his tutor for support Palm extended a hand to Jan and announced: 'We will come to your Cape as soon as we are ready, Jan, believe me, we look forward to that. But today something unusual has happened in my life, and I am only just getting used to it. One day I may tell you more.'

Although the sailor nodded he was becoming ever more bewildered.

If the truth were told Palm's thoughts and eyes had mostly been elsewhere, during these exchanges. Remaining in Stralsund may well have its compensations, as far as he was concerned. 'As to Headwork,' he thought quietly to himself, 'I have a surprise for my Minna: those 300 year old verses we came across last week, a loose sheet in my Professor's book, (we were studying the Slav rulers of Rügen,) written by a Minne-singer, a singer of love.

Palm was quietly planning an attack on his beautiful and unsuspecting victim. Had anyone ever before read Minna a poem? Might she be pleased I connect *her* name with *Minne,* meaning 'love'?

My, this ale is good...' He took another long swig.

Jan de Groote and Palm's mentor continued gossip about Spinoza, the learnèd man who appeared to be making prescription lenses for spectacles; 'what skills he had', and the strange views he took on life. The Professor showed knowledge and compassion, but Palm barely listened, took in just the occasional phrase, explanation, wondered about the name 'Spinoza', and 'why were they so impressed by such a man, who sounded like a rebel? Was this a grown-up thing? And Jan de Groote...why was he such congenial company? He was a sharp one! At first only a boy sailor, he was now conversing with my Professor on equal footing?' So it seemed. He must have studied in some fine school. He was only pretending to be a sailor.

Anyone could be a sailor.

Fate had to take its course, Cap Diavolo would have to wait. Palm's eyes were getting heavy after a long day and strong ale he was passing time by remembering words and sentiments of the 'Minna'-song:

Consolation in winter. Yes, she will like that. Especially now in the dark months ...

Leaves blow, from trees to the valley, branches are bare. Flowers fade, wreaths have wilted, those which decorated the dancing.

'I have never danced in my life, will she show me? I doubt my mentor knows such things. What comes next, ah yes…'the roots of trees, stiff with freezing and icy frost; my mind grows dull, my senses saddened. Come, pure dreams, bring gentle consolation to Winter. New joy must be practised'…what are such words really telling us?'

Let us greet a thousand joys at this hour, more than May can bring.

Roses blossom on the red mouths of women, let us sing of those!

Let winter rage; her face is strewn with all delights of scent. Raise her up!

There is no higher rapture than when the beloved delights me.

'Dancing, swirling ecstatic words, from a mind of someone buried for three centuries. What luck I remember things I read with such ease. Have thoughts changed so much that this song is now ridiculous? Will Minna laugh at me? What can it mean: *roses blossoming on red mouths of women*, roots, stiff with freezing'…

Palm's face was pale, there were dark shadows around his eyes. His head drooped.

De Groote and the Professor soon gathered up cloaks and lanterns, with sincere but improbable promises to meet again in two, not three years time, God willing...indeed, they nodded, and God speed! Letters of importance would be sent to the Dutch East India Company in Amsterdam on Nieuwmarkt, to be forwarded.

'….and indeed, Professor, I will send a message, through the Inn keeper, when I next dock in Stralsund. No, no, I will not forget, I have greatly enjoyed your company. Back to light and warmth, to the very tip of Africa, it is so cold, so very dark in Europe...too bad about the cargo of sheep's-wool and skins loaded for Sweden, the smell is not pleasing, but thanks be to God, only for two nights, perhaps three.'

They shook hands, heads inclined politely. They bowed. Then they parted company, not quite, but almost like old friends.

The November night was raw and still, but for a distant dog. Professor Ruetz carried the flickering lantern but Palm kept his eyes down.

They walked in silence. Stralsund was asleep.

***

Have I overslept?

Is it still night?

Perhaps not, I see small streaks of light by the window, so now, time to rise and set down on paper all the concerns regarding my pupil. My body obeys my mind which has brought the command: 'seize the day.'

Yes, I must, I shall…

The tutor sits up and carefully dips his quilled pen into the ink pot, wondering how to begin:

Notes to myself, Martin Ruetz, written in the early hours of Martin's Day… the 11th day of the 11th month and also the day of Martin Luther's baptism.

I have taken the plunge, yesterday, with the account of Palm's mother, daughter of King Christian 1V. My pupil was not as surprised as I feared. A curious one, this boy, with his dreams of queens and Vineta! And thus began the inevitable monologue, which must soon change into dialogue. Palm was amenable, but a little shaken nevertheless. I know him well enough now to see the signs. I must be careful what I reveal, also when and how it is correct to do so. He has a sensitive soul.

In the evening, dining in the harbour inn with our commendable Dutch East India Company representative, further but predictable problems have come to the fore: Palm has become too dependent. He resents when he cannot keep up with the conversation and it becomes clear how much work is needed to rise to the level of a gentleman, one who will be taken seriously. I see more clearly the long path ahead.

Furthermore, he shows signs of interest in a very young girl, who works at the Inn, lovely of course, but I foresee him losing his head. Above all, I must protect him from such troubles as I myself have suffered. My plain speaking should prove effective and disarming. When all is made clear, when I speak with an open heart, what has happened to me may not be such an outrage, perhaps not even a misfortune. And yet I beat my breast, feel ashamed.

I steel myself. I shall use my own experience as caveat, as counsel, for him. I have won his trust. My position alone, 'in loco parentis' is already in some sense 'reparation'.

He need not see it quite in this way.

This, my account, is not clear. My debt is not paid. I must make use of all that has happened to me to help us both. I am troubled, a profligate, suffering the sin of pride.

What can be done?

***

'Two years', sighs Palm, 'even three. Learning, nothing but books, and discussion! You spoke of horses, horse-riding during the long cold months, Professor, what has happened to your promise?'

The teacher, exhausted from lack of sleep, had tightened his lips, he nodded, eyes closed… but remained silent. Palm chattered on:

'St. Martin's Day, two years ago, I was still with my family. We were all content. We celebrated, always on the 11th November, an important time on farms when the harvest is finally over and the slaughtering of beasts begins. First it was the geese, by now full and plump. If they were not used for making payment to the landowner (many of us are still tenants on these lands), they were 'pierced' in the night, which is how one slaughters these animals, the blood was gathered in large clay pots and mixed with vinegar, so that it remained fresh,…it is called 'Schwarz-sauer', and my brother and I did not like it. But we Pomeranians say it is the best food in the world.'

Palm's teacher was leaning back, his eyes half closed, arms folded behind his head, legs stretched out before him. The boy, unused to the sight of an almost recumbent teacher continued his description of life in the country…one of the few things he truly knew about.

'A St. Martin's goose has healing powers, you know…its fat, rubbed in, helps against gout and its blood against fevers. My mother rubbed me once for a fever and also used the wishbone, because it fulfils wishes provided you get the right end. She usually did because I was always better the next morning…'

'…on the same night goose feathers and down were put up in the attic to dry. And the delicious healing goose fat? It was mixed with salt and herbs and onion….eaten spread on bread. The goose breast, which is hung up in the smoke-hut, will be prepared for Advent and for the Christmas feast. And then there was Martin's Day!

Martin's Day is *not* to celebrate Luther but another Martin, some apostle, no, a bishop, who lived over one thousand years before us. He was a good man who cut his cloak in half to give to a cold beggar-man by the roadside. I have not thought much about St. Martin, to be honest. Do you know about him, Professor?'

'Certainly Palm, none of this is new to me, but, pray continue your account. It pleases me to hear you open up, to hear you speak like this. Last night, in company, you were dreary and silent…continue, do continue!'

Palm, not used to praise, spun on with gusto.

'…during the second half of November it was time for the pigs. The men did all the hard work. We, the children, helped making sausages, holding the intestines and binding up the ends with string and then carrying them to the cooking-pots or to the smoke hut…but the women and girls sat around tables with mountains of feathers, to sort them for different uses. The young men knew tales to tell, either cheerful or terrifying, songs were sung, and if there was a pipe or a fiddle there might be dancing and merry-making. It was a pleasing time. And now? All I do is read. And discuss, and read again and so on. I miss the old ways, especially last night, after the harbour inn. How was it for you, when you were young, Professor? May I ask such a question? Will I be forgiven? I imagine the years ahead and see nothing but books, books and evermore books. I am afraid. I am a prisoner, with only one, now very distant goal: to be a gentleman who will, one day, perhaps, visit a magic mountain'.

They looked into each other's' eyes, then Palm stared at his feet, upset, embarrassed. The Professor turned slowly. He stepped over to the window, thoughts racing. He had failed. He needed an authoritative reply, one without loss of credibility.

'Indeed, Palm, yes, excellent. There is truth in your lively description: honest, good life, sharing company and laughter, and tasks as you described from your past. I sense how you feel, and, believe me, I am sorry for that. You are paying a price, now that your life is changing.

I have taken it upon myself to make you entirely comfortable in living the life of a gentleman, adding, believe me, not taking away, a dimension to your former life in the old Pomeranian country ways. Please do not lose heart; you are making huge advances. But yes, I both hear and I see the difficulty. I will try harder. I myself have become as dry as an old stick, without much enjoyment. There *are* reasons.

I am resolved to tell you, bear with me, this is difficult...'

Palm feels concern for his kind tutor. Has he gone too far?

'...I will arrange the horses. I will enquire about early morning choral practice. We must honour every moment we spend together, give an account of each day, of every hour. A new regime: after St. Nicholas' day, the sixth of December, later the Nativity; give me until then. There will be a new timetable for you.'

The tutor stepped over to the fireplace: 'Before that, I have something pressing we must talk about, a predicament, a tender spot, a thorn in my flesh.' He paused, agitated, seemingly gasping for air.

'Let us build up a fire, Palm, such a chill in this room! Will you collect a few logs from the store down in the cellar? I have a flagon of good wine. We will discuss as friends; feel free to question, to interrupt, as if *I* were in the dock. You may see yourself as judge.

What a chill to-night' he rubs his hands, 'it will be the first fire I allow myself this winter. 'Mens sana in corpore sano', one should never neglect the 'corpore'...it is only Latin, you know, but has found itself into all European languages, forgive me, Palm, I simply cannot suppress my urge to teach you all the time.'

'Corpore, corper....Körper' (*body*) sounds a little like it, I believe, Professor?' The teacher beams: 'and therefore...Corpus Christi means ...' 'why, professor, the body of Christ, one can but hope'.

'What an asset, you are, Master Palm. Your clear mind will stand you in good stead. *Mens sana* means healthy mind, *in corpore sano,* in a healthy body, *sano,* sanity is soundness, balance.

But now, I beg you, get those logs, and also a light...so we can discuss with healthy minds in comforting, comfortable warmth. Do not imagine I have been completely overwhelmed by melancholia, Palm!'

***

Palm's tutor, now on his feet, is striding to and fro near the flickering logs, his arms linked before his chest, as if to protect himself from hostile blows: 'how one wishes to forget,... but the past, it stays with us. So, Palm, I begin with *my* beginning:

Yes, it was pleasing enough! And you may be surprised to know my family has lived for centuries not far from Stralsund, on this side of the Oder River, but further to the south. My father was a Mecklenburg land-owner...a fine area with wealthy landowners. In *his* employ were several families not unlike your own, who helped run the estate.

Like most privileged boys I spent much of the day in the care of a tutor. My father and mother, with their large circle of friends, mostly landowners like themselves, enjoyed time devoted to horse-riding, or going for long walks or hunting game in the woods. I was taught to ride and read and also the names of plants and of stones, but especially to take aim and shoot correctly.' The tutor stared out into the cold night, a few windows still lit on the other side of the cobbled road.

'Our home was large, with a high tiled roof in which there were many attic rooms for the cook and maids and housekeeper. Stables and a coach house stood on the other side of a handsome paved yard with an ancient Linden tree at one end, a favourite place to sit and read. I was a healthy but somewhat dreamy boy who loved nothing better than to read.

My parents' wish was I should study in larger centres of learning, as soon as I was old enough. Aged eighteen I rode with father to Berlin; we found lodgings for my new student life and muddling through at the start I began to attend lectures. I was soon in control of my own daily routines, if not my destiny. Or so I believed.

Then, in 1656 a message came: 'return home at once'. Marauding soldiery or ruffians passing that way had, one night, jointly attacked our home and outlying houses and stables, as well as the farm workers. It seemed a planned event: they attacked from several sides at once, just like a battlefield. My father was badly injured defending his property, several dwellings were burnt down, workers were injured, three of them killed. Distraught but determined to hide her grief and their humiliation, my dear mother, now poor for the first time (as she saw it) obliged me to return and this I did, glad to be able to help. I suggested they might like to leave life in the country, come to the big town, but no, this was the family home, they loved the land, insisted on staying. And thus, having rolled up their sleeves and joined with labourers to bring fields and the property back in order, with the help of fair sums of money (my father had cleverly hidden some behind stones in the cellar), he hired help and got everyone back to work. From then on most of our labourers were equipped with weapons, should future attacks occur.

I stayed for one year, learned to think about practical matters, becoming friendly with the labourers on our land, particularly with one very lively young woman, an excellent cook and helper in the house, while my mother cared for father. The helper's name was Sophia. Five years older than I was, dark eyed with long lashes and brown tumbling silken locks, she asked about my reading and learning. Whenever there was time we walked in the surrounding fields and woods, exchanged thoughts and confidences. I became besotted with her, determined never to leave her or home again, and my mother, that brave and determined woman, was glad to have me there. I believed my studies were over. Real life had become more important. Then my father died. He never fully recovered his health after the attackers struck him down with swords. His wounds and broken bones had healed but his will to live was gone. He made my mother promise I should return to my studies, to become a judge or a man of science, rather than grow old as a landowner.'

Palm listened eagerly, aghast. His teacher's history was so unexpected, and so painful.

Then there was more:

'Sophia consoled me. We had become inseparable. She stroked my face, smiled, spoke kind words and one evening, after we had read that ancient elegy to passionate love, the one *you* were at pains to recall last night...in careless and carefree innocence...I forgot myself. Not long after she began swelling with child. Master Palm, imagine such a thing: *my* own child! I was not yet twenty. My mother remarked on Sophia's condition, questioned me about the possible father, but in my cowardly way I shrugged, looked away, pretending I had nothing to say. Sophia was carrying *my mother's* first grandchild. If my mother suspected she gave no hint. On the day of the birth she assisted Sophia, while I hid in my room, windows and shutters shut, drapes drawn, pillows over my ears, so as not to hear my screaming friend and lover, her agonies of pain, hour after hour. Why is nature so cruel? I wanted to die.

It was Sophia who died. I lived. She was no mere trollop, Palm, believe me, she was an honourable girl and neither of us meant to cause harm. Such events come from simple entrapment, a momentary delight of nature.

By the time I'd found the courage to confess to my mother she had already decided to take on the child as her own, to bring it up as her own daughter. She named her Maria. There was much whispering and gossip among the labourers, but honest country people quickly forget such things. Sophia appeared to have no known relatives so my mother cared for the infant while I was sent off to Heidelberg, to continue my studies. Soon, to earn my keep as best I could, I was tutoring young children in private.

For many years I have lived on my wits. Now my new responsibility is to you, and, of course, as long as I live, to my mother and to little Maria.

My own child, already almost two years old will believe me to be her brother. My mother wishes it that way. Now, no longer as strong as she has been, my mother begins to feel her age. Harvests have been poor. I send income to them as often as possible. I am responsible.

Master Palm, is it now clear to you why I must earn money, why I took on the post of being your tutor?'

Palm saw tears in his teacher's eyes but turned away pretending not to notice. He could not bear to see this. Why was his tutor so ill at ease; this strong man weakened by, well, what precisely?' Palm searched to find something friendly to say, and thinking of the festivities of St. Nicholas, so very soon now he muttered softly, gently, as he rose to warm his hands by the fireplace: 'we must both see things with, well, fresh eyes, yes, new, fresh eyes, to find good things in the present and the future. I will do all I can to make your teaching bear fruit, Professor, so you may take pride in being my tutor. I thank you for honouring me with such confidences.'

'I was not going to tell you any of this, Palm, but it came to me last night: I am in a strong position to use this cautionary tale for *your* very own protection, young man...I saw you eyeing that young woman last night...Minna? Is that her name?'

The windows rattled loudly with renewed ferocious gusts from the Baltic, underlining silent thoughts of both pupil and teacher.

'Look in my eyes, Palm! One should not want anything too much in this life. It is said God grants the wishes of those whom he intends to punish.'

Palm, alarmed, looked but smiled sheepishly. He thought it best to remain silent. As if born to diplomacy he solemnly advised his tutor:

'...there is a storm starting up, do you hear it, now, even as we speak? November rains, blowing in from the Baltic.... hear that gust shaking the window, Professor? The commotion will keep us awake. Poor Jan on his boat! May I leave you now, I counted eleven bells?'

'Indeed. God bless you Palm. How right you are, it is late. You have been a good listener. But try to think on it. Absorb and learn from my painful, shameful confession.'

Eight

First snows had settled on meadows and by rivers and roads, but not in the town. When puddles in town turned to ice, or when snow on roofs melted and turned to icicles…*then* it was Advent. All children knew this. Smiling happily they'd say: 'Soon it will be Christmas'. Grownups had to begin thinking about festivities.

A tale was told about an ancient bishop, Otto von Bamberg, who, having been baptised in Pomerania, was condemned to death by local heathens who worshipped false gods. Jeering bystanders promised a reprieve if the bishop could make flowers bloom during the night in the bitter December cold. On the way to the scaffold on the following morning the entire path was covered in dark-red blooms: Christmas-roses.

The condemned bishop, instantly freed, converted Pomeranians to the teachings and festivals of Christians. In later years the Christmas-rose was used as decoration during the festive season. The plant seeds had been carried to Pomerania by a rare bird, which nested and bred during the dark cold months but came from southern parts of Europe. Witches, but also ordinary citizens believed the plant had magical and medicinal powers.

***

Palm and the Professor were out riding stallions. Purchased by the Swedish governor from Polish lands further to the east, they were today on loan to tutor and pupil. Riding skills and general deportment in the manner of a gentleman, all such skills were part of Palm's development. He now reached forward to pat the neck of 'Satan', his snorting, prestigious silvery steed, a fiery, noble animal and full of tricks.

'So, in God's name, Satan, let us go', said Palm. He cracked his whip. Satan preferred a gentle pace.

'Fine, just fine' he thought proudly, 'riding on such a saddle; I've been instructed to saddle, to mount...and to guide a horse.

Last time I rode the neighbours' mare at home, a large broad horse, she did her best to shake me off...how I clung to her mane...she got the better of me, but now see *this* noble beast, so very well-bred, he's only snapped at me once, as we rode off. Satan has accepted me.'

Any lack of confidence soon vanished as riding became part of the new order. A radiant day, clouds swept away by night storms, and they were on their way to Palm's father and brother, bringing wine and cake, tokens for the Christmas feast.

Guards in the town-gate barely looked up, absorbed in throwing dice as usual....

To the riders' surprise they came upon a patch of those hardy Christmas blooms, on the side of the coast road. How peaceful, how heart warming: a sunny December morning...the air cleared last night; an eagle swooped gracefully, all sign of frosts melted away, and now a patch of dark royal red petals glowing in the pale winter sunshine. Palm was tempted to stop, dig some up to take along as a gift. But then he the remembered rules: if there were eagles flying overhead, it was a certain sign of death...best to ride on, this was no time to stop.

'Left here,' Palm was guiding the horse, while reassuring his companion, 'we take this sandy path, through the ferns, it is used by traders who serve the outlying farmers from time to time, the knife-sharpener, and also the only tinker in the district, he's known for his shoddy work, he comes this way and tries to please as best he can...it must surely be difficult to be a tinker, one's chances slim....' Palm was chattering happily, animated by this unexpectedly prestigious journey out of town. 'I have not seen father or brother for many months, what will they think and say when they see us arrive, and me in my new clothes... on such a fine horse?'

Palm's heart missed a beat: smoke was rising, it curled up from the chimney as always; he had come home. Tears came to his eyes: 'this will not do, no, not at all.' The horses snorted, shook their manes, stood scraping the hard earth, small clouds of condensed breath vanished into the winter air from their nostrils... noble equine heads lowered to test the partly frozen water trough.

Palm leaned forward, stroked the silvery neck of 'Satan'....and then his brother appeared by the door... wide staring eyes, ashen-faced, his clothing tattered, his hair unkempt; not expecting the noise of hooves and snorting horses he showed barely a flicker of welcome as Palm rushed to him, arms stretched towards the brother who, shaking his head, pointed inside the dark house: 'It is father, Palm, he fell from the roof yesterday...he is in pain, cannot move at all, he has broken his back, or his ribs, I fear, he barely draws breath, his lungs may be punctured...or his spleen...' he stared uselessly at the visitors. 'How is it you knew to come at this terrible time?'

Palm pushed his brother aside, hastened into the gloom to the shape on the bed; fearful groans and writhing, gasps for air, an injured man in agony. The young men stood, tormented, helpless, undecided; within minutes Palm's tutor turned back to summon the town's only eminent physician, a man shortly returned from studies with a famed Danish surgeon. The professor galloped off, taking both horses.

The boys clung to each other. Then Palm leaned over his step-father, grasped a cold trembling hand: 'I am here father, help will come, be calm, father, try to breathe peacefully...slowly, father, we will find a physician, a man of medicine.'

'Christmas flowers, bring the flowers'...'the injured man gasped, showing no sign of recognition. He was too far gone, in too much pain.

Palm soothed his step-fathers' head, stroked a cold, wrinkled, spotty hand. Then, turning about, peering into the dark corner where the fire was, he saw a woman's shape busying itself, leaning forward stirring a pot, intently staring, absorbed in her task.

'Ursel', his brother nodded in her direction. 'Remember, 'strange Ursel', the blue-eyed daughter from the neighbour's farm, the one we thought was touched in the head? She is still deprived of her wits but she cooks for us, helps every day, does what we tell her.

'Ursel...how can that be? She is unhinged, she rambles, Christian! Is this wise?'

'She does what she is told, obeys like a lamb and knows quite a few useful things, Palm, believe me, I understand her well enough...what no-one comprehends is how to stop father's suffering. The neighbours have looked in, the pastor will come soon. I have been up all night. Perhaps help will come from Stralsund? It is a miracle you have turned up at this time. I am so very weary, can barely keep my eyes open, will you sit with him, while I close my eyes for an hour or two?'

'Of course brother, I will stay right here, by his side, until help comes....'

But Christian had turned away, whispering: 'Our father cannot live, brother, he is barely connected with us. How extraordinary you have come, now, at this very moment, not knowing. He must not hear me speak like this...but he cannot live, of that I am certain, quite certain.'

***

'This is loneliness. Our father died in the night. We are left adrift in a huge silence. His death was real, it tore our hearts out. It snaps at our heels wherever we walk. It will be with us, me and my brother, forever. On the two occasions I've returned to my home...each time there has followed a death... I must never go again. My tutor suggests I am duped by superstition, I am misguided. I feel so lost: these new paths I have taken are crumbling. I am left in a lonely un-grounded-ness, with only two people in my life: my tutor, yes, real enough...and my brother, not kinsman by blood, as I *now* know. His new responsibilities, and his daily life with a woman, that 'Strange Ursel' who keeps him comfortable, strikes me as surprising, unaccountable.

We always knew Ursel, she lived near us with her mother, who guided her mostly silent, child...a girl who inhabited her skin lightly, yet to others, dangerously...her mind a dark unknown cave. She could not reason. We thought *for* her...she obeyed, she trusted us, but what can trust really know? We imagined her tenderness, joy, even shame. She needed protection. Our imagining gave us the confidence to love her. Now she cooks, she cleans, does what she is told. She feels, surely more than animals.

I ask myself...what is it that makes us human?

Should we be defined by our ambitions, knowledge, our destinies? What defines a human with a mind like Ursel's: might it be only hunger and basic needs in an empty cave, boundless darkness?

I have returned to my studies, left my brother behind with Ursel.

My thoughts bring ever more questions.

And Minna? She is my secret, the only soul who may have powers to guide me through that 'metamorphosis'... my new word, taught me during the studies of powerful foreign words. My tutor keeps a long list of these: from Melancholia to Metamorphoses to Nemesis...words which appear surrounded with threatening shadows; I dwell on their meanings, wrestle with their sounds. My former *special* words, the ones my mother, no, my stepmother taught me: 'Illyria, Venezia, Mercury'...those cheering sounds, like joyous music, I have yet to hear words to match those.

I am told St. Augustin believed that 'those who sing pray twice'. I have been thinking about this contrivance. It is pleasing but surely deceptive, perhaps only true of devout songs....such as those sung in Church.

I am to present myself to the choir master. At least there is that.

***

The day began well, although it did not please me to be up before the sun. A serving maid had to beat loudly on my door this morning to get me out of bed for the first meeting with the master of music at the Marienkirche.

During a private meeting in a small room containing a musical instrument on four legs the musician ran his fingers nimbly along narrow strips of wood, a row of differing tones he called his 'spinet'. Then, sitting before it, he stroked it like a beloved pet animal, filling the room with resonance and surprising me by bursting into song: just a few words, words that I have heard full well, and that I love dearly, a Christmas song often sung by the congregation in my village:

'Es ist ein Ros entsprungen...

Aus einer Wu-u-urzel zart...'

Studying my face as he sang, he supported the song by touching the strips of wood, all the while commanding me to 'sing boy, sing those words...just the first nine words will do,' and then he started once more, nodding at me with an encouraging smile.

My face became hot as I searched for the matching sound in my throat. He turned, remarked: 'Again boy. Boldly, with strength, if you please.'

He looked at me, struck the spinet with his left...raised his right arm, signalling to begin. I tried again. Quite loudly, I thought. His raised hand made graceful movements, followed the tune, first up, then down, as if drawing sounds from the air. I looked at the pattern, and stopped when his hand dropped. A strange compulsion, to draw sounds from the air. He turned, looked at me searchingly, and then frowned.

'You said you had never sung before? This I find difficult to believe: your voice is true, even pleasing', then, stroking his beard, 'perhaps not quite settled yet. The only hurdle you must overcome is learning to read such sounds on paper. Come closer to the spinet. Master Palm. Let me show you an example...'

A painless start; and such rewards…

'After some instruction in basic music vocabulary, terms, signs and symbols for reading, I now sing the line of the tenor at choir practice. Challenging as this is I must learn to read my own line while adjusting to the accompanying sounds. I can say I find great satisfaction fitting my voice into the harmonious whole, forming mysterious complex structures which hover pleasingly in the air and ear and continue to echo in the mind deep into the night. Then there is the magical trickery of accidentals, twisting sounds towards the light or back into the dark, followed by adjustments to new horizons, states of being.

Could it be true that *singing* and *being* a tenor are matters distinct from each other? One is a manner of existence, a means of expressing emotions in rising passages…showing resurrection, joy and heaven, and then the descending passages searching on the other side: hell, depths of depravity, suffering, even…death.

***

Being a tenor with other boys and men soon became a condition of strength and kinship. Those who studied or taught at the school, said little, showed respect for the choirmaster, but also for me, a mere beginner. Choristers were intelligent, punctual and disciplined. Twice a week they looked to each other, smiled, nodded and depended on each other as they practised in their church; not such a dark and mysterious place as the one in which Palm took fright less than a year ago. The sounds they created surged, swelled, swerved into the distance and returned. It was frightening each time, this resonance, even now that Palm's mind was made strong. There was always candlelight from stout white candles to the right of each singer. A smaller boy with long, golden locks singed his hair just yesterday.

Choristers asked no questions, were unfailingly polite. Perhaps they had been told Palm was 'a special case.' He would have liked to know who they thought he was but told himself to be patient. So much had changed. His great loneliness was now diffuse, scattered about. He met and befriended boys and men, even horses on each Sunday, after the service. From time to time he thought of his poor brother, now only a brother in word since they had but grown up together, suckled by the same woman. Always, hidden in a small corner of his thoughts, there was Minna. With less free time to visit the inn near the harbour she had surely forgotten his face by now.

Professor Ruetz claimed to have neither ear nor voice, and few friends. He had a great need to be alone, but was proud of Palm, he said.

***

'We, the singers, look very fine in special gowns when we sing in the Marien Choir; our next public event is in honour of the organist, Herr Buxtehude. He is in Denmark at present, but plans to visit us again; it seems he hopes to move here or to Lübeck. We must sing one of his settings as well as songs from our own copy of the Speiersche Gesangbuch of 1600, and also music by Praetorius, whose true name, I understand, is Schultze.

Three other composers, Schütz, Schein and Scheidt share the program...small wonder Herr Schultze changed his name to the preferred Praetorius...this clearly has a ring to it, does *not* begin with '*sch*' and is more joyful sounding than Schultze, although the meaning is the same, according to my tutor, the expert in Latin. Schultze, or indeed Herr Praetorious, wrote down at least one thousand songs and died not too far from here, creating voluminous works of reference dealing entirely with music. It seems hard to believe there is that much to write down about music.... but who am I to say?'

***

'Now the time has come, Master Palm: on to more serious matters. Remember Confucius? That man of deep and lasting beliefs and thoughts?' Palm looked at his feet, shook his locks from side to side:

'Not much, Professor. This is a word which leads me to nothing but *confu-sion*. Was he not a Chinaman? One who believed one should not do to others what you would not wish them to do to you, this much I do recall, and was his name not changed to our own language?'

'Forsooth,' smiled the teacher. The name among his own people and in his own language was K'ung Fu-tsu, the philosopher Kung. I like this; again you have shown me signs of a bright and lively mind. But before we move on: what do you know about the word *Philosophy*? It must go on our list along with *Melancholia* and the rest! I do believe we spoke of Confucius in connection with your true father, and all I said was to 'put him on our list.'

'Your list, Professor, is never-ending. I still wait to hear about Charlemagne, the man who was related to my father... this is what you said. At least I would get a little closer to the truth I so wait for!'

'First a time-scale, dear Palm, and more patience: Charlemagne lived a very long time before your father, when the world was a different place. And Confucius lived an even longer time before Charlemagne. Once we have traversed a vast amount of human thought and almost 1000 years, only then will you be ready to learn about your father. Trust me. Keep your mind open for commendable, seemly things, reap from the wisdom of paragons of history, bearing in mind even they can become limbs of Satan.'

'Limbs of Satan?' Palm's head was reeling. He had learnt *paragon* was a model of excellence and that *philo sophia* meant to love wisdom. 'And,' his teacher admonished: 'the ancient Greeks did not believe wisdom came readily to human beings; its possession was and remained a highly prized and rare but dangerous thing.'

'What then is this wisdom which I must absorb, Professor?'

Palm was told that Confucius advised his followers to return to former days; to learn from sages and return to principles of better times than the ones current in his own life: there should be no doctrine of God, nor any of spirits, nor of a future life. He believed religion was a good thing only because it promoted peace and order, so that he encouraged it as a discipline, not something to speculate about.

'Keep your mind for the practical matters of life: each man has a duty to cultivate his best qualities and to suppress the bad. Knowledge is the key to virtue...if men know what is wrong and the evil it causes, they will avoid it. And, please note, Master Palm: the means by which virtue is cultivated are: the study of poetry, the study of music and the study of ceremonial and manners. We are well on the way then, what say you, Palm?'

Palm remained silent. He had difficulty with such free-thinking over one thousand years ago. Even from his relaxed Lutheran background he was shaken to the core: 'Not believe in *any* God...is that what he said?'

His mentor nodded. Now very solemn, Palm betrayed no judgement.

'Consider yet more wisdom, Palm: before the time of Confucius lived a Persian called Zoroaster, a prophet from the 6th century *before* Christ, or even earlier, no-one quite knows. To most this is so long past that it is hard to grasp. The language of *his* verses lead us to believe he came from the east of Persia but it may never be clear when he lived on this earth; it is known however that he was only 30 years old when he was 'called' to become a prophet. With his followers he roamed and wandered about spreading his belief in religious purity, in justice amongst people and also his distrust of powerful men and corrupt priests. And yet, with such beliefs, he won over and befriended a king and his court and became the court prophet and writer, which is why we now have some of his preserved writing. Zoroaster, also known as Zarathustra, was never thought to be divine, he remained a man like you and me, but claimed inspiration from Ahuru Mazda, a name which stands for mysterious Eastern wisdom,...he was a wise Lord, who appointed Zarathustra to 'bring benefit' to humanity.

Look at it like this, Master Palm...at the beginning of time the world was divided into Good and Evil. Between these each man was, is, duty-bound to decide.

Each and every man, fully responsible for his fate! You, and I, the Swedish Governor, the Pastor and the Organist, your father and Confucius, to say nothing of Zarathustra...we all make or made choices.' Palm looked thoughtful.

'And women, Professor, you never speak of them and their choices?'

Your percipience pleases me, Master Palm. You might be perturbed to read lists and further lists of famed women, those who have been remembered since ancient times... I assume you have heard of Eve, the 'wife' of Adam. Now *there* was a woman...I have often wondered,...who had to make a *more* important choice: the dilemma of the apple before her eyes, the hissing snake, the 'tree of knowledge,' and then that backlash to her choice,...we could make a very long study to deduce the truth from this analogy. Furthermore we have copies of 'De mulieribus claris'...a book about the lives of 106 famous women, written some time in the 14th century by one Boccaccio... translated into German in the last century. There is an excellent reference to Agrippina, wife of Germanicus, (now this was a most famed man) and also to Venus, the queen of Cyprus, who was borne in much beauty from the ocean, floating on a shell, and many more, even about a woman Pope who gave birth. I have seen a woodcut of this event... a great shock to many one might say!

You grin, my young friend? The author, who wrote about female fame and achievement included not only their desires and longing, but also brought some of the oldest stories from the realm of myths to our advanced minds of 1668. I will try to find this book for you, but it may take a while. I fine entertainment, to read on a long journey, and please do not believe I am making light of the subject matter; know that I am personally much taken with a woman called Hildegard of Bingen, who has a long chapter and truly deserves it…'

***

We are invited, my teacher, and I, to a ceremony and a gathering in the home of the Swedish Governor.

The tailor has measured me for a set of festive garments the likes of which I find difficult to describe. He claims I have grown one hand taller and have broadened overall… that I am 'strapping'… perhaps on my way to 'imposing;' that there is need for much fine and costly material.

Best to stop growing any further.

There are stern looks from my tutor; in a 'fatherly' fashion he passes no judgement. I return for a further trying-on in four days from now, on my own.

Perhaps I might slip down to the harbour very briefly.

'…for some fresh air'….should I be questioned.

***

Nine

January, 1667. Reception at the Swedish Governor's House,

'Master Palm Uhlefeld, your Honour: a student of mine.'

Instructed to hold the left arm behind his back, to remove his cap with a grand flourish while leaning forward, to keep his balance on the right foot resting slightly to the front of the other, Palm now showed shapely legs, dressed as he was in finest hose and buckled shoes. Bowing correctly requires balance and grace: he had practised before a mirror, but he felt ridiculous...still, everyone was doing it, that is, those who were not clerics or military. It was necessary to distinguish one from the other. One must know and honour people of rank in the prescribed manner.

The Swedish Governor and his wife stood before a panelled wall. High above them a finely carved blood-coloured griffin reared up as if in battle, clawing the air with a ferocious look; Palm could not take his eyes off this creature, so aggressively proud and frightening. He resolved to question his mentor at the next opportune moment. For now he must bow and gaze attentively at each new face before him, show respect and interest. The Governor and his wife looked at the young man with approval and satisfaction, wishing him and his teacher a successful New Year, then they turned to personages following on.

Palm and his tutor moved towards others already clustered in groups. At first there was only disregard from the finely-clad guests: no-one knew Professor Ruetz, even less the young companion.

But then, in stentorian tones: 'Ah, young Master Palm, I have been told you would be coming and I am anxious to speak with you'....behind him loomed that very aged burgomaster who had led the interrogation many moons ago, the 'Ancient One', who had announced he was 'that small bloodied scrap...the son of Ulefeld.'

Palm, shocked, performed the carefully orchestrated bow of submission while looking into the Old One's eyes.

'Indeed, Sire, I am at your service'.

'You have changed remarkably, in a short time, Master Palm!'

The venerable burgomaster examined the tall young man before him, '...I am told you sing in our choir, you ride a horse with competence and you are able to read and write. Can this really be true?'

Palm nodded assurances. Then, thanking the old man for his kindness he felt the urgent need to explain he had lost both stepmother and stepfather since that day he was told about his *true* father, but that he still knew nothing about this most mysterious man...and how he longed for such information.

'All in good time, young man,' replied the burgomaster solemnly. Then, turning to Professor Ruetz he nodded and delivered another sonorous injunction: 'Perhaps the time has come'.

This resonated like a trumpet call under the high ceiling around the entire gathering. Guests turned their heads to see what the loud command could possibly foretell. Time stood still. In sudden silence Palm studied his fine shoes, embarrassed and blushing.

At this instant tall doors were flung open and the guests were ushered into an adjacent large room where stood two long tables, covered with white linen, plates, fine cutlery and glittering glassware. The time had come indeed: the guests must celebrate the New Years' Feast. Led away by a liveried servant, the 'Old One' with Palm and his mentor followed to be seated and served. He sat safely between his tutor and the choirmaster. No harm could come to him, so suddenly plunged into Stralsund's higher echelons. Palm was on his best behaviour.

‘This very year I will surely learn about my true father,’ crossed his mind. In the meantime he conversed with personages around him.

‘About that red gryphon, Sire, in the other chamber, is it really half lion and half eagle …can there be such a creature?’

Heads close by turned to hear the answer. A teacher from the Dominican school, sitting opposite, assured: ‘It was a symbol, Master Palm, used by dukes who ruled the Duchy of Pomerania, until 1637, when it was removed from the ducal coat of arms…

…. but the ancient heraldic beast, the seal of the Dukes of Pomerania, has been seen on documents since 1100, when it became the Coat of Arms for an entire dynasty of intermarriages with Denmark, Rügen, Mecklenburg and Poland.’

‘But why’, insisted Palm ‘should it *be* such a beast, a fusion of eagle and lion, had anyone seen such a thing?’ Guests to the right and left and opposite Palm were drawn into an absorbing discussion by the lively group: Palm, his mentor and the teacher from the school.

For some moments Professor Ruetz sat back enjoying the satisfaction of observing his pupil unexpectedly a part of Stralsund society. He continued in benign teacher-fashion: ‘I do not believe it has been seen, but it is thought to express hope in power and foresight, as do other mythical beasts; think of the Unicorn, which symbolises ferocity yet goodness, selflessness and solitary beauty, all admirable qualities’,… thus spoke the man never short of an answer…’and then, rather pointedly, ‘it is a symbol of chaste love, and fidelity, quite apart from the fact that its horn neutralizes poisons….’

Guests to the left and right of Palm listened in awe, nodded approval. Much wine was poured, roast goose, steaming potatoes, delectable goose-fat and pickled red cabbage were carried in through high double-doors and served generously. Palm looked up to see a serving maid in the adjacent room, loading up trays of the liveried waiters....surely, was that not his Minna? Her hair, the way she held her head...but then the grand doors were closed again.

Although filled and flushed with pleasure, good food, company and a modest glass of wine, Palm was distraught. Each time the door opened his head turned, his eyes wandered.

The tutor observed, kept a look-out, remained on his guard.

***

Later, at The Swedish Governor's home,

'Tak för maten min käre fru',...such a pleasing, delectable meal, my dear wife, and how very well served! Where did you find the additional staff for this occasion, we must surely use them again?' The Governor has put his feet up; social life always an exhausting and draining matter, however pleasing: all that polite remembering who everyone was, conversing fluently on various topics, including tactful remarks underlining one's own position, yet keeping an appropriate convenient but respectful distance, well, one knows how it is.

'Did you take note of the good-looking youngster with his bearded teacher? It is he I once mentioned: that new-born saved by our predecessor over seventeen years ago. And now...after just one year and a half in the care of the Professor we have before us a fine specimen of distant Danish royalty. Only, well, he is still not informed. Might it not be for the best if he never knew, better for his own peace of mind and for his soul? What possible good will it do to know about his iniquitous father? He spoke of the recent deaths of both step-mother and stepfather with great emotion; there remains one stepbrother, I understand...'

The governor reached for his meerschaum pipe, drew nearer to the candle, hoping for a quiet puff and undisturbed rest...but the topic of Palm Uhlefeld had not ended...'and yet, young Master Palm's breeding shone through, do you not agree, despite those early years on a Pomeranian farm...he moves like a prince-ling, his diction excellent, his manners perfect. I have to say; it is hard to credit such an outstanding tutor, what do you say, käre fru?'

'Indeed, indeed, dear husband! I saw them both and felt a caring disposition instantly. It will be a heavy burden for this young man, and I would not wish such a thing on any of our own children; the knowledge of an evil parent can surely warp ones spirit, make one lose confidence, turn one to despair and mistrust and all manner of sourness... it could cut one off from mankind completely. No, such circumstances would be most troubling.'

A worried look crossed the Governor's face. When his wife showed such agitation he had learned to take careful note, her insights invariably astute and far-seeing.

He sucked on his pipe, but removed it again. Then he tapped it out.

Head back, eyes closed and mouth dropping open he allowed himself a well-earned old gentleman's rest.

PART THREE
EXODUS

Ten

Spring,1667. Fruit-trees, flowering and greening, caught up in perpetual 'becoming', but my eyes are closed; weary, they burn ...as I too, endlessly 'becoming,'... see myself lying under an apple-tree, the tree of wisdom...plucking one fruit after another,...thus force-fed, from one day to the next... and this I can say: I am weary of the taste of 'wisdom.' How do I continue when I wish for little more than to walk by the sea, or to ride out in the countryside on 'Satan', or to talk to Minna. O world!' He drew a deep sigh. 'How worn I am. I ask myself how much longer I must be beguiled by lives and thoughts of others. It wearies me to understand people, the things they do, the words they say.
And all this because I am now condemned to mingle with those who have already lost their freedom: the nobility, the learnèd men of the clergy and those with doctorates, puffed up with knowledge absorbed from teachers to teachers and then on to the next ones, each adding something new of their own. I am to become a lawyer, my tutor suggests. I am plunged from one topic into another: each day I must consider who or what is good, who or what is bad: each day I wake, but my heart no longer sings. Will I ever be free?
I have walked with Minna. We met in the harbour, spoke about her life.

'I work in the Inn', she said, 'because of my ailing father; he depends on me entirely'. She is the same age as I and has no hopes for a future other than, one day, having a family of her own. She seems sober and sensible...but her natural edge is more blunted, without joy, than I imagined. I have offered to teach her to read, to write. She smiled.

Now I stagger about as in a dream, can't shake it off: where am I heading, why is this constant study so important? For the sake of.., I don't know how to say...my 'parentage'...so much above my fortune? To this moment I have no knowledge of my father. Still locked in that cycle of 'becoming' I impress the world with facts, and by acting the 'gentleman.' To what purpose other than to tower over simple good people who have little, but go about their business hoping to continue just that, for as long as possible.

I think learning belongs to everyone. Only my feelings are my own. I am trapped behind these walls, imagining a better life on this earth, a life with true purpose, whatever it might be. My mentor and I, we are *both* trapped by *my* circumstances...it makes my blood boil! I long to get away, get out, see other places and other people.

Life has become too serious...far too serious.

***

His teacher finds him, shivering, collapsed on the stairs. The housekeeper is called for help; together they support him, guide him back to his room, to his bed.

Palm's head is red-hot, still shivering, his teeth are chattering. He looks about with crazed eyes, stammers...'tis bitter cold and I am sick at heart, 'tis bitter cold and....'Professor Ruetz bending over the bed, wipes the young man's damp brow and, turning to the medicus, 'I recognize that! It is from Hamlet, the English play we have been reading and studying. What can be the matter, Palm, you are behaving so strangely... what ails you, boy?'

Palm groans, writhes, 'my head, my eyes, my teeth, my neck, my back, I ache.'

The doctor ordered cool compresses for the head and cooling drink from the school kitchen.

'There is juice from last autumn's pressed apples' he is told and so he nods approval; 'no food for a day, but let him drink as he pleases, I will call again in the morning, rest awhile, sleep, listen to the birds outside, Palm, be peaceful., no reading of any kind. Empty your mind....be still, allow your body, your neck, now your shoulders, your belly and your legs to feel soft, while you breathe deeply' ...stroking Palm's hands and shoulders he soothed the boy:

'Tomorrow we will review your symptoms.'

'Yes. I will rest, Herr Doktor, and I thank you...'

Two days have passed; Palm has refused all food, would only drink.

In need of sleep himself the professor sat with him, reading, or pacing up and down anxiously. 'And...what is this?' He had found some hurried writing, stuck among pages in the book they had explored together: a page of the boy's grievances and crazed complaints about the want of freedom, of company...and seeing the world.

The teacher was stung: again there had been renewed contact with that girl. It would be wise to get away.

Concern for the welfare of his student overwhelmed him: he decided to call on the Swedish Governor to discuss a complete change of environment for both him and his pupil: 'We need a coach, Governor, and funds...we will set out to Amsterdam, the boy needs a change.'

May 23, 1667.

...sun rising, fog rolling in, seagulls circling, squawking....... the first attempt at an entry in Palm's notebook for his travels; he was not inspired. However: his lamentations and his illness had borne fruit: a stage-coach stood before the main door to the school, with two horses, and two more, to be added shortly. They were leaving Stralsund.

To view new things and old events as they *truly* are is a universal remedy; the sudden change in Palm's life had come about thanks to quick thinking of his mentor, the magnanimity of the Swedish Governor, the handsome coffers of coins left behind by Palm's father 17 years ago, and by advanced beliefs in self-purification through observation and learning about the world. The young man's indisposition, numbness and depression needed to be lifted, for while he was afflicted with these symptoms there could be no progress.

Three large trunks were stored at the back, two containing clothes and one filled with books. Palm's much-travelled teacher had been all over the centre of Europe, knew what was essential. Palm stood by, hollow-eyed and pale, but also with a beating heart, excited, puzzled. An early departure then: four horses would bring them forward six to eight miles an hour, so they might reach Lübeck sometime tomorrow, with stop-offs somewhere, for meals, to change horses, and for rest. There appeared to be some delay, the coachman fussed: he needed a shave, and the guard who rode at the back with his blunderbuss and horn had to settle some private argument with his wife. But soon the journey began. Clattering over cobbles was a sensation Palm had not experienced before; he sat by the window and evaluated the prospect of a long journey ahead already feeling the springs beneath him. Just past the town-gates the coast road going west was deeply rutted in unpredictable ways...the coachman avoided the deepest ruts, stayed on firm ground as best he could. This was the road Palm knew so well, the one they rode horses on, but also the road to his former life.

'How is my step-brother.... and what would he think if he saw me passing by in a coach with four horses?'

Palm would not be the first to believe life was but a dream: 'All that studying, just a game...furnishing the bare walls of my existence with bright and colourful figures and visions that fly about in my head. Now, when I close my eyes there is another world which entertains me.'

They had all been up before daylight. Palm soon nodded off in his corner, with a rug over his knees. 'My tooth aches,' he thought, but said nothing.

'Palm, do rouse yourself, I have hot bread for our morning meal...freshly baked rolls wrapped in white napkins, still warm from the school kitchen!' The cook had also filled stoneware bottles, one with water, one with apple juice. The travellers broke their fast, chewed contentedly, while the teacher found further improving knowledge to pass on to his charge: 'Hear these reflections, Palm, by a man called Friedrich von Logau:'

Leichter trägt, was er träget,	*A burden is carried more readily*
Wer Geduld zur Bürde leget.	*If patience is added to the weight.*

Picking up crumbs Palm nodded numbly: 'Indeed, the man seems wise. One must attempt to act according to his little rhyme.

This 'von Logau', is he some friend of yours?'

'Alas no, he died some twenty years ago, in Silesia, near Breslau. What do you think of this one, Palm, he tries to describe 'Love':

Nenne mir den weiten Mantel	*Name for me that spacious mantle*
D'runter alles sich versteckt?	*Under which all is concealed?*
Liebe thut's, die alle Mängel	*Love will do, thus every failing's*
Gerne hüllt und fleissig deckt.	*Gladly hidden , not revealed.*

'Yes, 'love is blind'. I've heard that before. Are you fond of poetic thoughts, do you write them yourself, Sir?'

'I make attempts, Palm, but the result is mostly an embarrassment.'

The teacher closes his eyes to reach for further treasures stored in his brain. 'We value them, as they are short. But their message is strong, here, another of these epigrams, a famous one:' He smiles.

Gottes Mühlen mahlen langsam,
Mahlen aber trefflich klein;
Ob aus Langmut er sich säumet,
Bringt mit Schärf'er alles ein.

God's mills grind slowly'
But they grind exceeding small.
Though with patience he stands waiting
With exactness grinds he all.

The men are silent. The horses outside have fallen into a comfortable rhythm and Palm quietly reviews his own misdeeds, now being ground in those mills. He mutters 'epigrams, epigrams'; then, with a throaty chuckle his tutor reads:

Leser, wie gefall ich dir?
Leser, wie gefällst du mir?

Reader, do I please you?
Reader, do you please me?

'Yes, how close to us this feels... as if the man were in the coach with us, passing judgement! I must assume 'epigram' is yet another word for our list, professor?'

Palm knows how to flatter his teacher.

'Indeed Palm, when we come to a halt we shall make a note, also of the wondrous similarity of so many German and English words....here are some for you to think about and remember: 'forgive me' and '*vergieb mir*'...mother equals *Mutter*.... kiss and *Kuss, Haus* and house...burden and *Bürde, Mantel* and mantle, mills and *Mühle*...and this, pointing into his sleeve, is an 'arm' in both languages'. The teacher nods: 'These words may look different but sound much the same, don't you think...but above all, it means a German and an Englishman should soon understand one another, and this is also true of the Low Lands...the language there is an old form of German.....*das Pferd* has become 'die perd', I believe. I so hope our horses need water (or *Wasser)* soon, so we can stretch our legs a while!'

Passing through numerous places where horses were fed, watered or changed, the travellers read, wrote notes. They chatted and gazed at monotonous flat lands of meadows and moors. He saw peasants and vagabonds, some doffed their caps, others waved as the coach passed and he remembered doing just that when he himself was a small boy, strolling along the rough coast road with his brother, wondering where the important personages were going. But now, displaced, he found riding inside a coach even more painful and tedious than endlessly studying in his small room in Stralsund.

Suddenly the image of Ursel madly stirring dinners on the hot stove for his brother came to him: did they ever think of him, speak about him? He wished them well…as he nodded off….*into a dream-world of fiercely hot sun, directly overhead, he and his brother squinting up in the bright light, creeping out of the dark barn after a morning of cleaning out the pig-shed: 'There's hay stuck in your hair' shouts Christian.' 'You stink of shit' comes the reply.'*

'Let's run down to the lake to our secret place, we can swim and rest and catch a fish…the net is in my pocket.'

They stomp through the muddy yard, hens flutter and squawk, (avoid that bad-tempered goose), no-one sees them. Both carry an apple and a large clump of rye-bread folded in a cloth. Still filthy but free at last, to roam, to make traps…they reach the water, strip off, wriggle out of shirts and breeches…and rush into cool green water, slippery mud underfoot, squidgy and squelchy between toes…naked young bodies feeling their way warily, slithering forward, Palm wishes he was in the deeper end where one could pretend to be a frog, thrash about on one's belly, arms and legs propelling forward.

'Aaahhh, we are lucky to have a lake so near and we can do what we want; I'm nearly up to my chest….now I will kick my legs'…he sinks for a moment but reappears, laughing, coughing, more or less afloat. Christian stares, irritated. 'I've shown you before: come on,…even dogs can do it, keep moving your arms and legs, we've been doing it for three summers now, keep your head up,…no, up…come on, Palm, come on!

Birds and fluttering dragonflies hover by the edge of the water. Soon the half-drowned boys stretch out on a grassy verge, after cautious looks behind and under shrubs and ferns…. for adders and other threats. They bask, dry off in the sun, chew their bread. Gnats and midges swarm peacefully. A large headed fat frog with blank eyes emerges

from disturbed mud, 'eyes not unlike Ursel's' suggests Palm.

'You know…father is up on the roof again, this afternoon, he wants us to help; should we go back….or shall we hide in the wood, see if we can find the red deer fighting again? I heard one singing his special song, I suppose his antlers were falling off, we could bring them home…'

Looking at their wet glistening bodies the boys giggle at their shrivelled sex organs: 'we'd never be able to do what the red deer does to his wife, not with these small things …remember the large clump of ferns, let's go there, find him, spy on the big beast again, we could also look for berries…we're always hungry, aren't we?'

They were so very close, Palm and Christian, like twins, they knew each others' thoughts. They learned about everything together.

Still under the dreamy spell of a cool lake and carefree boyhood he re-entered reality with some regret: the coachman's horn! Palm's eyes opened with a jerk to the shock of arrival at a country inn just before Rostock.

They clambered out of the diabolical conveyance back onto solid, firm earth to stretch his aching, compressed limbs. His head was spinning, his bones ached.

Forlorn horses, frothing at the mouth, snorting, sweating, shook their wet sticky manes… they too needed water, shade, and rest.

'*Terra firma*, at last, and 'oh, my back,' muttered the mentor as their boxes were carried in by strong young menials. Palm was embarrassed as they bowed before him.

'Just incline your head', was the quiet advice from his teacher, 'in this instance that is all that is required. Tomorrow is the last lap: we should be in Lübeck by late afternoon. I've been planning ahead Palm: after our visit we continue our journey to Hamburg, but then it's across the sea to Amsterdam: which will give us an opportunity to explore conditions on a Dutch East India ship. This coach leaves much to be desired, even if it does belong to the Swedish Governor, don't you agree?'

While the servants staggered to and fro with trunks and cases Palm was told there was no need to bow to such young men, the correct thing was to acknowledge their presence, and pay them for their service.

'Next time *you* must do it. On arrival at the coaching inn in Lübeck, you will show me you now know how to behave like a gentleman...remember Master Palm, the *grandson of a King,* I often wonder if you have forgotten this...'I will stand back and observe,' warns the mentor .'You do have coins in your purse, Palm?'

'Indeed, Professor, I have a few.'

They were led upstairs to a dark room, a place to rest overnight: large oak beds with soft pillows and covers, a massive carved wardrobe and near the door a table bearing candles, a heavy pottery bowl and a jug of water for ablutions. On the floor was a pail. Palm stretched out on his bed, felt tears welling up... he re-lived his dream, felt he was floating, disconnected from all he had ever known. He missed his past and more than he could say, his brother. Never before had he felt so deeply unsettled:

'I barely know who I am, where I am. It is not manly to weep. I must wrestle with my fears, my uncertainties...while I am caught between vanished things, parents, separation from my brother, from Minna, and now this obligation to become a 'gentleman'. He drifted down and further down, a spiral without end.

'Where is this new destination, what is my destiny?'

During a modest meal his teacher reassured him: 'Keep that diary' he said, 'write down your thoughts, each day record all new impressions. You will have a new soul. Palm, trust me, believe in your resolutions...your horizons will expand. Remember your stepmother's wisdom: 'Say yes to life!'

Indeed. What good will come of it? Palm was close to tears; he turned away so the teacher did not notice. 'And dear God, there was Minna: I'd had no chance to tell her we were leaving.'

24th May. Late afternoon. The coachman's instructions were to enter Lübeck by way of the Holsten Tor, 'even if it meant riding around the Trave River a bit further.' The tutor explained: 'Master Palm *must* pass through this magnificent gate as we approach town, the 'Queen of the Hanseatic League'...an experience every visitor should enjoy. And please hold the horses now, just for a while, for we wish to count the seven steeples as we approach...'

They crossed the river, noted sailing ships and handsome salt-storehouses... admired the massive double-towered brick town-gate while Palm wondered about the Lübeck citizens who had such a poor reputation with the people of Stralsund: they did after all, have the audacity to burn Stralsund down three hundred years ago. Do they still suffer from their sin of pride?

CONCORDIA DOMI FORIS PAX he read on the gate. His teacher translated: UNITY AT HOME PEACE ABROAD.... a commendable thought, considering their past behaviour. 'I suppose we *must* forgive them now, as centuries have passed,' thought Palm, still bristling at the thought of *his* Stralsund burnt to the ground.....All he now saw from the coach window was great prosperity: narrow cobbled streets, fine houses, high redbrick churches, so many of them.

According to his tutor Master Buxtehude was here, somewhere.

'I understand he has chosen the organ in the Marienkirche....and may already have taken up his post as chief organist'.

'Do you know Palm, that Buxtehude's father was also an organist, somewhere north, in Denmark? Such skills are often handed from father to son. Tomorrow we must visit the church and find out if he has arrived. At least there will be one person we know in this town!'

The coachman took them to an inn near the Holy Spirit Hospital, famed in these parts, a home for the poor and the sick, designed by wealthy merchants in 1280..., only a few years after they'd burnt down Stralsund. Palm walked about filled with melancholy feelings about life but especially about the misdeeds of Lübeck's ancestors. Nothing brought a smile to his face, least of all the greedy merchants of 13th century Lübeck.

'I beg you to remember, Palm, bad things have happened everywhere but they do not have to remain part of the living. Try to recall how much time has passed, how many wars have been fought...then learn to open your heart to the new world you are privileged to know; just think: you are in a town which Charles the IV named one of the 'Five Glories of the Empire', by which he meant The Holy Roman Empire, a title shared with Venice, Rome, Pisa and Florence...yes, this very place you stand carries *such* a reputation...'

Still disenchanted Palm felt obliged to enquire...'and who was he, that Charles IV, when did *he* live?'

The teacher studied his pupil for a moment, before he dared sugar one further pill of knowledge: 'One of *your* own distant ancestors, dear Palm, a Holy Roman Emperor the first of whom was Charlemagne, the man we are yet to discuss. You may be cheered to know this Charles was followed by a string of Charles-es, seven of them all together: Charles the Bold, and Charles the Fat...' he paused for a moment, then:

'I forget the others, but the man who spoke with such praise about Lübeck was King of Bohemia, who expanded trade by buying or annexing parts of Germany...no doubt committing a number of cruel war crimes on the way.'

'War crimes? Killing people? Wars mean destruction and death, I know that... but *my* ancestors? My despair grows, Professor. Tell me it was a long time ago. And even that will be no help.'

'Certainly, Palm. But believe me: we must all learn to forgive.' The teacher gave Palm an encouraging look.

'And now, young man, it is time for our evening bread, and wine, or milk if you prefer. Time to rest! We have a busy day tomorrow.

'I would prefer wine, Sir, if I may. It will help me to forget, to sleep…and my tooth aches again.'

'If the pain continues we must attempt finding a cure: I understand roots of the Tooth-wart plant are very good. Learn to be more objective, Palm, and more light-hearted. But wait: allow me to close these thick wood shutters, they keep out the street noise.'

***

Palm slept; the teacher kept his own diary, by candlelight:

'The Lübeck inn is tolerable, but much noise outside, due to customers who have drunken, or are still drinking far too much beer. Palm is undergoing numerous deep torments. He also complains of toothache. Is it a wisdom-tooth? He is the right age now to be growing his last teeth.

He will become ill unless I take great care. But he has yet to learn to be free, challenged and responsible. I must be both mother and father to him, for he is unstable. I am certain he is not ready to hear about his father. Perhaps it will be easier in Amsterdam, where there is stimulation, entertainment and a great deal to learn about living. He will be speaking other languages and perhaps spend time with others, young like himself.

First the journey to Hamburg, alas again by coach! Then, on by ship to Amsterdam…

Palm is dead to the world, has forgotten his tooth… and also to blow out his candle. I observe his face, flushed with wine, but now more peaceful than during our journey. And so to bed.'

May 25th. The tutor's diary: 'Our day in Lübeck.'

A fruitful day: Herr Buxtehude was in the Marienkirche, having arrived from Elsinore where he worked in a church also called St Mary. We sat with many good people at the service, heard him perform on an even more majestic organ than our own in Stralsund and there was a fine choir, which moved Palm extremely, he could barely sit still, so pleased was he. The pastor spoke with resonance, for a very long time. As we hear similar sermons at home we were anxious throughout to be free of sermons and able to catch Buxtehude on his way out. And this is indeed what happened: we reminded him of his visit to Stralsund, and his advice to Palm and of the pleasure choir practice has become. The great man looked at Palm with paternal interest, put his hand on Palm's shoulder inviting us both to a concert on this very night: an evening of music for viols and harpsichord. Such music we are not accustomed to. We are to meet him before the event to drink wine and exchange news about Stralsund.

He told us he will soon marry the daughter of his predecessor, and they will have the use of a house close to the church. Herr Buxtehude mentioned it is not uncommon practice for organists to marry the daughter of the man whose work he takes over. His wife-to-be is called Anna Magdalena. He has two organs to play: a large one for important services and a smaller one for funerals. Palm and I discussed all these arrangements later and found them good, provided, thought Palm, the bride-to-be was pleasing to the eye, and also that there would not be too many funerals.

We had advice from the captain of a ship on the Trave River, as we wandered near the moored boats. 'There is a 'water-street' from the Trave to the Elbe,' he told us, 'which is a canal unique in its way, to transport salt from Lübeck to Hamburg'. I had no idea there were salt-mines near Lübeck. The canal would be just what we need for getting to Hamburg, but now we are told it would take far too long as the boats are very small and piled high with salt. We were advised to take the coach again as it is only 40 miles across land to Hamburg; all is arranged for the morrow.

Some time was spent admiring the magnificent City Hall, more impressive than ours at home. But words fail when one tries to take in the 300 year old Marienkirche . How they managed to complete it in one hundred years is impossible to comprehend, how they built it at all... a miracle, entirely from red bricks. We strained our necks to imagine constructing a ceiling thirty-eight metres above our heads, apparently the highest in the world. Standing dwarfed before the double-towered front, surrounded by town houses and the market, Palm has decided it was not unlike our St. Nicholas in Stralsund, so I did laugh at him and told him he showed poor judgement.

'How long do you believe it will stand', he demanded and I suggested 'At least another 300 years'....while Palm counted the total and suggested The Good Lord would be very much on the side of Lübeck if it lasted as long as 1950.

'That would make it 700 years old, a fine figure. Should Lübeck behave badly again he will punish the inhabitants and knock it down!'

We examined the famous organ, which bears the name 'Dance of Death.' It has a total of 5000 pipes! If the name is anything to go by it sounds even more terrifying complex and fragile object was the giant Astronomical Clock, finished only 100 years ago. It showed planetary positions, phases of the sun and the moon as well as the signs of the zodiac. 'How anyone can be clever enough to create such a thing is beyond all comprehension,' said Palm. Humbled, he now feels it is all too much, everything too difficult to understand. I told him we had an even better one in the St. Nicholai church at home, but he claimed not to have seen it.

Later: The viols. Palm could not tear himself away, wished he could take the sounds with him, hear them wherever he went. Again there were tears in his eyes. I must have a word with him.

Palm's toothache has abated but no doubt the coach journey will shake it back. I may have to consult the book of Phillipus Theophrastus Bombastus, who knew cures for such things. But *where to find this book? He is dead for over 100 years, is also known as Paracelsus. I prefer the other names. He had a theory that plants which resemble organs of the body will also cure those same organs: thus the creamy tooth-like scales on the roots of the Toothwart plant than our instrument in the Marienkirche, at home.*

Most pleasing was the bronze baptismal font, also over three-hundred years old and finely decorated with a double row of small saintly figures. As long as there are Christians the font will be there for them, being at least as strong as the pyramids of Egypt.

A rest may cure Palm's complaint. If not the herbalists in Amsterdam will know. Until then the cure may have to be more wine, which, in any case, puts Palm in a more pleasing frame of mind. We leave for Hamburg tomorrow, soon after breakfast.'

May, the 26th. Farewell to Lübeck.

Today we have a passenger. The innkeeper enquired: might we assist a scientist, recently arrived from Denmark ...to reach Hamburg by coach, he must catch a boat to London, most urgently...appears to speak English, also Danish and German. This may prove to be a challenge, on the other hand...it is only for one day and he *has* offered to share the costs. This clearly is a good thing.

The stranger, having appeared, clambered in clumsily, dressed in shabby garments. He was withdrawn. The matter of costs must be resolved later. So far he had fleetingly smiled at us both, and now finally settled, having drawn a book from his pocket, was immediately immersed in the text. We were less inclined to speak, for fear of disturbing him. One last look at the seven spires... then we set out across the river.

Palm was the one feeling most uncomfortable: 'This fleshy fellow-passenger must be English,' he thought, 'I can tell by his foreign garments. Do I try out English words? I could say *Good Day,* and *I trust you are well....* 'no, perhaps not. It is up to him to speak to us, I refuse to make a fool of myself…I shall smile but speak to my mentor. The man barely seems to understands German.'

'So, Master Palm… what has most impressed you yesterday?'

The Professor enquired in lowered tones, to allow the stranger undisturbed reading. Palm replied, also in a hushed voice: 'at first, the height of the Marienkirche, but no, on reflection: that massive astronomical clock, Professor, the impossible complexity of wheels within wheels. I cannot imagine any man with sufficient mental powers to put together a mechanism so bedevilling.'

Palm kept a wary eye on the stranger who had looked up, smiling and nodding his head. The man's stringy dark hair, flecked with grey and particles of dried skin, swung from side to side. His double-chins expanded and contracted.

'May I introduce myself', he asked, eyes twinkling, exceptionally long fingers smoothing a thin moustache,' I am Heinrich Oldenburg, formerly from these parts but now an Englishman by choice. I could not help hearing your admiration for the clock in the Marienkirche, and I surmise, Sir,' turning to the professor, 'that you are the tutor of this young gentleman?'

'Indeed, Sir, that is so. My name is Martin Ruetz and I am taking Master Palm Uhlfeld for a short tour to Amsterdam. We are honoured to have you with us and most interested to understand you live across the sea in such a distant place as England. How do you come to be *there* and why are you now here; perhaps come to visit relatives?'

Herr Oldenburg sat back smiling and nodding contentedly, arms folded over his corpulent middle.

'Yes, yes, relatives, but also work! I maintain an extensive network of scientific contacts, which means I must travel a great deal. I've just been on a visit to Elsinore, to the Royal Observatory Uraniborg where the Danish King has built a vast astronomical laboratory…I too was a tutor for a while, many years ago. Then, offered a post in

London, as theologian and philosopher, I became an early member of the Royal Society, at its foundation eight years ago I took on the role of foreign correspondent, which explains why I am here.'

There followed polite smiles from the fellow passengers, heads nodding, coach bobbing, hooves cluttering ...on such a very dusty road. After a lengthy silence Professor Ruetz enquired:

'And what precisely is this Royal Society?'

'We are a learned society for science, formed for the improvement of Natural Knowledge,' explained the man,' King Charles II has given us a Royal Charter. But to get back to your views on that astronomical clock, Master Palm, if I may call you by that name, have you perhaps heard of the scientist Tycho Brahe? No? His ancestors lived in a castle, his father, a nobleman was an important figure at the court of the Danish King....

(Palm glanced at his tutor, who nodded back reassuringly...)

...like you he was sent on a study-tour of Europe with a mentor, who allowed young Tycho to pursue astronomy during the tour. Aged only seventeen he already knew he wished to be an astronomer; he was so interested in the heavens he soon discovered the positions of the planets did not coincide with the positions as known at the time. Soon he went to Rostock University, to study astronomy and chemistry, just around the corner from Lübeck, as you well know. Imagine what happened to him there: during the foolishness of a duel... (do *you* enjoy sword-fighting, Master Palm?), he lost most of his nose! Yes...for the rest of his life he wore a silver and gold replacement which he attached daily with some paste. He was 19 years old, Master Palm...you see, even the bright ones can be foolish!

And there are many bright fellows from these parts, you may have heard of Johannes Kepler, who years later became Tycho Brahe's assistant? No? Well, there is no reason why you should know these men...'he paused to scratch his chin: 'Let me see, yes, Kepler, died about 30 years ago, it was he who was the true founder of 'celestial mechanics', as you appear interested in astronomical clocks...he discovered the elliptical orbits of planets, he explained how tides were influenced by the moon and he even determined the exact year of the birth of our Lord Jesus...such a religious man...at first Kepler wanted to be a priest. But in the end he felt more drawn to science. This happens, as you probably know.

We have recently had another insight into his fertile mind; he has penned a 'Dream' which describes a journey to the moon and the lunar inhabitants. Well, *over*-fertile, for such a thing could never occur, never, you surely agree?'

'To the moon! Impossible! There was much nodding from both Palm and his teacher who were now greatly entertained by the corpulent 'German' Englishman. They were beginning to enjoy his company.

***

'*Oldenburg'*, is this not the name of important German royalty, or is it just the town, from which our affable passenger has derived his name', wondered Professor Ruetz. The man spoke without pause, and his new topic was some 'very bright' fellow at his university in England called Newton, who had been elected to a 'college fellowship' a few months earlier.

Palm's eyes had closed...*bright stars, glittering on a dark background, a fellowship of brightness, glowing, sparkling, crackling, fingers reaching up, burnt each time trying to put out vast flames everywhere, an urgency...reaching out to stop the burning, a tightness, discomfort....a jolt of the carriage wakes him...*and Palm told himself he must remember to enquire what that was: a fellowship? Herr Oldenburg had so very much to say. Palm Ulefeld and his own admired Professor were stunned by the impressive flow of information.

Anxiously, aware of being the focus of not just one but *two* tutors...Palm began to *long* for the next stop. Not that the topics raised were uninteresting, no, not at all...but the man from London was making matters worse when he said Tycho Brahe was thought to have died from a burst bladder, during a Royal Dinner party in Prague:' Tycho Brahe, the 'Phoenix of Astronomy', died ...not wanting to disrupt a Royal Party...'

And the horses too must surely need watering. Please, we must stop. Now! Ah, yes, over there, by those bushes...

A refreshing break in the journey... they had reached...well, nowhere special. Lübeck to Hamburg was uneventful. There was, however, no lack of interesting conversation.

'And how did *you* learn to converse with the English, Herr Oldenburg?'

'Well, certainly not by reading that play about Hamlet. There are simpler ways, rest assured, Master Palm. But hear this: I have another pleasing coincidence for you. I once examined a grand engraving, the head of Tycho Brahe, which showed two ancestors engraved beside his portrait, created in 1530. Written clearly below their pictures were their names: Rosenkrans and Guldensteren.

Now, you may have reached the place in 'Hamlet' when England's great playwright used these poetic names? No, not yet? It is in the middle part of the plot, you will come to them, no doubt. Mr. Shakespeare will have studied the portrait carefully, noting those splendid names. Perhaps he went to Denmark and visited the famous Astronomical Laboratory? And was there not talk of a star at the beginning of his play? The longer I live the more I believe all knowledge is interconnected and the more we see and think and discover the more'...here Mr Oldenburg fell silent, having exhausted his own complex connections,...but not for long, '...for Tycho was so linked with stars and we are privileged to marvel at his vast talents, now bestowed on us, as we rattle along through our own lives. It is all there for us to enjoy, but so much passes us by, like the landscape flying past our windows, which we no longer care to see....''Yes, long coach journeys are a trial', said Palm, but also thought to remember the extraordinary things the large man was saying.

The coachman blew his horn: it was sunset, and Hamburg was in view. As they entered the prosperous city, having passed through grazing cattle and rich farm lands, they crossed a substantial bridge, the approach not unlike Lübeck in that it was a town surrounded by water: the rivers Elbe and Alster, with almost as many spires.

'One of the largest cities in these parts', assured fleshy Herr Oldenburg, 'the place took its name from the first permanent building on this spot: a fortress built by Charlemagne about 800 years ago, erected on marshland, between the two rivers. It was called Hammaburg...well, I say permanent, for where is it now?' He wrinkled his nose. 'It served as defence against the Slav and the Vikings, but not for long...a colourful history, Master Palm, no doubt your tutor knows more than I do.' Now he nodded at Palm's teacher. 'I can tell you there were even 'interventions' from two Holy Roman emperors, and also from Denmark, but by 1200 Hammaburg had found its feet, was making its own laws...well, here we are, you good, kind people, I thank-you most deeply for listening to me, putting up with me, for so long'. Looking left and right out from the coach windows he said: 'in a moment I must bid you both farewell.'

The coach pulled up. Herr Oldenburg staggered to his feet, then heaved and squeezed his vast circumference out onto the cobbles. Palm joined him and they stretched their legs for a moment, while a modest, beaten-up leather bag belonging to the passenger was handed down.

...'Just one more thing, Master Palm', said Oldenburg, pulling Palm to the side of the road...if you wish to learn English very quickly...*do* spend time with the pretty English girls in Amsterdam harbour area...they are most entertaining; it is known as 'night school'; you may be pleasantly surprised.' This was spoken sotto voce, and drowned by the noise of snorting horses, ready to move on in another direction. Palm jumped back up into the coach.

On then, to the official coaching inn, somewhere near the harbour, ('drop us by the inn on the Reeper Bahn', called Professor Ruetz,) they saw, in the long shadows of the setting sun, a width of the river Elbe with rope makers, stowing away their days' work for the boats in the harbour. It was a soothing sight.

'Tomorrow we will find a ship, one which calls at Amsterdam. Let us sample the famous Hamburg beer before we turn in for the night', suggested the tutor. They wandered about on Dyke Street, where most trading took place, and marvelled at such business everywhere, even after sunset. Not far off stood St.Michael, with its spindly spire, still under construction, but almost completed, lit by a splendid full moon. They were relieved to be alone again and in very good spirits.

'Oldenburg forgot to pay his share' remembered Palm.

27th May, 1667. *Master Palm no longer mentions his tooth…* was the only entry in the professor's diary. It was a radiant day. Seagulls squawking the same calls as those in Stralsund accompanied the visitors picking their way through docks stacked high with newly unloaded boxes filled with English textiles, barrels of finest Dutch herrings and French wines, baskets of raisins, capers, almonds and figs, jars of olives, oil and fragrant citrus fruits. Exports were more robust: timber, rigging, ropes and beasts; the entire harbour buzzed with questionable strangers of many hues and languages, every spot was filled with din, chaos, shouts and activity.

'They look like pirates here, in the docks', said Palm, 'I can't understand a word of what anyone is saying.'

'Yes, I dare say, it is not always easy to follow, most of them are from other countries; but patience, we've only just begun our enquiries.'They marched from ship to ship, and, as luck would have it advice was on hand: 'Along here, Sir, the fourth ship now loading logs, it goes to Amsterdam, why not try them. They leave tonight I've been told, or in the morning. Arrrrrgh!' The ancient sailor spat on the ground and quickly pocketed the proffered coins: 'I thank you, Sir, most kind, young Sir, and you can both trust me…for sure, you too, Sir, yes indeed, this is a good Dutch East Indies ship. He held his gnarled old hand by his head in salutation.

'Arrrrrgh...you can rely on the Dutch. For sure, they go far and wide these days........'

Eleven

And thus, accommodated in a modest cabin on the quarter-deck, with hammocks for two nights and a day, to arrive in Amsterdam... should the winds blow in the right direction for the time of year,...(it was all a little vague), Palm and his tutor had been invited to take the evening meal with the captain; an unexpected honour! After several jugs of famed Hamburg beer their friendly captain broke the news: 'the ship must drop off cargo only about 30 miles north from here at the Holy Land, or 'heylige land'...do take a look, gentlemen, here, on the left of the map.'

At first this was thought to be a joke by the attentive tutor. But, ever the diplomat, the unfailingly polite Professor Ruetz added:'....*now* known, of course, as 'Heligoland', Master Palm. There is a the legend about an ancient stone wall only five miles to the east of the island but covered by water about as high as five men standing on each others' shoulders, it was part of a city on a hill overlooking the mouth of the Elbe,... more or less where we are now.' The Captain nodded his head, enjoying the company of such very knowledgeable passengers.

'Why has the sea become deeper, Professor, or what has caused the old city to sink?'

'This is not known, alas. We are told the world changes over time and ancient treasures lie buried for ever. Think of our own Vineta near Stralsund. Much of the North Sea may once have been dry land for all we know. It is said this island belonged to a Germanic god called Forsite, who dwelled in a glittering temple of gold and silver and was the wisest and most gentle god, gifted with speech and wisdom, above all an awesome figure who knew how to keep pirates away. Sailors, even pirates, offered one tenth of their coffers to the hermits living there, to gain favour with the gods. Perhaps we should enquire, Palm, whether our captain and his crew have prepared their offerings on this journey...what do you say?'

The captain grinned, then coughed noisily while lighting his pipe: 'We leave very early tomorrow, gentlemen, I hope you will be comfortable.'

Professor Ruetz rose and smiled. One knows when one is dismissed.

'Must we believe in such gods, Professor?….As for pirates, well, yes, sailors in Stralsund have told me about Klaus Stoertebeker, but he has been dead for hundreds of years…they said his base was on Heligoland and that he captured Danish, English and Dutch, even German ships. Everyone feared him. When they finally caught him somewhere near Helgoland he and 71 other pirates were executed. Usually pirates were thrown overboard. But he was different. He was famous! The rumour of his last request, Professor, when he was about to have his head chopped off in Hamburg, do you really believe what people say?'

'Well, what precisely is this rumour, Palm, there are conflicting stories, first you must give an account of what *you* have heard!'

Palm was swinging in his hammock.

'I heard they were all lined up in the dock, Klaus Stoertebecker and his shipmates, the executioner standing by with a sharpened axe. At that point wicked Klaus requested the authorities should spare every man of his pirate crew if *he himself* would manage to walk, after the blow, headless, past his mates…

This request was met: the beheaded pirate collapsed only after walking past his terrified fellow pirates, so I was told. Professor, truly, he walked for some distance, without his head! Now, please Sir, what do you say: would such a thing be possible?'

Palm, white as a sheet needed reassurance, or at least a further half pint of Hamburg ale. His teacher hesitated.

'Well, I have seen chickens run about without heads, Palm, but not in a straight line and certainly not for long. Since all this happened over two hundred years ago I think we must take it as a myth created to intimidate onlookers who flock to such events and also by those who dispatch criminals to the other world. We can surely argue that hangmen and executioners are heroic figures, doing a service to their community?'

Palm's teacher was swinging in the hammock, eyes shut, speaking quietly with an unusually small thin voice. He looked very pale.

He was sea-sick, perhaps?

'This has not been a pleasing topic, professor. May I go up on deck for a while to see the island appearing on the horizon, or is it already too dark? It is, allegedly a wondrous sight, all red rocks and frightening shapes. There will be no pirates, of that I am almost sure.'

But his teacher had fallen asleep. The ship would not leave until early.

Nevertheless Palm went up to explore. Only a short while before sunrise Palm decided to creep into his hammock, underneath the rug, and close his eyes.

28th May. In the morning a huge racket on deck distracted them both. Their ship had cast off, hammocks now rocked even more perilously. They were sailing north extremely slowly, sails flapping listlessly, little or no movement, for quite a while. For the third time Palm clambered up narrow wooden steps, hanging on to whatever there was...up to the deck to watch the receding coastline.... low grey fog being blown away over the Frisian Islands. There were other stately vessels floating northwards on the Elbe estuary, accompanied by noisy gulls, while the sun rose through a haze of fog. By the time the glowing disc had reached its highest point the ship finally entered the North Sea, the weather was no longer calm and oh, such efficient sailors clambering, swinging, larking about like nimble monkeys among the vast sails.

'These boys are mostly my age: If only I could understand their shouts and signals, lucky devils.' Poor Palm: in the back of his mind loomed one headless pirate and pools of blood. What does an executioner feel when he receives and then senses the terror of his victim before the punishment? Palm had not yet shaken off last evening's discussion. His eyes carefully scanned the horizon for suspicious-looking vessels.

'Best to stay on deck for a while... my tutor is not himself and in no mood for conversation.' Palm, feeling responsible, reported to the captain, but was sent away with: 'Let him rest in the cuddy, find his sea-legs, young man, he will recover in a while…it happens to some land-dwellers. You alright then, Master Palm?'

'Aye, aye, Captain, Sir, yes, I like the ship, the sea air. I am a little hungry though.'

'To my cabin then, Palm, you will find bread and beer on the table, but my advice is to take very little. The sea will be rough today. We may not arrive before sunset. Be patient. Keep an eye on your tutor and report to me in a few hours time: he should feel better by then.'

'How long will this journey be, Captain, Sir?'

'Seven hours at this rate, young man, perhaps longer. After some sleep tonight, at 'day-blink', we will be on our way to Amsterdam. Tell your tutor, seven hours, seven knots….seven is our magic number!'

***

Professor Ruetz had resigned himself; it does no harm to abstain from food for a day.

'The loblolly boy has been in to see me, offered lumpy porridge, then ship's biscuits, but I declined. Now you and I must amuse each other with games of some sort. Any suggestions, Palm?'

Palm was in his hammock: 'A 'loblolly' boy, Professor, what is that?'

'A ship surgeon's assistant, in charge of herbs, medicines, and so forth… a young person much like you, Palm...sent by our captain.'

Palm could think of nothing other than those nimble young sailors, clambering about on deck, without a care in the world. While he considered going up once more, if only to watch and imagine becoming one of them, he heard his teacher muttering: 'seven is the magic number, magic, magic, magic...and seven deadly sins. Palm: tell me what *you* know of the seven deadly sins!'

A profound silence followed. The farmer's boy, groomed for over a year to become a gentleman has lost touch with reality and cannot recall a single sin other than robbery, the thing pirates do.

His teacher recited a list of all seven deadly sins, placed them before his pupil's innocent eye for inspection: 'Pride, Covetousness, Envy and Lust, to say nothing of Gluttony, Anger and Sloth.

Well Palm, what do you say: are you guilty of any of these?'

'No, no, Professor. I am not proud, nor have I wanted things that are not mine. I have been angry with my brother, but it was a long time ago. As to Gluttony, no, definitely never, and Sloth, perhaps a little, when I was very tired! I am left with Lust. This is a troublesome word. One has thoughts and longings, hard to control, how can one say, feelings that are pleasing but one tries to keep them in check...'

'...and is it not the same for most people, Palm? To have leanings toward one thing or another, then to reconsider the consequences and exert control, how strange we only *have five* senses, yet each one is designed to lead us straight *to* those seven 'oh so deadly sins!'

'Why should we call them *deadly*, Professor? Are they not the substance of living? Surely only very dull, very tired or extremely ancient people do not experience some or all of these so-called sins from time to time?'

'Master Palm, you surprise me. I have no answers. You speak like one of the seven wise men of Greece...Solon is the only one of those *I* can remember. There were also seven wonders of the Ancient World...and seven sleepers of Ephesus, those legendary Christians who fled into a cave and slept there for 200 years.

It all seems to add up: seven being a sacred number, a number of perfection. Even multiples of it are often mentioned in the Bible. Consider the seven days of God's creation, the clean beasts that were taken into the arc in sevens, the seven words on the cross, the seven ages of man. Even in Japan there are seven gods of happiness or luck…'

Palm stared at his tutor: the poor man had exhausted himself.

'But only just one more thing, Palm, your anger: It is touching you mentioned your small anger against your brother, Palm, at a time when you were only a young boy.

There is a quotation in the Bible you should memorise, as I have, for future occasions of *real* anger, because all men are like brothers, and some day one or many of them will drive you into rage and despair:

'Lord, how oft shall my brother sin against me, and I forgive him? Till seven times? Jesus said unto him; I say not unto thee until seven times; but until seventy times seven.'

Pupil and teacher contemplated all this, peaceably, in their gently rocking hammocks.

'I will note it down in my book of thoughts, Professor.'

Palm was smiling: for some reason he imagined his brother in their old home with that troublesome straw roof, and now…mad Ursel by the stove, pushing in another log to prepare the main meal of the day for Christian. 'Perhaps he will marry,' he thought, 'and have strange children with her.'

Then came sudden shouts and turmoil on deck: 'Heligoland in sight!'

Coaxed at last from their suspended position man and boy climbed up on deck to test their eyesight against that of the sailor boy's up in the 'crow's nest' on the mast head: *his* eyes appeared to be better than theirs, for they could see nothing whatsoever. It was probably no more than a miniscule dot on the horizon.

'Be thankful it is not you who sits in that basket,' muttered the recovered teacher, although still pale and protecting his eyes from sunlight. 'The danger of sea-sickness is multiplied a hundredfold sitting up there. The captain will send sailors to spend time in the crow's nest, those who are in need of punishment... and do you have any idea why it is called a 'crow's' nest, Master Palm? No? I give you until arrival in Amsterdam to know the answer.'

The passengers had conquered their sea-sickness. All was going according to plan.

29th May. 'They tied ropes around the logs on board today, to be dropped overboard and then dragged, before dark, by smaller boats into the harbour of Heligoland. I have never seen such a strange place in all my life. How will those logs be raised to the top? Unthinkable!'

'A red craggy monster in the middle of the ocean, such is this island, surely a place completely safe from attack, so high and separate from any invaders, who would have only one small path to clamber up, where they can be picked off with shotguns or anything heavy thrown at them. I see also a white dune-like sand island just across from where we are anchored.' The professor estimated the red stone main island was as high as an extremely tall church steeple.

'We do not disembark, there is no time. Our ship will sail south, or southwest, first thing tomorrow, to reach Amsterdam by early evening.'

30th May. 'Just look: we emerge from our hammocks as hunchbacks! Nevertheless, I've slept well, rocked gently by the water around us. How do you feel this morning, Professor, shall I bring that dry biscuit and water from the galley?'

'Thank-you, Palm, no need. I must venture out myself. Perhaps this is how one feels in one's mother's womb, safe and protected, before emerging into the world, to face the rough and tumble.' The professor's eyes remained closed. Palm stretched, shook his tousled hair and dashed up on deck leaving the tutor to come back to life in his own time.

'To think I was born at sea... small wonder it so agrees with me. How would it feel for three months on such a trip to the southern-most tip of Africa? If Jan de Groote could do it, so can I. But oh, my poor tutor…'

'Another fine day and a fair wind… we go full and by', shouted the captain, 'anchors ahoy, all hands on deck!'

There followed a flurry of activity.

Master Palm Ulefeld emerged from his cocoon, ready to tackle a strange city where he feared he would understand no-one. But he was getting to 'know the ropes' in more ways than one. Now there was new confidence.

'Yes, just like a crow from the crow's nest, that clever creature which knows to fly across the sea, through the fog in a straight line back to the land. Of course', Palm chuckled to himself, 'of course, of course, that's it, the answer my teacher expected to hear; it is what he hoped I will learn to do myself.' *A crow knows where it belongs: it will always find its way* 'And so will I.'

Twelve
Amsterdam.

Palm's tutor had recovered. Even before they caught sight of the Frisian Islands dotted along the coast Palm received the following essential instruction on the curiosities of the Low Lands:

'In 1287 a huge storm breached sand-dunes thus creating the Zuiderzee, giving the inland direct access to the sea. Large seafaring vessels could go straight into the opening towards the city, which of course had not developed yet, at first it was just like Stralsund close to that time, an area of marshlands and swamps from where adventurous fishermen arrived in hollowed–out logs and began to build dams and bridges across a river, in this case called the Amstel. We are speaking about the 12th century, Palm! Soon after came settlement and trade. Inhabitants called themselves the 'Amstelledammers', and wasted no time, creating dwellings and canals and began trading with others from further afield. In 1327 the settlement had its name: yes, indeed, you guessed, Palm, this was 'Amsterdam'.... Already then they had exclusive rights for trade with Hamburg; these cunning 'Amstelledammers' began exacting toll money from beer and herring traders, and even joined the Hanseatic League. An incredible success-story, Palm: Dutch sailors and dealers, they flourished more than most. Already during the 1500's the place emerged as one of the world's major trading powers, they never missed a trick. By 1300 they had built what is now known as the Old Church, right by the Dam Square in the centre of town where we will disembark. I tell you Palm, it is now the wealthiest city in the world....even though they have been through difficult times due to battles for religious freedom. All sorts of radical religious ideas found their way to this exciting city, causing many problems.'

Palm's teacher broke off: around them was intense activity: the crew prepared delicate manoeuvres required to sail a large ship into the peaceful entrance of Amsterdam harbour. Everywhere one looked were extensive systems of dykes reclaiming land from the North Sea. The Captain stopped by his passengers for a moment, told them more than one quarter of the country was *under* sea level, wished them well, while getting with on with his demanding job. In no time they had docked. 'Can this be safe?' wondered Palm, 'under sea-level, one doesn't like the sound of that!'

Hawkers and their 'assistants' were crowding around disembarking passengers. Palm and his Professor each carried leather bags heavy with books. Gulls swooped, screeched, sails flapped on the soon abandoned deck.

Now, feet back on terra firma beside the boat, Palm was alarmed. 'The ground is rocking just as the boat did,' he complained, while they counted their belongings and looked around for someone to transport their cases. What did this mean? The dock looked solid enough, Palm reassured himself, no, there was not a trace of water seeping up through the pavement, but uncannily, he felt the ground sway from side to side. 'De Wallen', which was the name for the quays, teemed with exotic life from foreign lands; black men, Chinamen, Indian men, pushing and shouting, offering to cart luggage wherever it must go. No-one else was troubled by the swaying ground.

'An inn, not too far from the Dutch East India Company!'...ordered his tutor, suddenly fluent in a tongue which Palm assumed might be Dutch. Houses along the way were handsome. It seemed a wealthy, open place, welcoming to strangers. They strolled, following their baggage, strangers smiled, waved, laughed, he heard languages, but for the moment not the one he knew. Palm's heart was beating fast, he felt exhilarated: something unexpected and unusual would surely come his way while he was here in this strange place, he was sure of that. But the pavement still rocked, perhaps a little less so.

After considerable travail, they found a set of rooms close by the Jewish Quarter in Graven Straat. One hefty pull of a bell-chain and the door swung open. Palm's eyes rested on a tiled floor: huge black and orange squares, heavy carved Netherlands kists with brass fittings, flanked by carved chairs with cane seats; a fine woven rug over the table, and a bronze chandelier gleaming as handsomely as those of the Swedish governor. The Pomeranian farmer's boy was impressed.

A parrot, allowed full freedom on his perch, gave a chattering welcome.

Mevrou Terblanche, the small delicate matron with startling round black eyes (not unlike those of her parrot fluttering nervously on a pole), was the land lady. The woman's skin was pale; from under a snow-white cap with long flaps hanging down to her shoulders there emerged strands of dark but greying hair. She listened attentively...fingers clasped over her ample bosom, to the requests and needs of her customers.

The Professor introduced his student: 'Master Palm Ulefeld, Mevrou, he will require a writing table, candles and a comfortable chair... for he must study in his room.' Mevrou Terblanche rewarded the young lodger with a maternal glance, nodded approval while her colourful bird flapped its wings on a perch near the window. Now dancing nervously along a pole, it emitted disapproving noises at the disturbance in the house. The landlady shook her head to and fro: 'what can I do...he's always like that with new guests.'

Standing by a tall window they could see down into the busy street filled with life: vendors, sailors, mothers with children all wandering about and shopping. There were dogs. There were many people with dark skins from sunnier countries. An entertainer on a street corner was scratching on a violin, wearing colourful, nonsensical clothes. Surrounded by smiling citizens...clapping in time to the tune his dog danced on hind-legs. Onlookers would surely throw coins into an upturned cap on the cobbles.

'It resembles Stralsund, but I see more bustle here,' thought Palm, with a twinge of mixed feelings and a slight presentiment. 'So many new things to learn...and now to carry up all our boxes; our own rooms are up two flights of narrow stairs'. Griet, a shy young maid servant, had already begun this arduous task.

Palm took a good look at little Griet.

Mevrou Terblanche smiled apologetically. Her faltering German with a strange accent was accompanied by rapid, encouraging nods. She addressed her customers with a long and complex introduction: 'Mais oui, ja, dear gentlemen, do not 'esitate to ask for anything you may need in this 'ouse , we are at your service throughout the day, you ring ze bell, we come, that is to say, my maids, Liesel, and Griet and, of course, my 'usband. You are most welcome, we enjoy guests from other countries and young Liesel also speaks German...and is an excellent cook,..' then, addressing Palm once again: 'Master Ulefeld, you are most welcome. We 'ave recently 'ad guests from up north, Ulefelds, a very old family, fine and noble, they keep 'orses and own lands, are they relations, perhaps?'

A bewildered Palm raised his eyebrows and shoulders and answered with one of the few short phrases in Dutch he had memorised: 'ek weet nie…mevrou.'

'Ah,ze young gentleman, he eez trying!' Tutor and landlady exchanged a conspiratorial glance 'It eez a difficult language. Yes? No?'

'We dine out tonight, Mevrou Terblanche,' smiled the tutor, now back in his element as Dutch language skills returned seemingly from nowhere, 'we thank you for your kindness. First I wish to show my student the town I loved so dearly some years ago.'

She nodded, flushed, eager to please and care for her new and delightful gentlemen lodgers.

'Bring fresh bed linen, Griet', she called to her maid 'for our gentlemen!'

***

'This town is blessed with everything a man could wish for. What do you think, will you like it here? Our rooms are also near the best inns and drinking places, where the locals and sailors spend their evenings.'

Palm had no doubts whatsoever. Mercifully the curious 'rocking' of the ground had stopped, at last.

They discussed their new routine: Latin grammar, English and Dutch in the morning, and after midday serious topics such as mathematics, politics, religion, philosophy and history in the mother-tongue, perhaps also a little French. On some days Palm would be left to his own explorations, while his tutor would take time off. So far this was an outline of the weeks, months to come. Now they strolled along their own busy road, found an inn to drink, eat and discuss the new life.

'First, Master Palm, allow me to give you an insight into the riches, the power and culture here. You will immediately feel its tolerance: the place has welcomed Huguenots from France and Jews from Spain, just look around you, it is bustling with merchants from many countries and of all hues and races, and above all... this town is a centre for free press mainly because of the Flemish printers who are active here. People say it is the wealthiest city in the world. Did you know the Dutch East India Company has even begun trading with its own shares, turning this place into the financial city of the world?'

'No, Professor. But '*ygeno's*...and shares, what *are* they?'

The farmer's boy from Pomerania could barely keep up with his mentor's enthusiasms. Where and how does one begin with a mind as empty and open as that of Palm's, at heart still a farmer's son with almost no facility of other languages, nor of finance, let alone an understanding of religious strife in foreign lands. The first great Reformation in Pomerania had been absorbed with reasonable simplicity...to everyone at home it was second nature, a fact of life. But now, surrounded by strangers, in a foreign country, came a wider picture.

Over a hearty meal of finest Dutch herring, freshly baked bread, washed down with beer as good as that from

Hamburg, Palm learned about the population of Amsterdam, (already 200,000 despite four terrible epidemics of the Plague), how nothing held back the remaining citizens, ever onwards, growth, development, high finance and above all art, and how this shaped the lives and influence of the Dutch world-wide. And those famous painters, known all over Europe, 'yes, indeed, one of them lives just around the corner, a Mr. Rembrandt....already famous but there are several others. However, one event that did hold Amsterdam back for a short time'...the professor examined his student with care: 'are you able to stay awake for another hour, Palm...tell me if you have had enough for one day, I have an interesting story to tell.' The tutor studied his pupil.

'Oh well, it can wait until tomorrow.'

'Of course I will stay awake, Professor. These 'ygenos' you mention...what do *they* do, Professor?' The professor began his lecture knowing it was high time they wandered back 'home':

'They are now just like any other resident here, perhaps they still speak their own language, but they have been assimilated. They like food and have many eating places. They eat frog's legs and drink good wine...I will tell you more tomorrow, but be patient, you have made me stray from one very important name: Ulrich Zwingli, born seven days after Luther. He also started a Reformation, another movement, which began in Zurich. Just like Luther he was a dynamic theologian and his belief, quite simply, was this: *The Bible is Truth,* anything *not* in the Bible, is not.

Straight-forward. Not so, Palm? Why and how could this possibly bring further dissent? Big questions were constantly being asked but many people had to loose their lives. Not just big but also ultimate questions...about existence and rules given by the highest authority, by God. Eventually this was to lead Zwingli to a confrontation with Luther, the man we Germans all know.

While Zwingli worked for 'reforms to the Reformation' two young people in his group of followers began the

'Anabaptist' movement. Their objection was that baptism should be for 'informed' adults: only people who had attained the age of reason and responsibility could *promise* their lives to Jesus and the Church. They insisted on adult baptism, 'ana' meaning 'again'.... by full immersion into water, like John the Baptist in the River Jordan. They established a religious community. Then the trouble began: the Zurich council decreed they were to be drowned. So they fled to spread their beliefs to other countries, like Germany and to Holland.

Existing churches showed no interest in treating Anabaptists with justice. Soon came persecutions, Palm... all over Europe these brought martyrs' death to thousands of people. The followers of this new religion were thought to be a danger to religious stability. Catholics, Protestants and even royalty pronounced death sentences. King Ferdinand declared 'drowning' to be 'the best antidote to Anabaptists... the third baptism!'

There are hundreds of stories about people killed for their beliefs, describing horror but also their bravery. Here, Palm, just around this corner for example, when twelve nude Anabaptists walked unarmed in the streets in 'honest nakedness' to proclaim the 'naked truth' of the 'new Eden...' they were burned at the stake and their Anabaptist bishop was beheaded. This was in July 1535. These 'naakt-loopers,' (naked walkers) were accused of gross immoral wickedness.

Needless to say, for a while, this manner of terror held back the city's growth. Later a milder regime followed: the Dutch advocated freedom and were opposed to religious persecution. By the end of the 1500's there was religious toleration in the Netherlands...'

Palm's eyes were glazing over.

'..and, do try to hear me out, Palm, all the while, not far from here, even on the island of the English, the Baptists had a history written in blood. Many Hollanders who'd fled there, during the rule of Henry VIII, were persecuted, and not only Hollanders, even English Baptists were considered grave criminals, persecuted and burnt to death. In England one official noted there had been 8000 executions already.

Some of them came here, to Amsterdam, exiled themselves from their home-country: One John Smyth, now buried in the New Church just around the corner from where we sit, called the 'Self Baptiser' because he baptised himself from a small basin, died only 50 years ago.

Palm's eyes had closed. A further small glass of Dutch Gin briefly raised his spirits sufficiently to weave his way back 'home'.

'Nowadays there is nothing holding back the people of Amsterdam', reassured the Professor. 'While we are here we will visit the studios of artists and your view of what truly is important in life will grow and be stimulated...and, I've been thinking about this, Palm: from now on *you* will be the one who pays for our meals. When we are back at the inn I will give you sufficient funds for which you are responsible and must keep account of after each week has ended'.

They had reached their new home. Suddenly Palm was wide awake.

'Do you understand, Palm? This is a most serious matter and I will show you how to keep track of income and expenditure.'

'Yes, yes, I will do my best. But tomorrow you will tell more about those 'ygnos', Professor? They sound really interesting. And now: how do I pull these wooden things down?' Palm stared up.

Professor Ruetz smiled to himself.

With the help of a long rod behind the curtain and by means of a hook he masterfully pulled down the handsome internal wooden shutters.

***

"Good morning, Professor: the 'ygnos'... you promised you would explain. You would tell me about their appearance and their vile food. You spoke of frog's legs! They must be extraordinary people. Are there still some about, here in Amsterdam? Have you seen them?'

'Well yes, good morning, Palm. And so have you…seen them, I mean.'

'No, no, Professor, you are mistaken. I have never seen an 'ygno', nor a Frenchman. Please explain. I shall certainly be on the look-out….'

Palm looked up expectantly: 'what does it mean, truly?'

'The word is pronounced 'ygno' simply because the French speak through the front of their noses in a strange way… it sounds different to the way it is written. And indeed, you have already spoken to an 'ygno' and will be doing so again shortly: it is Madame Terblanche…hers is an old French name. It means Mrs. *White earth*.'

'What! What do you say, Professor, she is French? She is an 'ygno'? Why, she is no different from us! She spoke to you in Dutch, and looks just like anyone else.' Palm, eyes wide and very agitated was a little disappointed.

'Indeed Palm. And now I hope you will begin to understand that all people are mostly the same as each other and that discrimination is a perilous, dangerous and sinful thing. You were almost trapped into believing that Huguenots were monsters, were you not? Note the spelling of the word Palm.'

During further silence, as his teacher wrote the name down with a flourish and in large letters, Palm admitted to himself he had been expecting something of vast significance.

But there it was: *Huguenots*….

'They *did* foster an identity that enabled them to remain aloof, a minority convinced of their language and their culture and they had a leader called Hugues, a religious leader and politician, which *may* have given rise to the name 'Ygnots'. These were the French Protestants in the time of the Reformation, they struggled for their freedom, became a state within the state, which made the Catholics feel threatened. And now consider the consequence:

A massacre took place on St. Bartholomew's Day: a hideous, dreadful crime: almost 25,000 Protestants killed in Paris alone. In France there were eight separate wars, all to do with religion. When the harassment continued the Huguenots fled to different countries. Some of them came here to make a new life, in Amsterdam.

Now, Master Palm...I trust you see more clearly how one must never judge, reject or mistrust people until one truly understands all the facts. I recommend you consider this discussion many times....ah, and here comes Madame Terblanche (or should I say 'mevrou') with hot milk and coffee and Griet has brought freshly baked pastry; how I love Amsterdam... a very good morning, Madame, thank you for all this!'

Then, turning back to his pupil: 'Today we resume English lessons. After that we make a start on Charlemagne.'

Palm studied Mevrou Terblanche from the corner of his eye. She had not changed. Huguenots, Anabaptists...his head was spinning.

And today was only the first morning of the first day in this New World.

***

'He's gone off, my tutor, after our 'English conversation 'with a breezy farewell. 'To my favourite university'...he said and I am left behind with *my* onerous tasks which include Charlemagne. I have little desire, the book has too many pages and the print is hard to read.

Before his departure we had a brisk discussion about the name *Charles*, and how there were far too many of them living even now: two Charles II, one English, one Spanish, the latter born handicapped at birth...and then, going back 300 years ago a king of France called Charles the Wise, as also Charles V who was a Holy Roman Emperor. After a short rest my tutor retrieved from his memory another one named Charles 'the Foolish', who suffered from fits of madness in the 15th century. He was followed by Charles the Victorious, who did rather better than his predecessor as he helped the French rid themselves of the English invaders. And Charles IX, an evil man who authorised the massacre of the Huguenots...I had heard of him before, if only yesterday. At least he was haunted by that evil deed until his own death about one hundred years ago. So it is written. Now that I have met true 'ygnots' I can join all those others who heartily condemn him. Not quite, there remains Charlemagne, or Charles the Great.

I sit, alone, condemning, staring at the pages before me, reading about a man who lived almost one thousand years before me and who is thought to be worthy of such careful scrutiny. It says here:....... Palm's eyelids had drooped and his thoughts were straying:

'Alone, in a country with another language, abandoned in a room in Amsterdam, well, I do not like it. Of course Mevrou Terblanche is here too, just downstairs and her Liesel, and that Griet, and somewhere also an 'ygno' husband whom I have not seen.

And yes, there is money in my pocket.

Later...no, sooner or later I can, I must, step out to look around, buy food, perhaps fruit, or cakes, like I did at the old merchant's house near my school. Yes, I must. Mönch Strasse,..just saying the word makes me miss Stralsund. I never thought I would so miss it. I will jot down what I buy, and how much I spend and also how much remains... It is called *Book-keeping.* Last night my tutor explained the need to be methodical in all matters, but especially in finance.

...Now, where was I with this Charlemagne? He had a father called Pepin the Short. Can this be the man my 'true' father claims to be related to? Pepin's eldest son lived unimaginably far back in past times; all the more surprising I must waste time being instructed about his life...'Grimly Palm picked up his pen and wrote:

My account of Charlemagne. He had German blood and German speech. We know this because of ancient documents ...Even though he could barely put pen to paper himself;.... he learned late and probably had scribes and he was a great fighter: 18 campaigns against the Saxons who had burnt down a Christian church. He gave them a choice between baptism and death and then proceeded to behead 4500 rebels in ONE day. Defeated Lombards and Arabs in Spain. (Who are these Lombards?) Fought just about everybody and took control of central Europe. A Pope crowned him Emperor. He controlled a vast empire and promoted Christianity, education, agriculture and the arts. He had four successive wives, five mistresses or concubines and eighteen *children.....truly a Great Man,......* Palm's essay breaks off....He walks over to the window, looks down at the busy road and longs to be out in the sunshine, to wander about, to explore. He sits down again, scribbles hastily:

'I have no desire to write this, I do not know who I am...so why should I know this Charlemagne? Who is my father, that is what I need to know and what is this downward spiral I feel presently? Homeless I must become a gentleman, withdrawn and pumped full of knowledge and must also remain humble as the monks of St Catherine's Monastery: I have knowledge of their perpetual training to dedicate their lives to God, their asceticism, ,... basic rules made 1000 years ago. But I am Palm, and need to see the world and be in it now. What harm can it do, what will it do to me? Should I abandon this heavy book? Yes.

and yes again. I wish to find enjoyment in the real world, yes! There, a blot of ink carelessly spilt and I no longer care: 'I must get out of these lodgings..."

...opening the window he peered around, got his bearings: 'There, that must be Nieuwe Kerk, I will keep my eyes on it, the spire will guide me. I can return later to study Charlemagne. I will feel refreshed. I will find the grave of the English Anabaptist; his spirit will be with me as I explore.'

With a jacket in one hand, his cap in the other, Palm stormed down the stairs, out into the sunny street below, and marched briskly towards the big church, wandering round it he turned back heading for the Waal and Dam Square, breathing deeply, savouring freedom, and suddenly curiously alive, yet perturbed: those naked Anabaptists had been slaughtered right here on this very spot for testing the boundaries of religious freedom.

Meanwhile Mevrou Terblanche had raised the curtain slightly, noted her young lodger apparently heading for the Church and also that he had, so far, spoken to no-one.

For one Taler I can buy, (in Stralsund)

2 pairs of shoes	1 castrated ram
5 geese	13 pounds of butter
2 bushels of barley	10 pounds of honey

Palm had his notebook with him, was writing down prices of goods available in Amsterdam, not quite sure why, still, one never knows... it might be of use to know such things, proof that he was taking matters seriously.

Such strange objects! Fruits he had never seen before, yellow curved things and orange prickly ones, and everyone was speaking Dutch: it did sound almost like German but not enough to be sure. He pointed at the yellow fruit while the vendor made incomprehensible sounds like a small child, 'bababa, drie pfennige'... Palm drew coins from his pocket, studied them at length, then pointed and paid for one 'bababa'...while observing another customer peeling off long soft strips to reveal a naked rude centre, which he stuck into his mouth and then chewed contently.

'Goed' nodded the customer and smiled, 'goed en soet'...and within seconds Palm had learnt that 'goed' and 'soet' could only be the equivalent of 'gut' and 'süss', and that the man had devoured a 'banana'.

This market was not unlike the one at home: he saw wooden wheel-barrows, trestles heaped with purple onions, glistening like rare jewels in the sunlight, next to these were stacked king-size orange carrots, and heaps of familiar greens. He saw a row of bloodied pig's heads, the butcher doing busy trade with cooks and maids sent out for fresh supplies, arguing, sniffing, prodding goods for quality, everywhere much banter and laughter.

'Good-natured people, these Amsterdamers, that's how they seem; and everywhere pigeons, white, grey and speckled, making a nuisance of themselves. But I...no, I am making huge progress.'

A word he heard and picked up soon was the guttural 'grachten'; these were canals and they were everywhere, with lordly names easy to remember such as 'Herengracht' and 'Keizergracht' and 'Prinsengracht', the first of these marked the line of the town walls, which enclosed a tower with a worrying name, the 'Schreyers-toren' or Weepers Tower, by the old harbour, as well as the Oude Kerk and the Nieuwe Kerk beside a palace by the Dam.

After several hours of solitary wandering he passed an inn with a large sign proclaiming 'De drie Fleschjes', along with a picture displaying three bottles. Now tired and thirsty Palm spotted, across the large dark room, a colourfully dressed lutenist performing with astonishing skill.

Customers craned their necks to see the young man playing, while Palm gulped down a tumbler of what appeared to be water.

He spluttered, blinked, deliberated for a moment and raised his arm for another. Awash with feelings of pleasurable abandon, waves of wishing to put his head down someplace... and gazing vacantly at the beams on the ceiling, he emptied a second glass, choked a little, and coughed. He did not know Gin. The smiling waitress stood before him; she appeared to be swaying from side to side; Palm shook his head slowly and said 'ja, noch ein Glas,' thus revealing he was a customer from across the borders, more than likely a Hamburger, judging from his clothes. Again he held his hand aloft, waved it about in time to a merry gig from the lute then, by and by, confronting the third glass... he slid off his chair after several gulps and fell to the floor, with a loud thud, smashing the glass.

The publican, swearing to himself quietly(in English,) had dragged the comatose customer to a back room, where Palm spent a good three hours kept warm by a cat... with an occasional comforting lick on his face from a dog.

Some four hours later, Palm returned to the living. Bewildered, after a very long sleep, the youth staggered out into the back yard, found a pump and took huge gulps of water while washing his face. Chickens fluttered cackling at the disturbance and a maid, wearing her white *kappie,* grinned saucily, hanging up a vast basket of washing. Palm remembered as good as nothing, apart from the musician, who had been playing so peacefully in a dark corner. When he returned indoors he found this cheerful individual packing up to go home.

He studied the young lutenist: a rare exotic bird, dressed in a black jacket with heavily gathered orange stripes, and a matching cap pushed down on thick brown locks. Sitting near him were customers, eating, drinking, chatting and calling out, wishing the musician 'Farewell, Piet, but please come back!'

Piet picked his way across the room to Palm. Carrying the lute under one arm he shook his head in the direction to the door saying, in almost perfect German: 'Kommen Sie nur mit, I will assist you to get home.'

'To the Nieuwe Kerk, with Madame Terblanche' explained Palm, giving all the information he had. The two walked silently for a while. 'Ah, yes! Graven Straat, I remember now.' The lutenist smiled.

'We are almost there, Mynheer. I am Piet, and I play the lute for my living. I trust you have recovered?'

Palm was very touched. 'I have found a friend,' he thought to himself.

'I will come again to hear you play, but I will drink only tea, Piet. Please call me Palm. Thank you for your kindness. Goodbye, tot siens.'

They bowed, they smiled, waved and parted.

The vendor of bananas had gone. Palm found someone selling cherries, large and mouth-watering, on the corner near his lodgings. He paid for a punnet, filled to the top, carried it back to the home of his landlady. By the time he found the house he had eaten every one of them and had spat out at least forty pips. He lumbered up the flights of stairs to his room, empty-handed, with red lips, tired and feeling a little guilty.

His teacher was waiting: 'Well, Master Palm, out and about in Amsterdam? Does the place please you?'

'Why, indeed, Professor, I have learnt a great deal. But apart from a banana, some cherries and a drink I have had little to sustain me. I would like to go out again soon, but in *your* company, to enjoy a hot meal.'

'Of course, Palm. And you will tell me about your studies of Charlemagne. Allow me to finish my notes for today. We will go out in one, perhaps two hours. Until then I beg to be excused ....'

***

On the following day, again and yet again, he agreed to immerse himself in the life of Charlemagne. He tried to take in all the incredible activities of this super-human ruler. But on the hour, each time the church bell struck, he was drawn away from his studies to the window. Long before midday he'd head off to Dam Square. The place already felt more familiar. He hoped to take lunch with his new friend, the lutenist. 'I shall never touch gin again.' 'At most a beer,' he had promised the professor.

Piet Hals was there, hard at work. He managed to whisper to Palm he was not allowed to stop playing until customers left after their midday break. 'I must perform to make them enjoy their food...only afterwards the management feed me. Then we can talk.'

'Musicians have a good life,' thought Palm, deciding to return later; he would explore Amsterdam until the man was free. 'I will seek out the Dutch East India House. It is on a side-road, not far from here.'

After awkward gesticulating, questioning, he found his way to an impressively large brick building with its own shipyard at the back. 'At last, here it is,' he muttered to himself, 'the famous organisation my sailor friend Jan de Groote works for...it does look very fine. I will enter and enquire after him'.

This took courage. He climbed up seven steps and pushed open a heavy black door of impressive dimensions. On the walls inside he studied splendid maps displayed in frames, in the corners the proud signature of one

Willem Janzoon Blaen.

'Blaen,.... Amsterdam?' Palm, having caught the eye of a German-speaking official, pointed at the picture, enquired casually, trying to appear knowledgeable. He had heard the company went bankrupt in 1656, but as his eyes darted about at marble mantelpieces displaying blue and white Chinese porcelain....fittings, furnishings and portraits of wealthy worthies... the current grandeur told another story. The place seemed even grander than that of the Swedish governor in Stralsund. He remembered full well how to behave in such surroundings.

Master Ulfeld understood how to create a good impression at the venerable headquarters of the Dutch East India Company. Soon the polite member of staff had not only located the approximate whereabouts of Palm's young sailor friend but now also gave account of regular sailings around the Cape and that passengers could be taken onboard, assuming they were able to pay a handsome sum before they left: 'a return journey would require about a quarter of the sum paid for an average house, shall we say 250 guilders.' Frowning, Palm entered this into his notebook, acquiring *gravitas*, as he jotted down information about the journey, also approximate dates of sailing in the foreseeable future, that is, in the coming year 1668.

The Dutch East India Company, better known by its Dutch abbreviation, the VOC, had assumed Master Uhlfeld to be a prospective customer...not only a traveller...also an investor, perhaps?

Palm enjoyed himself in this new role: 'One is treated as a gentleman', he noted, 'it must be the clever tailor in Stralsund, he knew what he was doing when he last measured me...what will my Professor say to all this...?'

It was tricky to find one's way through the crowds on the Dam market back into the heart of Amsterdam. As he passed vendors, sailors and travellers from arriving ships, luggage carriers, pretty girls, beggars and musicians, carriages and wagons, horses and dogs, a great mixture of life and noise and smells... he tried not to stop, apart from the renewed temptation of another ripe banana. He attempted various words in Dutch, to the amusement of the vendor who today carried a colourful parrot on his shoulder. The bird intoned, 'ba nan a...ba na na...' with remarkable accuracy, as well as 'good day' in Dutch. 'Ja, goed!,' the vendor grinned and nodded approvingly.

'My lutenist must surely be finishing his performance in the Gin parlour by now,' reasoned Palm. His teacher had informed him there were at least four-hundred distillers of gin in Amsterdam, that it was used to cure lumbago and gout and was best avoided.

Bursting with renewed confidence Palm strolled into the Inn, hardly aware of yesterday's disgrace. He apologised to the landlord, who, well versed in German, English, perhaps *was* English, or indeed French ...laughed and assured his customer that both cat and dog had taken good care of him: 'Their names are 'Cavalier' and 'Roundhead,' he stated proudly but Palm, still ignorant of history, did not see the joke, merely hoped to renew contact with that 'colourful' musician, surely not much older than himself? And there he was, still in the extraordinary outfit from the previous day, but sadly about to leave.

'Piet! Palm! With cheeky grins they greeted one another as old friends...'how about some 'peekle haering? Yes? Wonderful, it is my favourite dish, especially with new potatoes...and with beer.'

Palm nodded but was overwhelmed with homesickness. What a discovery: the Dutch eat the same things as Stralsund folk: pickled herrings, sliced onions in cream sauce. He sighed.

'Over there, Palm, follow me, they know me, they give generous portions...'Palm gazed at his friend with admiration, dazzled anew by the colourful garment and hat. This lutenist stood out in the crowd, people stared as he passed. Yes, he seemed well known and loved. The two young men were soon seated in a small eating house and had asked for food.

'Piet, why do you dress like this, the strange hat, this jacket? Everyone is looking at you...'

'Because I am a Fool, Palm, that is why.'

'You seem no fool to me, Piet, you are an artist and also a thoughtful and helpful person, of that I am certain!'

The lutenist grinned at the youthful stranger from the depths of darkest Germany. He took a thirsty swig of foaming beer and then looked well satisfied with what he was about to tell:

'It was my father, Palm, who gave me this idea: he is a painter, he enjoys the company of publicans and drunkards, mixes with *'disreputable'* people. He painted a picture of a lute-player and called it 'The Fool'. It was my idea I might make myself resemble this Fool in every detail...as you can see, people know me and like me like this, and my poor father, old and unwell, enjoys my success in his own quiet way. I tell you, you've never seen anyone who paints so speedily, with animated freshness, his style is informal, life-like. When he was young he was also known for his coarse humour and fluency in producing many famous pictures...you should see some of them: 'Singing boy with a flute' or 'Two boys singing' or even the 'Young man in a hat',.... in fact, that is the one who looks a little like you with his white lace collar and cuffs...my father's pictures often make me feel a real thinking being is looking back at me.'

Piet has had his say. Grinning and pleased with himself, he took a deep swig of beer:

'Well, now my father is old. He has his failings as a man, always broke. He lives in Harlem, and the municipality gives him a stipend, but only since 1662...so, you see, although I have several siblings we all try to help him and I work each day to support not only myself but also him,'...Palm interrupted the lute-player at this point:

'I no longer have a father, nor a mother, Piet. *You* are the fortunate one.'

'Fortunate, yes, but poor,' he replied. The one balances the other! Just think how it would be to have riches as well...riches Palm, not fame. For that is what my father has: 'our famous Frans', people say, sounding respectful....now *there* is a man of talent. But he remains poor, so very poor.'

Palm had fallen silent. He too had a father, but he dared not say so, since he knew nothing about him. Was he famous or infamous? Palm suspected the latter.

After a silence he plucked up courage to present an improbable and unexpected request.

'Could you teach me, Piet? I am here for some time and it would be a great pleasure to play such a pleasing instrument...I would so like to try it. I could find a lute, perhaps with your help? I beg you?'

'Ha! Such an instrument costs a small fortune, my new friend. Besides, time is money, I would have to charge you...and what if you showed no talent?'

'If you help me find a lute I will find money *and* talent. Will you agree?'

'Well, Master Palm, my father always likes to say painting is an endeavour for the strong-hearted, but it is equally, if not *more* challenging, to learn a stringed instrument. Do you really mean what you are saying, or are you just trying to fill your time? Believe me, this is *one* thing that truly demands time. It lives on time.'

'I mean it, I truly do,' was Palm's enthusiastic reply. I will discuss this with my tutor. We will meet again here and I will tell you his response.'

'Well, if that is so!' Grinning happily they leaned forward to attack platefuls of pickled herring, and steaming new potatoes. Life was good.

***

Amsterdam, 29th June, 1667, My dear Mother, little Marie,

I so lose track of time, now I write to you from Amsterdam. Who knows for how long I am here with the young person I told you about. I guide him through as many interesting experiences as possible, so he may mature and understand his future position in life. It has to be said: he makes phenomenal progress, surprises me with his clear mind, enterprise and appreciation of new experience. So far we have paid short visits to Lübeck, Hamburg and Heligoland, and are now safely established in the home of a thoughtful Dutch lady in Amsterdam, who has taken us in as paying guests. We reside in the very centre of this wonderful town. My pupil appears to have no fear of the foreign language, it is so close to our own. He will soon be sufficiently comfortable speaking Dutch and also English so he can fully benefit from lectures I hope to expose him to at the University. The Swedish governor in Stralsund will dispatch this by messenger. I am still able to send you the greater part of my salary each month. May the Lord keep you both safe.

Your devoted son,   Martin Ruetz.

30th June. 'Please do calm yourself, Master Palm. We have discussed this at length. I believe you have no understanding of what is involved in the art of playing a lute. You have already joined the choir in the Nieuwe Kerk, That is sufficient time spent on music. I must insist you do as I say. I repeat. Palm: I insist.'

Palm is aghast. This is the first time his tutor has stood in his way…not counting that sudden departure from Stralsund.

'I wish to bring Piet along to Madame Terblanche's establishment. She will no doubt become pale and look distressed by his wild hair and strange apparel, and I do not wish my new friend to be made uncomfortable. You talk me out of learning to play the lute… is this not something fine gentlemen do? I am irritable with being told what to do. I will not eat tonight.' Palm rushes to his room, slams the door and throws himself on the bed.

Of course Palm was unaware of the requirements, stipulations, all the Professor's plans for him: that dense programme of study, to be absorbed as soon as possible, along with mind-expanding travel, the linguistic skills, all the hallmarks of cultivated men. To begin, at this stage, with the study of an instrument such as the lute would draw on time and energies required to get through more serious disciplines: 'Mathematics, languages, religion, sciences and history, and now the lute,' agonised the tutor, 'where do I draw the line?'

Even in music there must be intense discipline: a lute will devour years of valuable time spent doing nothing but training fingers to dexterity, to pleasure and dreaming. 'No, there is not enough time. Palm, you are seventeen years old. Such skills must be honed before you are ten. It is too late. Besides, such activities are for dreamers, to be employed by wealthy men to give pleasure to guests, dignitaries and damsels... *real* men have more serious things to think about.'

'I must tell Palm about King Christian's orchestra', thinks the professor when he wakes the following morning, after a restless night. 'Yes, not only will it break the ice, it will open his eyes to the musicians' lot. His behaviour pains me, he has locked his door, he refuses to eat. In *his* eyes I have failed him. He thinks I am a bad teacher.'

In the morning there was, at first, a frost between them. They broke their fast in silence. Palm had appeared, but with dark shadows under his eyes, looking distant and forlorn. Still, he knew: he must apologise.

The tutor had also considered his own position and now made a peace offering: 'Master Palm: Let us work together this morning: some science first, or even Philosophy: about a man called Descartes who also lives here and resolves to find the truth in nature and in himself. 'I think, therefore I am', he says, then repeats it in Latin: 'Cogito ergo sum'. Now I ask you, Palm, consider and memorise this short phrase. Later we will find your friend and invite him to dine with us. We can discuss the entire matter, about the music lessons, all three of us. What do you say?'

Palm looks up and manages a courteous but worried smile.

'You will not show excessive surprise at his appearance?' Palm is now pleading protectively, 'my friend dresses for his performance; he has his reasons.'

'Palm, do not concern yourself, I look forward to meeting your musician.' So, with renewed trust and energy they resume the serious morning study sessions. 'Cogito ergo sum', Palm....find the truth in yourself, and in nature. Repeat it! Yes, that's it. Just open your mind!'

Later, on the warm summer's day, they arrived at the 'Drie Fleschjies' to listen to the last of the colourfully dressed artist's offerings, see him take a bow and then watch him wrap his instrument in a soft fleece.

'Will it be safe in a large wardrobe at the back of the inn until later,' Piet asked the owner of the inn, while Palm took a sideways glance at the teacher's face to judge his surprise or consternation. There was none.

The lute-player's audience, as before, had given Piet a rousing farewell and soon the three men were standing outside, away from the guests; they bowed politely, spoke German, there was no difficulty. Palm escorted his Professor to their favoured spot, a quiet corner, and instantly a lively discussion arose about the difficulties of keeping such an instrument in order.

'I have heard of the immense tension of those strings stretched across the belly of the lute; could they not cause the middle to sag or crack, and should it not be kept in a 'bed' when not in use?' As always, Palm was astonished at his tutor's knowledge and jealously noted his new friend fully taking up the attention of the older man.

'Indeed, Sir', nodded Piet, 'a cradle: for a lute is like a delicate child. It is a problem. I have no such thing. I worry each day, as my instrument is the only thing of value I own. Some famous French lutenist in Paris, I forget his name, claimed the cost of keeping a horse and a lute is about the same. Still, I have no horse so I couldn't say. The strings are made of cat gut and their tender charm is much appreciated, although devilish hard to keep in tune. It is believed good lutes are mostly made in Germany; I know however, the finest come from Italy. Mine is such a one, a pitiful, old cracked thing, but its value equals that of a house...and it is all I have, left to me by my teacher, who came from Nürnberg, God rest his soul! My teacher's instruction was that the Arabic word *al'ud* is of oriental origin, we now call it a 'lute', and it came to us during the Crusades. Only the Portuguese 'alaude' still retains the more ancient name. One so enjoys these mysterious historical connections!'

'He is unstoppable', thinks Palm. Then, frowning: 'is it truly *cat gut* you said, Piet...do you slaughter cats to make your strings? I am very fond of cats.'

'No, no, rest assured, Master Palm, the word is only a shortened form of 'cattle' gut, and this comes from the natural fibre in the walls of animal intestines, usually sheep or goat, even hog or horse....animals which are slaughtered for other reasons. Never a cat, no, not at all, there is a superstition they would bring bad luck.' Palm pulls a face, imagining the processes, killing, cutting, and all that bleeding.

'Yes,' continued Piet, 'an unpleasing thought and the choosing of lute strings is a great art and responsibility: 'they must be fresh and especially treble strings should be 'faire and clear, whitish-grey or ash colour'. A well-known Englishman has written a treatise about strings; an excellent player I'm told, my teacher knew him well: John Dowland, himself a composer of note, my own teacher knew him, working together in Denmark, in an orchestra of the King, Christian IV.'

Palm turned quickly, eyebrows raised, and looked at his teacher, who in return gazed steadily at Palm. For a moment they communicated, without saying a word: a moment when their own special bond was affirmed and re-assured. They said nothing further, knowing they could talk later, when they were alone.

Palm had not forgotten, but having no knowledge of this orchestra, he shivered, conscious suddenly: his own connection with a real King marked him as something, someone special. Breathlessly he pressed Piet Hals to tell all he had heard about the King's orchestra and the honour bestowed on the lute-player from Holland, and how it felt to be in the employ of such a King.

'Did your teacher earn good money? Was it a great adventure to be in Denmark, was the King pleased with his musicians?' Palm and his tutor stared at the lutenist in his garish costume, wishing he would stop chewing with his mouth open, and to stop swilling ever more beer. At last Piet wiped his mouth on his sleeve (Palm knew, this was not the correct thing to do) then turned to the tutor with a cheerful wink, 'if I may, gentlemen, I do so enjoy repeating this history my own beloved teacher told me...'

'The sooner, the better,' replied Palm. Both he and the professor, rubbed their hands and encouraged the musician with friendly smiles. And so Piet told the story:

'The orchestra, made up of players from all over Europe, fiddlers from Italy,...from Germany a viol player, a French cembalo, two lute players, one from England, the other, my own dear teacher, from here...a motley bunch, found themselves, to their greatest surprise, not in a fine hall but in a dank, dark cellar, below the King's quarters. This was not only their home but also where, for some unknown reason, the King's hens were kept. Climbing down roughly constructed, winding stone steps into a cold, stone cellar, with small ground-level windows and a low ceiling, and only a few torches and candles... reading and playing music, also simply passing time in a more general way, became a questionable task. There were not only cages with hens, but casks of wine. These at least came with a pleasing resinous smell, helping to mask the odorous hens. Several musicians could not bear it and ran away, depressed by the cold dank darkness that enveloped their bodies and souls and made their lives pitiful. Yet, others were aware of the honour of being in the employ of a king. They stayed on and made the best of it.'

Palm and his tutor exchanged a glance.

'Through a system of hollow pipes running along the wall up into the King's room, the 'Winter Room' as it was known, the sound of music could pass up whenever it pleased the

King to open a trapdoor in the ceiling. It was his greatest pleasure to invite guests and see them marvelling at the invisible source of heavenly music. Players in the Royal Orchestra had to be ready to play for the King both day and night....'Piet stopped his monologue for a few moments and looked at his captive audience.

'My poor teacher became ill after one year and asked to be released from his duties; the performers were not well paid. Very few renewed their contracts. So he returned to his homeland having earned no more than the average wage of a craftsman. But worse was to follow: his chest was heavy, he had begun to cough from the chill of the cellar, and he only lived another year before he had coughed himself to death. His instrument, well, he bequeathed it to me with only one bit of advice:

'Remain inventive, Piet,' he said, ' think hard what it is you have to offer the world and make it special, so no-one can take it from you.

I had to think for a long time what I had that no-one else had, and it was this: my father's picture of the boy with a lute...his 'Joseph's Coat' costume and hat, which I have copied and wear when I perform...it makes people happy to see me. They remember me, they welcome me and I now earn enough each day to eat. I still have this picture. Perhaps one day a rich man will offer me a few gulden for it. And my lute....it is probably also worth enough, but I depend on it so it is not for sale. My former instrument is in a sorry state, however, I could lend it to you, Master Palm, just for trying out how it feels to hold and touch the strings.'

'And your charge, Piet, what is the cost?' enquired the Professor.

'Sufficient for the purchase of one meal, such as this one, yes, that would be most satisfactory...for each lesson, with no time limit. After two lessons Palm can make up his mind if he is still so eager to learn'. The professor cleared his throat, clasped his hands before him and nodding solemnly stated: 'As long as my student continues his other studies with the same diligence as before! And one more thing, Master Piet, I beg you, speak only in Dutch to your new pupil. He must become more used to your language....'

Palm's wish had been granted. He had won.

Yes!

DÜRER'S THE DRAUGHTSMAN AND THE LUTE (1525)

THIRTEEN

'It is too cold to go out. It is even too cold to practise the lute. I have asked Madame Terblanche to send Griet with hot food and drink later. 'Palm: this is the long awaited day! You have waited patiently, I know.'

Professor Ruetz, his cloak around his shoulders, was standing near the fireplace, already lit in the very early hours by Griet. Rubbing his hands to generate additional warmth he studied his pupil seated by the table. Palm seemed eager to write down all he was about to hear. Only recently he had even sharpened the quill of his pen.

'My heart is beating faster than usual; I feel warm enough and only a little apprehensive,' he assured his tutor.

'What you *do not* know, Palm, is that I have *not* been at the university day after day'...the tutor appeared to hesitate with this revelation: 'I have devoted my time to research government departments, embassies and many other sources, even the military, trying to assemble as much information as possible about the 'official' truth concerning your father. Our helpful Swedish governor in Stralsund has done the same, but his report only presents the 'truth' from the Swedish viewpoint. You must see, a fair amount of time has gone by and somewhere in this assemblage of truths, and I say the word with caution, there may be an 'absolute' truth, or one that you shall find to become your own personal explanation.'

'I am astonished! Why did you not tell me? Truly astonished! But pray continue, professor, I am ready for this day. I am bursting to know...I long to hear it all, do begin if it pleases you, I beg you.'

'You might be honoured, Palm, to hear the family *von Ulfeldt*, or *von Uhlfeldt,* has been known back to the 14th century... the name appeared on old documents in places from Holland up to Danish lands and in the areas known as Brandenburg and Mecklenburg. The original holders may have been 'robber-barons', but also peaceful land or mill owners and all had a consistent coat of arms showing a strange hat, some sort of military helmet atop a shield displaying two crossed battle axes. Spelling of names was variable. As you know, Palm, the art of writing is not widespread in these parts...so we see *Ulvelde, Uhlenfeld, Ulfeldt,* and even *Ilenfeld,* which may be a more realistic way of the northern pronunciation of ü....The teacher stopped, drew from a folder a picture of the coat of arms of an ancient Ulfeld family and handed it to Palm who stared at it in wonderment.

And then followed facts about his father: Born in 1606 his first name was Corfitz; ancestors had lived on an island called Fyn, where their ancient seat was Uhlfeldsholm. 'How grand was that', thought Palm.

'Corfitz, the seventh child of seventeen children, had also been sent to travel in other lands, guided by a tutor, Palm. Some things never change! He travelled as far as Italy and remained for some time to study in Padua. He knew many languages, he understood mathematics and wrote poetry and eventually became the headmaster of a school. *His* own father, a chancellor in the employ of Christian IV, introduced his son to the Court, where he made such a good impression he was instantly made a Knight of the 'Order of the Elephant.' Soon seen to be restless, he was sent on diplomatic missions, his knowledge of languages proving to be a great asset. Greater honours were soon bestowed on him. The King offered him a prospective bride, although she, his favourite daughter, was only eight years old: Eleonora Christina, was her name. 'Palm raised his eyebrows but was quickly assured: 'your parents married 1636, when she was fifteen and Corfitz was thirty years old.' The professor cleared his throat noisily:

'The first thing she did was to sell all her jewellery so she could help to pay her husband's numerous debts. By then Corfitz had become a member of the great Council, Governor of Copenhagen and even Chancellor of the Exchequer; he was sent to Vienna as Ambassador and Emperor Ferdinand III made him a Count of the German

Empire. By 1643 he became Lord High Steward of Denmark...he was at the summit of power and influence.'

'Now Palm, don't look bewildered!'

'But all these titles Professor, and what is a *diplomatic mission*?

I should make a list of such things.'

'We shall stop for a while, Palm,' announced the Professor, 'perhaps to call for Griet to bring refreshments? I will try to answer your questions, while you make your list.'

'Yes indeed, thank you, professor!'

Palm bounded down the stairs, calling Griet's name: he liked Griet, her shyness gave him a feeling of power. She curtsied each time he addressed her. Rosy, fleshy lips, usually half parted as if she had something to say, beguiled him, but being modest and earnest she wanted only to please without speaking... to nod and smile was all she felt brave enough to do.

Soon enough Palm had absorbed his father's titles of Governor, Chancellor, Ambassador and Steward, but then came a confrontation with damning news: the man had bought estates, land, jewellery, lived in great comfort and splendour, but, (solemnly stressed by his tutor,) the money he used for these luxuries was not his own: it came from state coffers, he had been pocketing illegal profits...in 1640 alone he swindled the crown of 100,000 rix-dollars, shady deals were concluded under his code-name 'il Unicorno'.

'It seems your father was known as one of Europe's leading money-lenders, Palm, loaning generously to poorer monarchs. Even worse: your father struck 'base coin': using a mixture of cheaper metal, while the crown was in need of money he neglected the defences of his country. Now this was shameful behaviour...'confirmed Palm's teacher.

Palm could only nod. He frowned and his face was pale.

'Then there was a moment of truth: Sweden, engaged in the Thirty Years War in German lands, launched an unexpected attack on Denmark. A disaster, Palm, imagine, your father unable to back his own King with the necessary supplies, and needless to say this very King losing confidence in his chancellor. Even so, your father *still* kept his important offices, was even sent abroad again, with your mother, and everywhere they went they were received with flattering attention. However, by the time the Ulfeldts returned to Denmark King Christian IV was no longer satisfied.

But in 1648 this King died.

Then came a new King, the second son of Christian IV. *His* wife, a Saxon princess, hated your father; even more she hated your mother, who was more talented and beautiful than she was.

Your parents secretly ransacked the late King's archives in a fruitless attempt to document their children's claim to the Danish throne. Yes, indeed, I see your surprise Palm, you did not know you had numerous brothers and sisters! There were further troubles when a former mistress of Corfitz, now pregnant, spread rumours the Ulfelds were plotting to kill the new King with poison. This woman was interrogated under torture and hanged in 1651'.

At this point Palm put down his pen. There was no pleasure in writing all this down. Black clouds had gathered over his head. The teacher continued:

'Count Ulfeld of the Roman Empire, High Steward of the Realm in Denmark, your father, Palm, still closely connected with the political events in northern Europe, published a defence of his political conduct in 1652. Again your parents were sent to Holland...your father held his position as diplomat, and this time he was to negotiate a tricky subject: you've heard about the levies imposed on shipping that had to pass through the Sound, an age-old, permanent cause of conflict between Denmark and all Baltic traders, as well as between the ships from the Dutch Republic and other nations. By the time he returned from these diplomatic negotiations abroad your father's past conduct had been investigated, condemned and his powers curtailed. Nor was anyone in favour of his recent hard-won solutions to the problem of the shipping levies.

The new King had also closed in on former titles and honours bestowed by Christian IV, even those given to his numerous children. This so irritated your father he refused to go to Court. Of course there was an immediate official enquiry: your father was absolved, but his enemies did their best to keep suspicions alive,' the professor looked up,'and, at this time your father was advised to leave Denmark.'

Palm hopes were dashed. He turned away, stared out of the window. He had already heard more than he could bear.

Encouraged to ask questions he did not know where to begin. 'Levies, what are levies,' he wondered...but in the end neither cared nor wished to hear any more. His own father was a scoundrel, this much was plain. There had been answers to his questions but the answers brought understanding he could not enjoy. After a while Palm asked only one question: 'What was his appearance?'

'Your father's, Palm?' The disaffected son nodded disdainfully, 'well yes. This 'Corfitz', how did he look?'

'I have seen but one portrait', replied the tutor, 'painted by a court-painter in Denmark (there is a modest copy in Den Haag)... He had long, curly hair like you, Palm, but darker, and a large moustache with a neatly-shaped beard...a pleasing face, contrary to what one might expect.' After this information Palm fell silent. He tried to persuade himself: 'Since my father was so very poor and found himself admired by the King, he did perhaps feel he could help himself to as much money as he needed...since the King had coffers filled with coins. Besides, he *was* the king's son-in-law. Perhaps he did not wish to trouble the King? It was after all his own responsibility to keep the coffers full...but that business about minting valueless money, well, that was a rotten thing to do, but did the King not own a silver-mine in the north of Denmark?'

Suppositions, justifications, endless explanations teemed like wild mushrooms in Palm's head. He had wanted to admire his father. But now? He sat by the table, rested his head on his arms and fell asleep...to be woken when Griet knocked on his door.

'Hot soup and fresh bread rolls, for you, Master Palm' the servant girl whispered, not wishing to intrude. One side of Palm's face was red, the side that had rested on his arm. She grinned at his distorted features. He praised her for climbing all those steps without spilling a drop. It pleased and consoled him to see her blushing. And he was hungry. Almost, yes almost, that famous 'black dog of melancholia' had been pushed aside.

The Professor, hearing them speak, re-entered and settled himself.

'We could continue here with your father's life, Palm. By now,' the tutor assured his student, 'you have heard the worst.'

'So be it,' sighed Palm.

'Corfitz had spent some time in Amsterdam, hiding. No longer free to roam as before, your parents stayed with friends, their lives were now those of fugitives. At times your mother was disguised as a man, yes, Palm, indeed, an extraordinary woman! But when threatened with arrest from a Danish pursuer she managed to escape at gunpoint. They left Amsterdam, travelled by coach and then by sea trying to get to Stockholm, where Corfitz would be engaged with Denmark's enemies, offering treasonous services to Sweden. The King of Sweden had invited your father to enter into *his* service. By accepting such an offer your father was naturally seen to be a traitorous 'collaborator' by his own country. Now hear this, Palm:

It was during this journey by ship, Palm that *you* were born at sea just off the coast by Stralsund. Your parents had at least nine children already. Little is known about them, two or three died young. They were raised by others, perhaps in Denmark with relatives, or even in other countries. You were the last.'

Here the Professor sighed, shuffled his papers and studied his pupil who sat head bowed, pale and withdrawn. Palm no longer knew what to feel about his father. He had learned about a tangle of evil. He wished his father was never born. He began to wish he too did not exist...for now it was he who would have to bear his father's guilt.

'Your father was unstable, Palm. His lust for power ended in megalomania and madness, his character blemished by greed and lack of conscience. The Swedish king condemned him for double treachery...but there was an amnesty: your father was permitted to return to make peace with his own King. Not surprisingly he was promptly imprisoned: He (and your mother) were locked up in a grim castle, a medieval fortress on the coast of Bornholm, a small island near Stralsund. Around this time you, Palm, were growing up peacefully in the countryside outside Stralsund, only a short trip by boat away from them.

Your father began to think of revenge. But first your parents ransomed themselves by deeding over most of their properties to the King of Denmark. Your father had still not learnt his lesson: he planned a rebellion and offered the Danish crown to Frederick William I, the Elector of Brandenburg. This man was no fool, passed on the treasonous plan to the ruling monarch in Denmark and in this way, I am sorry to have to tell you, your father was condemned to be beheaded and quartered. He, and all his children, wherever they might be, were 'degraded,' all his property was confiscated. When your parents returned to Denmark they were imprisoned in the Mantel tower, until 1661. But they escaped...'

'Stop, Professor, please stop!' Palm's hands covered his face. He was shaking. 'There is no end to the disgrace, I cannot bear it!'

'Yes Palm, I know. But it is not over. Face the facts: Your father was never caught but His Majesty ordered him hanged in effigy (as mockery) in 1663; his descendants were forever exiled from Denmark.'

'My poor mother, Professor, did *she* know what was for the best?'

'Palm, whenever she was cross-examined she refused to speak badly of your father, refused to sign away any family lands for *her* freedom. She seemed to harbour blind devotion to this unworthy man.

'Cross-examined, professor, you frighten me, what is cross- examined?'

'Calm yourself, Master Palm. It is a means of questioning by various questioners: one of numerous ways to arrive at a truth. I also discovered your mother travelled by ship to England, to get repayment of loans your father had made to various princes and noblemen, such as a distant cousin, later to become King Charles II. But instead of receiving the money she was turned over to the Danes and instantly imprisoned in the 'Blue Tower' next to the royal apartments where she had grown up. She was never charged with any crime. After your father had fled from place to place hunted by men anxious to earn the reward put on his head he finally hid in Basle for a while, then, not feeling too safe he took a boat, alone, on the Rhine and drowned, now some three, perhaps four years ago.'

Palm's face was white. There were tears in his eyes.

'No-one knows the circumstances of this death, nor where he was buried, or where your brothers are...there are other versions of this story...that he had a chest cold, the night air killed him, a boatman brought his body on shore, his sons came to bury him, but the truth, well, who knows.' The Professor stepped over to Palm, put an arm around his pupil's shaking shoulders and speaking softly he said:

'I see your pain, Palm. Time has a way of altering our perception of events that occur. I often fear history may be a ragbag of distorted facts. New insights may be born. Officials and writers of these accounts were reluctant when I pleaded with them to reveal nothing but the proven truth.'

Pupil and teacher were enveloped by a very long silence. Eventually, after hiding his face behind his hands, Palm looked at his tutor:

'Do you suppose, professor, I could change my name?'

'If it consoles you, Palm: that is easily done. There are already Ahlfeldts, Ihlefelds, Ohlfeldts in all their permutations; there is even a small river in Mecklenburg called the Ihle....no-one stands in your way if that is what you wish. We can make enquiries.' Then, with a sigh: 'enough for today. I suggest we get out for a brisk walk along the Damrak, find a pleasing inn with good wine, what do you say?

Might your lute-player be performing someplace?'

***

A week later Palm stood by a window, staring down into the dismal back yard where there was no life, no birds, no hens, no dogs, no children playing and shouting, only some washing on the line, hanging stiff and motionless from the frost...

'To be the son of such a man'! Palm felt he had changed. He now wandered about dishevelled, unwashed, slovenly, unsociable, unfriendly. He would sit for hours alone in the church near by and try to talk with his God. He found no relief. His questions had no answers.

He had dutifully completed his task for the day: the professor recommended reading chapters of Monsieur Rabelais in French. These satirical tales, an immense rambling foolery of wild extravagances and grossly indecent adventures of mythical giants called Gargantua and Pantagruel had come as *some* relief: the giants were father and son, who saw life with fresh pairs of eyes, said outrageous things and made much of the 'good life': of eating, drinking, and of breaking all rules.

Gargantua stated nature did not suffer, advocated only one rule in life: to *do what you will.* The professor was hoping this outrageous account might help Palm to recover from the shock. *Life should be lived according to free will and pleasure, because those who were well-bred and free had a natural instinct called honour and therefore would be guided to do only the right things.*

The author, dead for over one hundred years, had not only been a Benedictine monk but also a doctor of medicine. Critical of medieval philosophy he wished to attack clerical education and all the strictness and repression of monastic orders: his riotous and outrageous vision of true freedom remained that of a humanist scholar. Might it be possible to ease Palm's disturbed mind into a more powerful understanding? Could there possibly be acceptance of the frailties and evils of mankind, by struggling through the French version? A German translation was not available.

But despite the antics of Rabelais, Palm's newly acquired knowledge of his father's left him perturbed. Distaste, disappointment, dismay and shame weighed on his innocent mind.

'Slubberdegullian', is what his tutor had just called him. According to the famous Rabelais this was the name for a filthy slobbering person. Palm saw no humour in this, nor in much else.

He was encouraged by his tutor to put it all on paper:

This is what I know about my father: He has wandered about here, in Amsterdam, with my mother and.... but none of it would flow. Everything had gone sour. Not even Griet's smiles and curtsies pleased him; Palm felt besmirched by his father's deeds and bearing the guilt with his name he had curled up like a frightened hedgehog. He had been shaken to the core.

This lasted from morning to night for, well, at least ten days.

After ten days of a hermit's life Palm emerged from the blow. His tutor was out.

Realising he had already missed several choir rehearsals in the church across the road Palm left the house to find the choir master and apologise for his absence...('I was not able to sing with a painful throat'...) but saw little Griet emerging thoughtfully from the Church entrance.

He nodded and smiled, she smiled and curtsied, and they strolled together, back to the house. She appeared to be returning from an errand with a basket heavy with potatoes and carrots over her delicate arm. The sun emerged from behind a bank of clouds just when Palm offered to carry the load for her.

Soon Spring would return. He was feeling better, yes, just a little better.

He would return to the church some other time.

***

Amsterdam,... early Spring 1669

Your Honour,

Looking back on events and changing seasons I am content to report that my student Palm Uhlfeldt is well, and having absorbed experience and knowledge, is finding peace and his place in society, even here.

We appear to have overcome the greatest hurdle: revealing the truth about his father's life. I have gradually introduced him to those unpleasing events which are now history to those who care to know. At first he was thrown into a troubled state, but now he has become stronger and appears less like a boy, more like a man. What I hope may help Master Palm is the effort of writing down, in his own words, and coming to terms with those events which eventually led to his father's death.....'

Here the document to the Swedish Governor in Stralsund ends abruptly.

Had there been some crisis? The letter was neither completed nor despatched, but found later in between the pages of a large atlas... next to a map of the Atlantic coast of Africa.

What had been delivered was a message for Professor Ruetz, received by special delivery from the Swedish Embassy in Amsterdam:

'Will the recipient come to the Embassy as soon as is possible. We hold news from Stralsund of a personal nature.'

***

The tutor wasted no time. Fearing the worst he presented himself at the Embassy where a bowing junior official carried the recently arrived letter on a silver platter and stood by politely ....awaiting a reply:

Professor Martin Ruetz,

'We regret to inform you, Sire, about a fire which occurred on the first day in the Year of our Lord, 1667, burning down the entire cottage of deceased farmer Michael August Sack......(Step-father of Palm Uhlfeld)... inherited and inhabited by his son Christian Sack.

It is assumed this fire occurred due to accidental flames from either a candle or from a brick-oven left glowing at night. The entire property was burnt to the ground and two bodies found within the rubble were those of young Christian and Ursula....'common-law wife' of the above. We do not suspect foul play. There is suspicion the woman was with child.

The remains of these young people have been interred by the village priest. We ask you to express our condolences to Master Palm Uhlfeldt.'

This news had come at a bad time.

'Allow me to pass the information to my pupil. I will return with a reply as soon as possible', said the teacher with a heavy heart. He wandered back to Mevrou Terblanche's establishment, seeing and speaking to no-one along the way. 'What was the correct thing to do? His pupil rarely spoke of his stepbrother, but the news would add to his current distress...'For days the melancholy secret was filed away in the tutor's head. 'Will it serve any purpose to tell Palm, on top of recent revelations? How can I even *begin* to protect him?'

Master Palm and his tutor, despondent for different reasons... neither with any great desire to go out and eat, did finally decide to find somewhere new. Wandering in silence further afield, close by the docks for larger ships they saw a welcoming, solid inn, quiet and comforting, not too far from the Dutch East India Company building.

Palm hoped for simple sailors' food and a flagon of Dutch beer. As the door opened wide they faced a departing guest, adjusting his cloak, staring blankly for a moment: it was none other than Jan de Groote, last seen in Stralsund some eight months ago, not quite recognising them...but no, he stopped, chortled and exclaimed: 'is it truly *you*, Master Palm, what brings you to *my* home town? And the Professor! I was just leaving. May I join you? A wondrous coincidence! Please do tell: I *must* know what brings you here?'

'And *we* believed you to be in Africa, Jan de Groote!'

'Ah, the same old story: recruitment, and ever more of it...the Cape needs Dutchmen, or indeed any men, Germans, French, who are willing to take a new life, offer their skills, build up the beautiful place by Table Mountain...the Commander encourages, even helps new burghers and the Company will assist with wages until one is settled.... But hear this, gentlemen: I have a title now: 'Recruitment Officer de Groote' and I tell you both, you would not regret going there, the place becomes more interesting from month to month; the Commander seeks teachers and gardeners and all manner of expertise. The Dutch East India Company has even reduced the high cost of the fares...but here I go again...what brings *you* to my home town? I do remember trying to talk you into visiting us, how pleasing to imagine you are here on account of *my* inducement? Can this be so?' His eager sunburnt face was turned toward them.

'Here, the beer!' Palm and his tutor were looking more at ease. They proposed a toast, stretched their legs and smiled at 'their' sailor.

Is this meeting with de Groote's divine intervention? Just when it was most needed... the tutor asked himself, observing Palm returning to his old self, eyes alert and eager. But still he did not put his cards on the table. Instead he enquired:

'When must you travel again, Jan, will you stay a while and show us *your* Amsterdam? While Palm said: 'I suppose we must return to Stralsund...I leave all planning to my Professor...well yes, I know, I am soon eighteen years and should think for myself'. The tutor nodded: 'Yes, indeed, Master Palm.'

'But I *did* visit the D.E India Company', even without my tutor, and they treated me with respect when I enquired about travelling on one of their ships. What is the cost now, Jan, still *as much as a house*?'

'This depends on *which* house, *where* it is, how many rooms it has' de Groote grinned. 'In Africa one can have large houses with much land, but they will cost very little...compared with small buildings on valuable land won from the sea in Amsterdam. Yes, I'd say as much as a small house on the outskirts of Amsterdam...come and see for your selves, gentlemen! The journey south lasts just over three months...the cost of the journey includes food, drink. Sometimes, I should say often, there is illness, but look at me, I have been there and back since I last saw you ...do you see any signs of decay? No, we are mostly fit and the only sickness I saw lately was that of sailors who took time to 'grow their sea legs'. We did not see pirates either although I was told there were some about. Our ships are well armed, there is nothing to fear....I have even heard of occasional entertainment: an English ship carried a group of actors on board once, who were trained to perform plays of Shakespeare...the ship was named 'Dragon', and I was told they performed 'Hamlet', a play newly composed by an Englishman, somewhere off the coast of Africa, near the Equator. Think of that, gentlemen!' There seemed no end to d Groote's enthusiasm.

Palm had never seen a play, but had read excerpts of 'Hamlet' with his tutor. Now, chewing thoughtfully, they half dreamed, half listened to the flow of information about the new world, down there, somewhere on the other side of the globe. Jan de Groote knew he had lied through his teeth: men died like flies on these journeys, from illness and untellable disasters, but he could not surmise what thoughts were passing through the heads of his old friends from Stralsund, and he must play his role, right to the bitter end.

'A pleasing evening,' was all they said to him.' We must meet again after some days have passed.' They had made no commitment, no promises.

But there it stood, a real possibility: an escape into a sunnier world, obscure and unknown...somewhere to forget ancient troubles and to allow the 'seedling,' which was how Professor Ruetz saw Palm, take root and develop a firm inner core, to bear desirable fruit high up, amongst a crown of firm leafy fronds, in the near future. In *his* view his charge *was* a delicate plant, one which had now been badly bruised by a severe frost: that of his father's history, his mother's cruel fate and now also by the shocking and unnecessary fire-death, not yet revealed to him, of his step-brother in Stralsund.

On the very next day they called on the VOC for urgent enquiries about costs, funding the journey, monies for their needs, clothing and nourishment and above all permission to cross the seas. Life had made this big decision *for* them both. Or so it appeared.

In the end the painful revelation of fire and death in Stralsund was received by Palm with disbelief: 'My step-brother would not be so careless; to leave the fire burning, *and* go to sleep! No, never! And what of the animals, the geese, his hens and sheep...did *they* escape? Our straw roof covered the shed as well. What if that fire was started by robbers who took the animals for themselves, leaving the place to burn down, roasting the sleepers inside?'

'We cannot know, Palm. Farmers have their own rough justice. Your life is now on a new and different course. Let it be, Palm, what is done is done. In the distant future, when we return to Stralsund, when a few years have passed, you will be a different man, wise and understanding justice. You may even, by then, have some influence. Already now you experience a growing recognition how it is to become a valuable member of society, one who can prevent injustice, punish evil doers. Yes Palm, we shall do our best.'

One event led to another, like an arrow released from a bow, flying without hindrance: a carefully planned journey, packing of books, clothing and supposed necessities, and now farewells to and from a handful of new friends. Piet, the lute-player, toyed with the idea of having such an adventure, but lacked the necessary funds; besides, he was in mourning for his father who, poor as a 'church-mouse,' had just passed away, leaving his son one chair, some books and two paintings.

'Perhaps another time,' Piet said to Palm, 'you must let me know how it is...you must write to me: I too would like to see the world one day... leave-taking is so painful. It may be years before we meet again.'

***

Complaining calls from low-sweeping gulls on an overcast, drizzly March day made for a melancholy departure. Poor grieving Griet, trembling all over, wept into her white apron even though Palm had left her a small velvet purse containing two gulden. Sadly the words he had hoped to say to her had remained tangled inside him...

Later Mevrou Terblanche shook her head:

'Do not be foolish, girl, Master Palm is a young gentleman with his life before him... he has no time for the likes of you! He will marry a lady with an education and a fortune, when he is much older, and remember: he is not even from our country!'

Griet remained damp-eyed, sniffling and inconsolable. 'There, there, poor thing.' Her employer gave her an affectionate hug. 'Now pull yourself together, Griet! Go, clean out the rooms upstairs. Then wash all that bedding for our next guests…'

FOURTEEN

'Punish the evil-doers'.

This phrase, his tutor's words, resonated in Palm's head as they left Amsterdam on an open lighter, with their boxes and trunks, to board the 'Hof van Breda' anchored at Texel Roads.

'There! The masts of their vessel, vast sails bulging tentatively, were barely opened by the south-easterly winds.' The travellers breathed in the sea air, the tar and linseed oil on freshly treated ropes and wood; they heard the gulls.

'Our ship must wait for favourable East or North East winds...only then the Low Countries will retreat over the horizon. For now we wait, with all the others. This is where there was a powerful storm about half a century ago, Palm: A thousand sailors were drowned and forty ships were lost, just waiting. Fear not, we will make head-way for sure, although there are still so many waiting.'

Palm was constantly haunted by his father's death: presumably a death by water more chilly and choppy than to-days'. Was it inflicted by someone with a grudge; had he been tracked down by a murderous emissary from Denmark or Sweden: one evil atoned for by another? And his own *true* brothers and sisters, those remaining Uhlfeldt sons and daughters, would they have hunted down their own father ...for shaming them and all his family? Must they too bear their father's guilt?

'My father, was he pushed overboard to drown, or was he stabbed, robbed, tied up, weighted with heavy stones and thrown overboard,... or knifed and buried hidden away in some hole in a dark forest, never to be found ...perhaps he took his own life, a pious propitiation, overcome by his own worthlessness?'

Embittered and lonely, Palm stared into the churning waves of the North Sea, heard the groaning of the ship's timbers: the more he summoned up all he had been told, the more incensed he became: that treacherous Corfitz Uhlfeldt, and his ignoble dishonesty towards two kings, those doubly dubious standards of the riches he could get away with while lining his pockets with monies from state coffers...'a negligent, perfidious, thick-skinned monster... cunning and caring only for himself. And still my good and saintly mother adored him. How could this be? Now she suffers alone, locked in a tower. I must rescue her, help her. But here I am, leaving for another continent. Why am I doing this? Who knows when I return. One day, back in Stralsund, I will root out evil-doers like him, for my father was surely not alone? Traitors, thieves and liars, are they not everywhere? I will take a horse, ride to the Danish King, bow before him and plead for my mother's release. What big round eyes she will make, when she sees me, her Stralsund son! I will go to her, tell her who I am. She will not believe me...unless I can persuade the governor in Stralsund to write a letter on my behalf. Yes, then she may believe, trusting a Swedish Governor rather than me and my strange tale.

But when she is released I will care for her until her dying day.'

Palm looked at the murky sea below; he felt the chill of early March, he shivered in that breeze from the south-east. The sun was low. Tears came to his eyes, tears of sorrow and loneliness and despair. 'Generations rise and vanish' he thought, 'just like these flecks on the waves, deeds and thoughts vanish, are even forgotten, and then new forms and actions take over. Can good make up for ungodly acts? Is it not my duty to overcome the evil he has done, undo evil in the world, some sort of penance on his behalf? Should I not ask God's forgiveness for my father so he may rest in peace?

The Professor appeared on deck, unsteady, but concerned.

'Still brooding, Palm? Come now, it is time to think about the new life we have chosen, not to dwell on those dark things we have no control over. Consider this... I have had words with the captain: he has a proposal entirely in the interest of your strength and well-being. Do you wish to hear about it?'

Palm sighed, eyebrows raised, nodded, with scant enthusiasm. He knew his teacher.

This did not bode well.

'Tomorrow, Master Palm: to tackle (I trust you will not let me down on this challenge) basic tasks, perhaps...learning the ropes, or some other work and also to become acquainted with other young men on board....'

Palm looked up politely, nodded. His eyes were distant, his brooding thoughts still elsewhere.

'Come inside, Master Palm! You are pale; we will warm ourselves with Grog. I had withdrawn hours earlier to my comfortable bunk... that unsettled stomach, despite the well-intentioned potion made up for us by Madame Terblanche,... but I have nevertheless unpacked a case of interesting books for our studies, mostly legal cases from the past...but there *is* another matter: from tomorrow you are signed up for training under the guidance of various members of the ship's staff. Only on some of the afternoons will we be able to read, discuss and study. You have enough to learn one way or another and our journey may take more than three months. I trust you are prepared, it will not be easy.'

Heads nodding there followed a contemplative silence...then:

'Yes, yes, I hear your words', Palm sighed, 'would I were dead. What is the point? Why was I born, why is there so much to learn, what good is a voyage to the other side of the globe... and now I must become a sailor; how they will laugh at me...so ignorant about everything.'

The tutor handed him a man-sized tumbler of hot grog. He then disappeared to return with steaming fish-soup and chunks of brown bread. The boy, already in his bunk, was snoring lightly. Professor Ruetz covered the tortured sailor-to-be, enjoyed the hot soup himself and went off to find the captain for further discussion on methods that should be applied to his charge, the vulnerable, frail landlubber, now so greatly in need of strengthening and acquiring a general taste for skills of seafaring men.

***

Yawning, not too gracious by the early start: Palm Uhlfeldt had been woken at sunrise by a sonorous recitation of: 'mens sana in corpore sano,' the great Juvenal's saying. Are you awake? Absorb this wisdom, dear Palm, be guided by it....'

There followed further silence, yawning, stretching and scratching.

'What does it mean...who is Juvenal,' *should* be your response, Palm! I will go into all that later. Come on now, up, up, hurry young man, your days of soft living are over: the first bell has rung, all hands on deck and the captain is waiting. Hurry boy, punctuality is of the essence on a ship!'

Too sleepy to argue Palm jumped from his berth; he had slept fully clothed and hurried up on deck to see sailors shuffling to line up, the captain standing before them. The wind seemed favourable at last.

While others received orders, Palm, not knowing where to stand became conscious he was barefoot: a ridiculous unkempt boy in yesterday's crumpled clothes. The captain glanced at him, frowned, then commanded him to proceed to the Great Cabin. Palm was offered a hot bitter brown brew, not much to his liking, which he clutched to his chest, standing uneasily but respectfully, while the captain's eyes studied the young man before him, slowly, head to toe.

'I understand you have not sailed before, Uhlfeldt,' the Captain stated. He sighed, and continued: 'Hof van Breda is a merchant ship but we do *carry ordnance* as we are subject to piracy. Your responsibilities will increase from one week to the next but let me begin by giving you some facts about the vessel you find yourself in: tonnage is 600...and the ship's company of 180 includes myself, two master's mates, four carpenters, a master gunner with nine other gunmen, two stewards, two cooks, a chaplain, a surgeon and a medical orderly, also one hundred and fifty men and boys. There are eight passengers, and you are one of them, however, as from this day you become one of the sailors, without training....and also without footwear it seems, therefore,' he stopped to take a swig of coffee: 'I propose you start with something very simple: have you worked in a kitchen before?'

Palm nodded. He felt wide awake. 'Of course Captain, when I lived with my mother.'(The captain smiled, he must be a mild, reasoning man, who shows forethought and kindness...) 'I see. Kitchen duties will give you time to settle into the routine of life on the ocean.

And Master Palm: no smoking on board, I trust you do not use a pipe!'

Palm was not sure whether he was being found wanting in muscle, manhood and general appearance or whether the Master of the ship was perhaps a father of sons himself. 'So far,' he believed 'I've got off lightly.'

'Report back to me after seven days with the cook. You work from dawn until midday, also on the Lord's Day. There *are* no Sundays for cooks. After that you return to me for your next assignment. And now, make your way to the cauldron, just follow the smoke...it is everywhere. Good day to you.' The master of the ship turned smartly and left Palm to it.

Palm had to find the kitchen; it was on the lower deck.

There was Cook, muscular, red-faced, cross and sweating by a massive cast-iron cauldron over flames in a brick fireplace. He was expecting Palm.

'I will call you Cabin Boy Two! Here, wooden pails, fetch water, boy, no, no, *not* drinking water. Start washing these platters. First, you scour out that great copper kettle, the peas pots and frying pans, see this sand here...that's what we use. Then you rinse. You will need help with these, they are many and large enough...we serve one hundred and eighty people. Hans, you! Over here, you know what to do!

Cabin Boy One, show Cabin Boy Two how to work with you this week; he does speak German.'

Cook clapped his hands briskly: 'No standing about then, get on boys, stop gawking...action! Let me see action, every minute is precious here. First: cleaning. Then down to the store room for provisions, both of you will help to carry the foodstuffs...,now do *not* forget the Steep Tubs: the salt beef is ready to take out after soaking all night, when the copper kettle is cleaned....' Palm's heart sank.

But then he saw a friendly face, showing the beginnings of a small beard, whistling through its teeth, quietly to itself, showing how completely comfortable it all was: those never-ending tasks in and around the kitchen. This face belonged to Hans, the same height and age as Palm, but with a healthy suntan.

Safely out of the way of bronze cannons and guns on the battery deck Hans took Palm to see trunks, hides, firkins, bales, chests and parcels, stacked high in a locked store-room on the lower deck. Down in the dark they viewed, holding a candle aloft, several dozen vast Dutch cheeses, barrels of meat, bags of salt, sacks of barley, sacks of flour, barrels of green peas, of grey peas, two sacks of mustard seed, a mountain of groats and quantities of 'pepper-root' a specific against the dreaded scurvy. He stumbled over a cask of butter which had slipped out of a row of other casks. 'Above all, see these prepared bottles of lemon juice. Remember where these things are, cabin Boy Two, for you must run up and down and bring things Cook needs during the day!

And here, meet 'Meerkat', the ship's cat, an important member of Hof van Breda's crew!' Two eyes in a mass of dark fur examined Palm; for several pleasing moments the cat purred, rubbed up against Palm's leg. In passing Palm caught a glimpse of sailors cleaning and preparing weapons against attacks by sea-beggars, and wangled a promise from Cabin Boy One, who knew about such things: 'Why yes, pirates, my favourite subject, I will tell you all about them, much better than the 'Schweinerei' in the kitchen, but later, much later.... hurry now, Cook will not tolerate any slackness!' He whistled, kicked the cat, blew out the candle and then young men both hurried back to drudgery: that washing-up was never-ending. Palm longed for midday when he would be released from the steaming, smelly, smoky hell and permitted to rejoin his tutor.

***

A scrub, clean clothes...and a sigh of relief.
Palm and his professor were re-united to wander about on deck while planning the topics of study for the afternoon.

'White cliffs, Professor, look, see there, on our right'. Palm was immediately beside himself: 'We have travelled the wrong way, we are back in the Baltic, the white cliffs of Rügen, Professor, here, before us...on our right!

'Calm yourself, Palm. Look to the opposite side... do you not see the coast of the Dutch: flat, windmills everywhere? What you see are the *English* chalk cliffs, the land of Herr Shakespeare. With favourable winds we may observe their coast for three, perhaps four days: it is only a small island. And strangely we will soon pass a port with the same name as our own Stralsund: 'Stral Sund' denotes 'Dart Mouth': the English put together words just as we do....and for once they are not at the throats of the Dutch, although they have wars often enough!

Only last August a treaty of peace was signed between the English and the Dutch, we are fortunate. As for their pirates, those outrageous rascals, they have a multitude of them: let me tell you about one John Adey who stole 130 negroes from a plantation in Barbados: he locked them into the hold of his little ship and soon proceeded to sell his 'cargo' back to the original owner. Famed for his notoriety and extortion he was hanged on this very island, which we now see on our right, in about 1600. Not unlike the fate of your favourite, sailor, that wicked Störtebecker!'

'Yes, yes, I remember. But rest assured, we are well armed, Professor, I saw our cannons and guns, oiled and ready, and the Company insists that we, the crew, can assist in defending our ship...I look forward to instruction and also when I will learn about celestial navigation and how to understand the azimuth, and helping the surgeon. Today's scrubbing and carrying has been extremely tedious. Cabin Boy Hans has promised to tell me all *he* knows about pirates tomorrow...

Is it true that Dutch Naval power is the greatest in the world, that the Low Lands reign supreme? Hans tells me he has seen warships escorting outward-bound fleets of five to ten East Indiamen and soldiers on these warships were mostly from German lands, also that his own family comes from Würzburg; he seems very proud of them, they are wood-carvers: from lime and linden-wood they create decorative objects for churches. Hans claims he has no talent for it. He speaks Dutch and German equally well.' Palm looks up, frowning.

'This main mast is 120 ft...'

The professor, surprised by his student's need to talk, looks up too; they imagine the length of rigging...'nine sails on three masts, I think, professor....but the rigging, well, impossible to say. Did you know we are so stable because of the ballast: there are tons of lead down below deck...I should ask the boatswain; a kind man, most friendly, he will know about the rigging...the mizzen, the fore-and-aft-sail, the after-mast sail of our ship...you see, I have learned all this today. You will not know me by the time my week in the kitchen is over!'

'By then we may have reached Kales, Palm, or as the French prefer: Calais. This port was Dutch once: the people spoke mostly Dutch. Then Edward the Third of England captured it in the 1300's and for two centuries the citizens were obliged to learn English. One hundred years ago the French got it, that is, they fought hard for it...and the English Queen Mary was desolate; 'When I am dead and opened, she wrote, 'you shall find Philip (her husband) and Calais lying in my heart...'

'Ah, such an unhappy lady!

Speaking of 'Aa,' Palm, did you know of a river near Calais which is called the Aa? It is Old Dutch and means water; you will not have heard this singular word.' Palm nods, suggests it is not unlike the 'aam', a measure of liquids...'but no, Sir, I have not. Speaking of liquids: at Calais we take fresh supplies of water for the next lap.'

'Now Palm'...the teacher feels relieved he has finally regained his position of authority, 'we are so stable because the sea is calm. But once we turn the corner into the Bay of Biscay it will be another story. I doubt you will see much of me during that time! Before that is upon us I would very much like to meet your friend Hans, perhaps on deck after your work, in these coming days. This friend is doing you good, Palm, you have absorbed so much in a few hours of kitchen work, you barely stop speaking, Do enquire if he has heard of the great ship Vasa, a gunship which sank and now lies rotting in the Baltic close to Stockholm...but enough, we really must return to our books, I have a sense of uneasiness, as if I may never be able to catch your attention again! An afternoon of Geography, so you will know how many lands we pass, and where Barbados is... that's what is needed, and perhaps an hour or two with the English language, far, far simpler than our own. Then a walk on deck to study the night sky, find the North Star.'

'Your sense of unease is nothing, Professor, to my own shame and sorrow constantly haunting *me*, now that I am unable to speak of my own family. Friend Hans has already told me about *his* father, the descendant of a woodcarver of some renown, and how the entire family works together, making an honest living. But I must remain 'stumm' about *my* father, for all time'.

'This may be true, Palm. I suggest you say he was a nobleman, long dead. Instead speak of your brother, and your step-father and stepmother, and no-one will be any the wiser. Good honest people; you must honour them, their example will help you bear your burden.'

***

In Calais water was replenished and further supplies of fresh foodstuffs were stowed away. Palm soon graduated from kitchen duties to a different field of enquiry: that of practical medicine with the ship's surgeon.

Medical studies: (Begun on my journey to the Cape), Week Two.

'I am fortunate- the change from the kitchen to the doctor's cabin is more to my liking, although I miss Hans, my new friend.

The Ship's surgeon is elderly, I should think at least forty years, with calm blue eyes, numerous folds of skin atop his broad nose and, when he smiles, one chipped tooth in the front. At first, on entering his domain, he studied me for a long time. While we gazed at each other he spoke most earnestly: that he could see I was strong and healthy, that I would not faint at the sight of blood, pus and excrement, or worse, when assisting at operations. How he sees this I cannot explain. Perhaps he knows I helped my father when pigs and geese were slaughtered; there was much shrieking and blood then.

'There is no-one unwell yet' he informed, 'so I would like you to read to me... from this book, which is alas, in English, written by, let me see, one John Woodall of the St. Bartholomew's Hospital in London.'

'But Sir, I have no English,...'

The doctor appeared not to hear this remark.

'It is a book which surgeons of the Dutch East India Company must possess and although it was written in 1639 I have not found a Dutch translation, besides, my eye-glasses are not as effective as they once used to be...'

'My English is still at an early stage,' I ventured again, 'I must ask my tutor for his dictionary'. 'Very well', spoke the Surgeon. 'Let him accompany you, if he would be so kind, for with his help we might make excellent progress.....'

'Should I ask him to come directly, Doctor?'

'No, not today, we will speak of other things: .... the importance of foodstuffs and provisions against illnesses, for the Dutch East India Company does not believe in leaving its men to the Mercy of God....we are here to prevent illness if at all possible. Which illnesses have you experienced yourself, Master Palm?'

'I know little about the body, but I am acquainted with melancholia, fever and toothache, these are afflictions known to me....'

The surgeon's eyebrows went up, perplexed by my reply.

The book he then spoke of was called 'The Surgeon's Mate.' I saw a small portrait of the author, his pointed V-shaped beard below a large nose.... a fine man in a high-layered lace collar who is not only a surgeon, but also a chemist, business man, linguist and diplomat, who spent time working in Hamburg. Perhaps he met my true father, then in his role as diplomat? Tomorrow I am to translate for the Surgeon...and yes, my tutor has agreed...I am most thankful he will attend!

Ergo: Palm's first day with the Surgeon was restricted to a discussion of scurvy and the adequate diet which was required at sea to prevent it:

'Gums and teeth, that is the worst of it, young man: sailors lose their teeth and suffer excruciatingly with great debility if they do not have fresh food. Mouths become swollen, putrid, teeth fall out one by one. Also the legs swell while muscles, sinews, shrink, the skin becomes black or spotted...it happens quickly, even after two or three months at sea. We, the Dutch East India Company have learned the hard way; Dutch sailors carried oranges already one hundred years ago, not quite understanding their curative effect, we now bring supplies of dried apples, dried grapes and pears, and wherever we stop for fresh water we also purchase lemons, fruit and vegetables. If you have the disease you must fast, and only drink lemon juice...as you recover you are obliged to strengthen your muscles...we allow a morning draught of wine or ale...'

'...a pleasing cure then', interrupts Palm, not intimidated by the discourse of the Surgeon. 'Indeed Master Palm, but know that crews are often decimated: firstly on long journeys and, at times from diseases caught on the coast, not only scurvy, but also dysentery and malaria. If there is dysentery the filth of the sailors' quarters can become unbearable.

But there is more to it: venturing out to sea changes us all; it is a transforming experience, everyone on board will be challenged, some more, some less. There will be fights, falls, accidents with heavy equipment; some sailors begin to have visions caused by fear and isolation from the land...the ship becomes a stage where the perils of living and dying, of guilt, disgust and loneliness are lived out. A ship's doctor, surgeon, and his assistants must be ready with more than lemon juice, that is to say, there may be anything from amputation to death, even sailors losing their minds.....

Later this morning there is to be a flogging, for one of the sailors has been caught stealing from the Captain's Cabin. You, Palm, will witness this event. You are to escort the young sailor back to my cabin for we must see to his wounds, if indeed there are any, but yes, what am I saying, there usually is some blood...and painful swelling.'

Palm closed his eyes. He was not accustomed to such purging of guilt. For him this will be a Rite of Passage.

***

A powerful six foot, flaxen-haired Dutchman, now helpless and tied spread-eagled to a mast, was about to receive twenty lashes. His upper body was bare. Sailors not on duty had been ordered to watch. At first Palm's eyes strayed to the foaming waves and the gulls, then he forced himself to observe the muscular man who would deal out the punishment; seemingly unconcerned he tested the whip against a bollard, while looking around the assembled crew for approval. His duty was to punish severely. Palm's duty would be to bandage the wounds.

Already nauseous, he knew he must show no feelings. The lashes tore into the flesh and blood flowed, after only five strokes. There were no signs of remorse from the punished sailor ...all one heard were waves lapping against the ship, cawing seagulls, the crack of the whip. The punishment came to an end and the stony-faced crew shuffled off. The ship was still within view of the coast. The evil-doer, his face like a mask, was led by Palm to the ship's Surgeon who washed the wounds with saltwater and demonstrated how to tie a bandage securely over the damaged flesh. Hardly a word was spoken during this proceeding.

Later, with increasing gales and storm clouds on the horizon, the crew cleared the decks for working the ship, to batten the hatches. 'We are on course...but heading for a big one' they said. 'But then, what do you expect, it *is* the Bay of Biscay.'

The crew instantly went through routines of fastening and stowing away. The sky turned from grey to black, gusts whipped flecked waves into monsters who rose up to the deck, invading the spaces where only a few moments ago there had been a ceremonious purging of evil...

'It all makes sense' thought Palm: 'such washing away of wickedness.'

***

He was stretched out on his bunk unable to raise his head for two days. The ship had become unmanageable. Palm's sickness due to rough seas was so powerful that bandaging wounds, even translating the Surgeon's book, was out of the question. On the third day the shaken 'Surgeon's assistant' was back on his feet and ready for more work...as well as stroking and teasing the affectionate 'Meerkat'.

During an entire week of translating medical matters from English into Dutch Palm's head brimmed with new skills and information.

In the meantime two crew-men had died. Palm was obliged to witness their bodies 'buried' in the waves.

***

The captain received a report after one month: Master Palm had acquitted himself with full honours. Two further weeks were requested 'with his young assistant who was showing natural skills for treating wounds, supporting broken bones...and general insight into the frailties of the human body. This young man could readily find a life-occupation in the study and application of medicine.' Such was the verdict of the surgeon, after only a very short time.

The professor and the captain put their heads together: Palm's fate could not be assessed readily: he must spend time learning the skills of an ordinary sailor, which meant climbing, cleaning, pulling and winding, scrubbing and lifting, roughing it out on deck, to gain confidence and muscles, to think ahead and to persevere, but also to obey. The time had come to be toughened up: sleeping rough with ordinary sailors, eating with them and obeying orders from a new superior: he would have no special treatment nor privileges for two months. Confined, obedient, Palm Uhlfeldt ate, slept worked, received orders, reprimands, and payment, like the rest of the crew.

Occasionally he found time to scribble a few lines in his diary:

'Amsterdam to Lisbon...twenty-five days. Now, after the Bay of Biscay, none of the early terrors, no heavy gales, just a pleasing

voyage.... I am kept busy, busier than I have ever been in my life. The only time to regain strength is in my hammock at night. At first I feared I would surely die. We, the crew, are mostly foul, dirty, noisy and rough... the smells below deck are unspeakable, and there are mice and lice and roaches everywhere. The weather is fine. My muscles grow more powerful each day, my skin is dark and my hair is long. We, the sailors, eat every crumb on our platters. The ale is good. Sometimes we sing and dance on deck. Now, as it becomes warmer, we take blankets and sleep there as well. Hans, my only friend, still labours in the kitchen. There is hardly a task on this ship that I have not done. There is no time to think about my father. As a novice to this life at sea I do the best I can. I see my professor from a distance: he appears to be keeping an eye on me. He has befriended a sombre man called Borghorst, a Commander, no less. This man will also disembark at the Cape. At Lisbon we took fresh supplies. We now head across to islands off the coast of Africa. Our ship ploughs through Atlantic waves.

I have seen flying fish: they are sea monsters which raise their wings when they see our ship and try to keep pace with us. There will be whales, I am told, beasts of huge size who draw in and spout out water and make high waves, also playful fish called dolphins. There has been a succession of calm winds, my bare arms are changing colour...we have spent over one month travelling due south most days...

The west coast of Africa was interminable. Long before reaching the Equator Palm had been released from duties on deck to spend mornings learning to mend sails. He showed no aptitude.

After sweaty days of wasted effort and damaged fingers he was moved on to the tutelage of an officer: his mornings would be free, but afternoons were for calculations, and the dark hours would be spent studying the stars, weather permitting. During this stretch he jotted down notes on harbours where they had anchored for supplies of fruit and water.

At the fifth stop the Dutch East India Company has established a fort called Grèvecoeur. The Danes, not to be outdone, have built Christiansborg Castle, only two miles east of the Dutch fort. But the Portuguese got there first, already in 1482. A fortress, Elmina, (the 'mine') has given the area the enticing name of 'Gold Coast'. The settlement, known as Accra, is where trade in slaves, gold and palm oil is available to passing ships. We also picked up the latest news of other Dutch vessels which have passed by...

Illnesses, damage to the ship's side and the need for replenishing fresh foods and water had been holding up progress. Palm watched as some of the crew rowed ashore in sweltering heat to assist in the purchase of black prisoners, who, chained together by their ankles and pitiful enough became even more distressed to be taken on board, knowing they would be not going to see their home country again. For the entire journey they remained chained, locked in the smallest possible space below deck.

Many will die, said the crew, in the foulest conditions imaginable.

'Dear God, what a show of injustice and cruelty.' Stress was bringing hallucinations and guilt to Palm, who had to carry meagre supplies to the slaves and who felt their suffering and hopeless fate. He witnessed unpleasant scenes: sailors carrying stiff black corpses from dark recesses inside the ship to be thrown overboard without ceremony. These dark-skinned people perished from misery and despair, quite apart from their illnesses.

'How fortunate we are compared with such men, desperate souls whose black bodies wither, and are then thrown in the sea. Can this be the Lord's plan? I remain strong and whole, only my soul is in pain because of my father's misdeeds. Now there are these misdeeds. My pain is a lesser one.

Week after week, gliding south, he saw on his left unchanging green vegetation. Then, one morning, a complete change: the shifting shapes and colours had become dusty and curiously pale. Dense night fogs enveloped everything.

'Skeleton Coast', whispered the sailors and, at sunrise, when west winds dispelled the fog they stood in their ragged shirts, staring at the stark beauty of shifting sand dunes, desert lands mysteriously dead, deceptively still.

'A Jacob's ladder, I see it here, in this dry place, for angels and for the lucky ones of this earth, to find the true path to bliss and redemption...for souls to travel after death to the light of God, away from all suffering', babbled Palm, wide-eyed.

The sight of barren wastes had carried the Pomeranian peasant's soul to unknown regions of the mind...to some mystical oasis offering escape from human suffering.

'Unhinged, bewitched,' the sailors whispered behind his back. He watched a contingent row out to land in a small boat: there were said to be sweet water streams inland, and game.

But they returned empty-handed.

The 'Hof van Breda' continued its journey as speedily as possible: there were very few barrels of water left as the emergency supplies created by distillation were not plentiful. Palm, who had been moved back to share a cabin with his tutor remained unhinged when he had to spend hours with an irritable officer who tried to explain complex relationships of the positions of stars and the angle of the sun. The mathematical requirements remained depressingly unknowable under the circumstances. Advanced problems and solutions were no longer to Palm's liking, although there was some fascination in viewing the Southern Cross rising into view each evening, on the horizon.

How the sky sparkled in the Southern hemisphere!

Professor Ruetz resumed private coaching: 'hear these frightening tales, Palm, of earlier Portuguese sailors who landed along the coast 200 years ago... local people threw stones at them while these in turn shot back with their crossbows before sailing on. The Portuguese were really searching a sea-route to the source of gold which was coming across the Sahara on camels driven by Muslim traders.

It has taken two generations to establish this route down the west coast. Sailing around the Cape of Storms many lost their lives...but it has opened up the way to the Far East. Believe me, Master Palm, sailing into Table Bay has caused much trouble: In 1510, a tribe called the Khoi instantly drove back sailors trying to land, killing 65 men. Passing ships stayed clear of the Cape after that, until a few years ago, our own Dutch East India Company sent the right man out... the famed Jan van Riebeek, a man who had the right ideas. He climbed the famous mountain and wrote to the authorities in Amsterdam: that there was pasture everywhere crowded with cattle and sheep, also that the Khoi people claimed it as their own. He gave account of about 6000 'Khoi-Khoi' (which means 'men of men'), semi-naked nomads who lived in small reed huts and cultivated tobacco, and how they intended to bring their houses close by...they lay in thousands by the Salt River...'

'These tales about the nomads, Professor, I can't wait to see them...' claimed Palm, yet seemed unable to suppress a yawn.

'The Dutch exchanged goods with them', his teacher continued soberly...'alcohol and tobacco was much favoured but also brass and copper, iron and beads in exchange for meat and livestock... above all, just a month after stepping ashore, only about the time you were born Palm,...van Riebeek wrote to Amsterdam and asked for vines to be shipped out, for he believed they would thrive on the hill slopes as on those of France and Spain and indeed only ten years ago wine was made for the first time from Cape grapes....'

But Palm had sunken into a deep sleep, snoring like an ancient sailor. It seemed a reasonable thing to do.

CAP. DE BONA ESPERANZA *BY WILHELM STETTLER, GERMANY 1669*

PART FOUR
Lamentations

Fifteen

June 1667. Imposing mountains against a radiant sky... gulls swooping, swaying, screeched in greeting, while the men on deck raised a cheer and shook each other by the hand: 'God was with us: we have yearned and now we are safe and our journey lasted just over three months!' They stood on deck overwhelmed by the immense mass of grey rock. They blinked into the rising sunlight, spirits uplifted.

The Hof van Breda was sailing, serene and proud, into Table Bay.

'Have you heard of Admiral Drake, Palm? No? He was an English sea-captain, a great hero to the English...and *his* words, when he saw this very sight, were: *the fairest Cape in all the circumference of the earth'*.

Palm nodded: the foreign admiral was right. Now that they had covered half the globe Palm felt strangely changed and healed.

Tempus omnia sanat...and *mens sana in corpora sano*...Latin words seemed appropriate when days were as important as this one.

***

Jacob Borghost, the new Commander, stood by the professor. Palm's future was under discussion, bearing in mind the young man had come to work, to mature and find a profession. There seemed little to fear for the moment: a new world lay before them all, raw and full of challenge.

'So! This is the Cape winter,' exclaimed someone, 'just look at the weather here. 'Well yes, friend,' shouted an 'old hand', 'but just you wait, it is most changeable!'

Now came two challenges: unloading and getting ashore. Six ships already anchored, were preparing to unload, or perhaps to leave.

The beach seemed a long way off; there was not much to see on land.

One barely believes one's eyes: Here it stands, that 'monstrous table' looming before us. We have dropped anchor and await small boats for unloading. My head spins. It is all true: the hill on the right resembles the rump of a lion ...the one on the left is conical and as a group they stand waiting, patiently, for all eternity. These mountains must be the work of a supremely loving God. Already I have feelings of affection for them...I cannot explain, even to myself. The middle one shows strength and concern, it offers safety and permanence, like a father, yes, like an old, grey father.

I will think of it in this way. As this is my Private Diary, and as I have no father, there is no need to be ashamed of thinking such a thing....I wish to walk close and to lie down, by his feet, gaze at the impassive, massive grey rocks, the small rivulets pouring down and the incredible blue sky above everything: the closer I get the more improbable it becomes. Never have I seen such light as these rays in the lap of this Mountain. To my surprise there is, near our ship, a small rocky protrusion in the Bay. It lies to the right near the rump of the lion. Greenery, small beasts...workers are there, digging and loading up small boats with rocks or shells I am told, to be used for building.... they may be slaves or some local inhabitants of this land....or just sailors. We must remain onboard until unloading is done: hard work and concentration is required; slaves and sailors are being prepared for the task. For now my mind is numbed, stunned ...to the left sandy beaches as far as the eye can see, small round huts and in the distant haze another mountain range beyond a sandy plain...., also the beginnings of a settlement where we are to step ashore on a primitive wooden jetty. I must oversee and count what is carried up on deck and then down into the small boats, for several hours today. I am told Jan van Riebeeck instigated the making of these first coastal vessels in 1655; in doing so he used up much of the Cape timber. So, we remain onboard for some days yet...

There were several whales close by, in the bay this morning. The professor has already disembarked, along with the Commander and two officers. He said he was 'paving the way' for our future and that I should not concern myself with anything other than the orders I have been given. The ship must be emptied, first of slaves, then of all supplies for the Cape, but not of the packages for the Indies, all decks must be scrubbed, topsails and yards taken down to be cleaned after those months at sea, wood rubbed with linseed oil before...

...here Palm was called to action. Teamed with Otto, a young Dutchman who had spent months in the employ of the VOC, but lived in the settlement on shore...they now must to work together, organising the task of unloading.

For several days they were fully occupied. Should any item be lost after unloading they needed to give a full account. So far only one heavy case of ammunition had slipped from its ropes... appeared to have sunk. This was a disaster. A diver had disappeared below the waves for anxious minutes at a time but claimed he could not see it.

‘They subtract this from our wages, you know’, sighed Otto. ‘What treasures there must be lost here already. One needs a diving bell.’

In clear sunlight, with a north-east wind across the choppy bay, Palm squinted at his new home...but, of course, only in those rare moments when he was *not* observing and noting down each unloaded package, sack or case.

'What do I see there, Otto,' he asked, pointing, 'a rectangular patch of land, of a different colour to the rest, it may even be fenced or walled, could that be the famous Company Gardens, the salvation of us scurvy-ridden sailors?'

‘Yes, yes, quite right, Henrik Boom, the devoted gardener, was brought from Holland,’ Otto informed, ‘to lay out beds for lifesaving vegetables and fruits...many hectares of hard work, day after day....and he has planted an avenue of oaks along the side of it, with seedlings brought from Holland.’

‘Most appropriate,’ Palm noted, ‘for a gardener to be called Boom, which means a tree,’...the one-sided account was making it difficult for him to keep his mind on the task of unloading; he pondered his own name, a tree of sorts, especially now he was in a hot place where such plants were thought to thrive. ‘Might it be some message: was I meant to live near such excellent trees, symbols of peace and victory, with their coconuts and sap...?’

‘A complex soul, this young man from Pomerania,’ passed through Otto’s mind.

They did try to concentrate on the unloading. While *Otto* told about van Riebeeck’s employees, released to become farmers, free burghers, all fifty-one of them now owners of substantial plots along the Liesbeck river, and this already ten years ago, and while still counting and noting the packages, boxes and trunks, he also managed to regale Palm with tales of horrendous fighting against aggrieved tribesmen, problems which had to be quelled and resolved, over and over again, with cruel bloodshed. ‘Now’, assured

Otto, 'all is well: new farms are protected by a wild almond hedge with watch-towers to exclude the Hottentots from water supplies and grazing lands.'

Palm learned how, sixteen years ago, Van Riebeeck had been ordered by the VOC to found this fortified trading station. A small fort made with timber and mud was deemed sufficient protection and every burgher was required to have a gun...liable to perform military service if needed. The settlement was not even a colony. Van Riebeeck had established trust with the natives by simple barter, offering brandy, tobacco and various metals in return for cattle and sheep...

All they'd found on arrival was a small group of 'beach-rangers' at the Cape; they lived on fish, but soon there were hunters, herders and outcasts, all trying to make profit from the visiting ships from Europe. Their lives benefitted from helping with 'refreshing' of ships, from acting as messengers to other fleets and acting as middlemen when herders brought their cattle.

'Their acknowledged chief, Autshumato, spoke excellent English,' Otto told Palm, 'but I must tell you his unusual double life: he fell asleep on deck of a ship, which just happened to sail off back to England with him, a sleeping, unknown black man onboard...then years later, when he returned to Africa, he had been renamed 'Harry', and could no longer speak his own language! From then on, known as Chief Harry, he concerned himself with bringing livestock to Van Riebeeck, but also to enrich himself. Ah, but then troubles began: 'Harry' murdered a Dutch herd-boy, and deserted with all the Company's animals.

Despite all this he was re-instated. Later 'Harry' did end up in prison, first in the Fort, then on Robben Island. He died a year after van Riebeeck left the Cape, just six years ago. He will not be forgotten!'

'It was only last year we had the first Malays arrive as slaves,' Otto told Palm, and what a wonderful addition to our small settlement they are: excellent workers, such fine, clever men and women!'

‘But Otto, those tribesmen, do they still claim their grazing lands, their rights?’ Palm felt for them, spoke his mind: ‘They do have a just cause?’

‘Well yes, Palm, from the earliest days the directors of the VOC, the famous ‘Seventeen’, you must have you heard of them, laid down instructions: local people must not be treated too strictly: beach-rangers, the men who live only by fishing, and Hottentots, also known as Khoi, were not to be molested. If they stole cattle only the same number should be taken from them in reprisal….that sort of thing…but now things have changed. Any offending attackers, trying to reclaim the lands they see as their own, are caught and chained, then imprisoned on that island you see over there, Robben Island, the home of seals, along with criminals, and made to work for the Dutch East India Company, hewing black rocks and shells for the new fort: our castle of Good Hope made of brick, stone and cement, not mud, clay and timber as the old one…, look carefully, Palm, you will see the new foundations, see, over there, to the left, just by the Company Gardens….’

‘And ‘Boschjesmans’, as the Dutch call them’ asked Palm, ‘are they the same as the ‘Khoi’ and those ‘Hottentots’, it is confusing, these names; such a muddle to remember them, how do they look, these tribesmen?’

‘They are dark all over, they wear skins and beads, they carry weapons and speak a different language. We must try to learn some words as they do try to speak ours! Try it, Palm just say it: ‘hautitou, hautitou!’ ‘Yes, that’s it, louder and faster’…the two young men nod their heads, repeat the sounds stamping their feet, grinning happily…’hauttetou, houttetou, hottentou, hottento…’

This usual greeting from the locals was a dance song in which the word ‘hautitou’ was repeated at the start, in the middle and also at the end… …such performances of welcome may have been misunderstood by visitors, not used to dancing and singing wild men. It is really a collective name given to local people by travellers from

Europe. The locals call themselves 'Khoikhoi,' which means 'real' men.

'Soon you will meet them, Palm, small dark-skinned men, they are everywhere, they live in bush or barren lands extending across the vast Kalahari Desert, you will be surprised to see their straw huts, how quickly and neatly they put them up wherever they go. Some have cattle, some are hunters and it is best to treat them kindly, to trade with them.

....at first, when the Dutch landed here, they found 'strand-lopers', men who lived on seafood, they were few in number; Strand-lopers were permitted to make a kraal by the Lion's Head, near the sea, and there they lived in a miserable manner. For brandy and tobacco they would collect a little firewood, but they had no wish to work for any other reward. Now they have vanished, we never see them...

Skirmishes between other tribes are frequent, like the Gricqua, and Cochoqua and Chainouqua who all belong to one clan, worship the same god, believe in an after-life...we know this because their burial customs reveal cairns when there has been a death, where passers-by must put a stone to remain in contact with their forefathers. And I can tell you, Palm, these people seem resigned to our presence: we, the white men with our complex clothes and strange needs. We trade with them: *we* want their cattle and sheep, but in return *they appear to* want nothing but brandy and tobacco...'

'And the Company, is it always on the look-out for trading partners?'

'Of course,' Otto grinned. 'They grasp what they can, carefully protect whatever they already have. When, four years ago, the directors in Europe considered an imminent war between Holland and England, and the possibility of an attack on the Cape with that old mud fort and its constantly falling walls after the heavy rains...a resolution was passed to erect a strong stone fortress in Table valley, with heavy guns and room for a large garrison. Ag man! You should have seen the activity, Palm: three hundred soldiers were landed and set to work quarrying stone. Convicts and slaves had to gather shells to be processed in lime kilns. I, a mere farmer's assistant, was paid four gulden a day for one wagon with oxen and only two years ago the first stones were laid...there was great festivity that day, a day of pleasure...I remember it well: two oxen and six sheep were slaughtered and one hundred loaves of bread specially baked and washed down with vast numbers of casks of Cape ale. Still, it will be years before it is finished. When Khoi traders come to the old Fort now there is much bartering and even beginnings of Khoi labour on free-burgher farms. Do remind me to tell you about the first Khoi Christian convert...she is a brown woman now named Eva'.

Palm's head was reeling. He heard Otto's account while also writing down the number on each package, then passing it on to the next sailor, who carted each load to the edge of the ship. A different team lowered goods into primitive vessels swaying on rough waves, bumping against the salt and shell encrusted ship. The task seemed endless. Two days passed, the weather changed, became stormy: it was winter after all. Shivering sailors longed to take shelter. But no, work had to be finished before dark.

'Tomorrow, Palm, thanks be to God, the sloop takes us to the jetty ...no doubt your Professor will be waiting for you. A day of rest, but everyone is expected to attend Service on Sundays; it takes place in the great hall of the commander's house inside the old fort. For the time being we have a 'dominee', detained from a ship by the council of the VOC... I will look out for you, Palm.

Have you some place to stay? Annetjie de boerin, wife of Henrik Boom, has recently opened a house of accommodation...a very kind woman she is, her place might be, just the thing for you?'

***

And so it came to be: Palm's new home was a room in the house of the head gardener. Further along the road was a baker, a grocery store and four canteens. All business prices were fixed and controlled by the government in Amsterdam. At last count there were twenty free families living in Table valley, and countless slaves from the Far East and West Africa.

Palm looked up: today 'his' grey, craggy mountain seemed imponderable, even indifferent. Palm felt abandoned and alone.

New arrivals, together with Mynheer Boom, strolled across to the castle where a Sunday service was to take place in the great hall of the commander's lodgings. Skins of lions, leopards, and horns of dead beasts decorated the walls, opposite the entrance stood a striped horse-like beast stuffed with straw. The windows had been recently glazed when before there'd been only calico screens. 'Sufficient light, at last...' said those who could now read their bibles, follow their hymn-books. After Sunday service Palm met numbers of residents; the only man not present was new Commander Borghost.

'He is in ill health' announced Cornelius de Cretzer, the fiscal, who today was acting deputy. One of the leading men in the settlement also came over to welcome the newcomers, wishing them success and courage, but mainly enquiring if they might be interested in milling, perhaps on his newly granted plot of land,...'should you be passing my way, just around the mountain, do call in, you are welcome, you know.' Similar kindness was extended by Mynheer Cornelissen, a former ship's carpenter, who had been assigned a narrow strip of forest at the foot of the mountain to cut timber, 'but most of the best timber now comes from around the mountain, even the kloofs over the Rondeboom-bosjen will soon be exhausted' he claimed. 'The forests here are composed of many varieties growing side by side. We are giving them names, you will not know them: Stinkwood and Cape Chestnut, also the Cape Coast Cabbage tree and the beautiful Silver-trees and the Keurboom...there already has been such reckless waste; pathways must be constructed to reach them, teams of oxen are needed to bring them to the sites needed. How prodigal we have been with supplies...'

'I see no Palm-trees here, I thought there would be many,' remarked Palm, as casually as he could muster.

'They are to be found elsewhere, Master Uhlfeld, we have planted seed from Mauritius, but they are slow growing. You will not believe how much timber is needed for building, I can barely keep up supplies and I am constantly on the look-out for strong young men. I pay a fair wage, all fixed by the council in Amsterdam...'

'What are your plans, will you stay long?' Everyone was asking the new arrivals. For the moment, if there was any answer, it was a short one:

'One is not certain.'

***

The new commander had taken to his bed, a deputy was appointed. The man chosen was currently the Fiscal, a magistrate dealing with offences against revenue. For now he was the able, unbribe-able, capable, perhaps even likeable Cornelius de Cretzer.

Palm and the professor stood before him: de Cretzer, head down, was studying their papers. Small, rotund and aware of his new responsibilities he tried to bear them nobly. Bestowing a solemn smile on both newcomers he nodded, and announced:

'Professor Ruetz and Master Uhlfeldt, welcome to you, gentlemen!

We are fortunate, not only to have you here but also because it is an *un*eventful time: there is little to worry about other than trade with incoming ships. We *did* have to cope with a strong band of Namaquas last month who made a foray upon some small kraals of sheep at Saldanha Bay, further up the coast. Oxen and sheep belonging to the Company, grazing in the neighbourhood, also fell prey to the raiders: two or three Europeans who attempted a rescue were wounded with arrows. Three Namaquas were shot dead by firing muskets, but an amicable peace has been restored in a short time.'

He wiped his brow; it was a warm day, even in winter. Palm and the professor nodded, muttered words of respectful appreciation.

'Do you know there are strong regulations forbidding trade between freemen and the natives? No? This causes difficulties. But we have time to help and advise all newcomers.' He had stopped smiling at his guests; instead he wiped his brow again, with a snow-white kerchief.

'There do remain, of course, endless challenges with Hottentots and the new lands which have been taken from them and prepared for farming.... we've trained oxen to draw timber and we have learned to cope with wild animals,.. lions and leopards invade our cattle kraals by night and leopards even attack in broad daylight, carrying away sheep. Especially poultry is not safe; there are wild cats and all manner of ravenous beasts. Do not look alarmed, gentlemen! These are small things.... we manage, we all learn, and so will you, with each new challenge, rest assured. You are most welcome here. You have nothing to fear: you will carry arms, every burgher is required to have a gun, and you are liable to be called upon for military service...one occasionally practises the necessary drill. Also, you must meet our farmers, our craftsmen. Some of them are now free to sell produce to the crews of vessels after arrival. They are at liberty to trade with foreign vessels, something the VOC has not allowed in the past. Grain and cattle are for the Company's own use, and can never be sold without special permission, not to anyone. If at all possible the VOC tries to keep foreigners like the English and French away from the Cape.'

De Cretzer looked them up and down, then walked proudly to a richly carved table to pour three glasses of white Cape wine: 'Produce of the vineyard planted by Mynheer van Riebeeck over a decade ago, the fruit was Muscadel, you know...he had this vision. Such a vision!

Taste it, gentlemen? Yes? I see from your faces: it pleases you. Excellent.' He wiped his brow. 'Now, inform me, if you will, in which way *you* hope to spend your time here. How long and where will you stay? There are lodgings for strangers, licensed canteens, also some to be found in Rondeboorn-bosjen, but I understand you may be well cared for in lodgings, newly opened not far from here.'

'Indeed Mynheer, we are housed, we have taken two rooms. Palm Uhlfeldt has spoken to the head Gardener and will be glad to begin tending the Company gardens, under instruction, of course. We both hope to find useful occupation, serving the colony in any way you might suggest, Mynheer. There is no decision as to the duration of our stay, but we would like to make *some* contribution to this unusual settlement. For myself: I am interested in Jurisprudence. I am a teacher and can put my mind to most things in life, with the exception perhaps of religious matters...and Master Uhlfeldt, who remains my responsibility until he has reached his twenty-first year, has taken a risk: he has left the northern hemisphere to expand his understanding of the world.'

Palm stood, looking down at his feet. He remembered the globe at school in Stralsund. He was now standing right at the bottom of the ball which represented the world, listening to his mentor's description of himself. 'Our heads must all be pointing south' he decided.

'According to the ship's doctor Master Uhlfeldt has shown skill in tending the injured and persons who were unwell. He has also revealed interest in the rights and wrongs of the state. He understands plants. We are both flexible and put ourselves in your hands in the hope there are tasks to be done.' The Professor bowed, with an unusually sombre expression. And the magistrate, both elbows on his desk, stroked his nose by raising and lowering his head:

'Gentlemen, allow me time. Sufficient time to make enquiries, get guidance. I will consult the surgeon, the legal department and also the school and other organisations. I will have suggestions in two days…three perhaps.' Then he frowned, addressing Palm:

'And now, Master Uhlefeld, lest I forget: I am given to understand one entire box of ammunition was lost through your careless unloading when your vessel arrived. Is this correct?'

Palm inclined his head.

'I'm sorry to say the VOC demands a fine to the value of 15 gulden. And it must be paid in full within the month'.

De Cretzer gave Palm a stern look and wiped his brow again, most thoroughly, after he had spoken.

Palm stood corrected. His face had flushed red.

'Mistakes catch up with one…let it be a warning,' the tutor nodded.

***

On the following Wednesday De Cretzer offered numerous suggestions: 'For Master Uhlfeld: there is a vacancy at the school, where children of the Hottentots, slaves and the beach-rangers are taught to speak simple Dutch phrases and numbers and the rudiments of reading and writing, if only their names. Now this would require strength and patience on all fronts'…he looked at Palm.

'Also for you, Master Palm: assistants are required for services offered in the hospital, now in a proper building, no longer just a tent, ranging from laundry, cooking, burning waste, carrying patients, to bandaging their wounds and holding them down during operations.

Half of the days of the week, not on Sundays, you have been assigned to assist Mynheer Boom in the Company gardens…and it goes without saying, Professor, we would be honoured if *you* spent time in our legal department…you will have a seat and vote in the 'Court of Justice'. If this were to be the correct route for Master Palm he could also be attached to you, for keeping records…this might prove to be a strain but you would without any doubt be able to monitor his progress.' He looked at the two men before him.

'Is this of any help, is it clear, gentlemen? Your respective salaries would be calculated by the Company and I can assure you will be comfortably provided for. Gentlemen, I wish you luck with your deliberations.'

De Cretzer has had his say. He turned to go... but then remembered:

'Ah, yes...we also work on the production of ale, a product indispensable for scurvy patients in the hospital. We grow the barley but the hop will not thrive, despite the greatest care...definitely an opening here...should either of you be interested, this could become most lucrative...I am certain you need time to consider these suggestions. You will find me in my office when you have decided and when you are ready to sign any contracts. Good afternoon, gentlemen.'

The Professor was content. Young Palm was crushed by choice:

'In the end it may be best to compromise: the Law department each morning, but I wish above all else to work in the Company Gardens, to smell the air, to hear the birds, (ah, there are such birds here; have you seen the orange-breasted sunbird, shimmering, blue, green, a miracle)... to feel the Cape winds and to assist Mynheer Boom after noon. He has already mentioned experiments he makes with exotic plants: coconuts and cassava, rice and hops, olives and mulberry trees... plants I have never even heard of... but alas, they have all failed!

I will learn and become strong and brown, just as he is, and I will know all the strange plants, discover how to seed and sow and reap and plough, all things my stepfather knew when I was a boy in Pomerania. I wish to feel the heat and sweat and befriend Hottentots and men from the East and other parts of Africa and in the evening we can drink and learn to understand each other.

'Wondrous! New life in a new world! Your situation will be reviewed each year', Professor Ruetz, reminds Palm soberly. I shall see how you progress.'

SIXTEEN

1672. Palm keeps a diary during stormy winter months:

'...after the full-moon in April the rain began with violent winds and did not stop for seven days...now trees are uprooted, paths washed away. I have no true desire, and usually little time, to write down all events experienced since I have come to this strange place five years ago. There is at all times a feeling of unease, of impending danger. That early promise of security from my 'grey Father', being cradled and protected by his vastness, where is it now?

I am twenty-two years old and five of them lived in the Cape. One hears rumours of a battle between the Dutch and the English and also of the French marching into the heart of the Dutch Republic; perhaps we are fortunate so far from all that.

Funding from the Swedish Governor in Stralsund has come to an end. My tutor, no longer responsible for my welfare, must in any case soon return to Pomerania to fulfil duties towards his mother and his daughter. We both earn fair money here: the VOC is generous, within reason. News of unfriendly conduct from the English Court has alarmed the Dutch and we understand the directors of the East India Company consider it advisable to strengthen the defences of all their possessions. In Table Valley there is already a garrison of three hundred men and we, the white men, feel more secure than ever before, although relations with the Hottentots are often tense.

For sheep-stealing and assault on herdsmen Hottentot prisoners have recently been brought to trial and sentenced to be flogged, and three most guilty ones branded and banished to Robben island for fifteen years. Just yesterday there was news of shooting a Hottentot by a lawless character called Willem Willems...who has managed to escape on a Danish ship. There are strict regulations over the years prohibiting dealings between burghers and Hottentots, but forbidden traffic continues to carry on. Laws are issued frequently but to no avail. It remains a capital offence to supply arms or ammunition to a Hottentot. Furthermore it has become a penal offence to pay natives in money, for any services offered: it is thought they do not understand the value of it. The government fears that farmers or burghers foolishly create serious difficulties. How will this end? Scoundrel Willems is bound to return to his family and his property: the Hottentots are rightly clamouring for justice. We shall see.

My Professor still has a seat and vote in the Court of Justice. Now he scratches his head as to the treatment of this criminal.

He has approached me: he could pave the way, feels I would benefit from staying by his side, not just half day but all my time, to learn first hand the difficulties in this increasingly complex new country, while he is still here to help me. He tells me the Company wishes to draw up an important binding contract with the *so-called Prince Schacher, (are they aware his name implies he is a scoundrel and a haggler, for it is a German word I know well...)*

He is in fact a Hottentot Chief (among themselves their old names are preserved; when they speak to white men they employ corrupted names) laying down rules and clauses in precise legal language and I am to assist during the entire deliberations. The agreement is to be preserved in the registry of deeds: 'that he, the first Hottentot prince, agrees for himself and his heirs, in perpetuity, to sell the Cape, including Table, Hout and Saldanha Bays, all its lands and rivers and forests, to be cultivated and possessed without remonstrance from anyone. But that he and his people and cattle shall be free to come anywhere near the outermost farms in the district, where neither the Company nor the freemen require the pasture, and shall not be driven away by force.'

There is much legal work to be done. I must leave my duties on the new vine settlement on the southern side of the mountain, although I do have a horse which could get me there and back here if I set out early enough.

The 'Kasteel van Goede Hoop', the new fort, the building of which had been suspended for some time, is to be completed according to the original design, but will not be ready for at least another two years. Woodwork for various buildings connected with the castle is being prepared in Amsterdam and sent out along with large quantities of bricks and tiles and skilled handymen.

*In total there are now 421 white men and native slaves in the settlement, also 64 free burghers, mostly tavern keepers but also shopkeepers and craftsmen. There is still no church, but we are buoyed by the hope that one day there may be a place of worship in the settlement. I close my eyes, imagine a fine church with a tall spire near the Company Gardens; this place I cherish, filled as it is with wondrous plants and trees, even Mr.van Riebeeck's tree, the Saffron Pear, which he is said to have planted himself; it is now as high as a very tall man. Such trees can live for hundreds of years, Mynheer Boom assures me. Experiments are being made in the cultivation of various useful plants from other parts of the world: sugar cane and coconut trees, brought from Ceylon, cassava plants from the west coast of Africa, but these have all failed. The olive is still regarded as the tree that will ultimately succeed. The gardens cover 18 hectares and the **V**ereenigte **O**ost-Indische **C**ompagnie can be proud of their achievement, or might I say, of mine as well, since I have played my small part in this: it was my first choice, working under Boom, when so many years ago I planted, dug, watered and nursed tender plants and vegetables. Only in the afternoons, when the sun was hot, I spent time studying the laws brought from Holland to rule this new country.*

My years here already feel like a very long time......

Palm is much alone. He dispels loneliness by writing down all he sees and experiences:

The garrison is again to be increased and the administration entrusted to a class of men superior to those employed in the past...thus the handed-down wisdom I receive from my Professor, the man I rarely see now, for he is so very occupied in the law-court. We live separately, he is in lodgings near the Gardens; at first I felt I'd abandoned him when Boom sent me to help with planting of vines near the woodcutters' station, by the south side of the mountain, but I now see through all that: I am to make responsible choices for <u>my own</u> <u>developing life</u>. Will I ever return to my homeland? So much has happened in these past four years....there were unthinkable suggestions at first: we should sail, (when we had only just arrived), in some laughably small ship on a 'journey of discovery'....a tempting offer. We heard later, after the men had returned: the yacht reached no further eastward than St. Francis Bay, where they feared they had sprung a leak in a storm. No discoveries then, although we now know they missed much wondrous scenery and only a little further they would have come upon forest-clad hills and valleys of the Tsitsikama and other tribes of men called the Attaquas.

Such events most interest Palm: almost each day there is some unheard of challenge. There had been two changes of governors, Peter Hackius and Albert van Breughel....but with troubles in the mother country the numbers of ships in the bay were falling greatly. A quarter of a century since the Dutch arrival there seemed to be little change in the life of the natives. There were more of them, one saw their kraal in Table Valley, on the upper side of the rump of the lion, but mostly they were found idling about outside the houses of the burghers; the men only wishing to tend cattle, the women gathering wood for sale. Young black girls, dressed in sheepskin or cast-off Dutch clothing depended on rice in return for services offered.

'They have become fond of arrack and tobacco...too fond!' This is what most settlers think.

On the 18th of October Sergeant Cruythof and twelve men were to ride across the Cape flats to Hottentots-Holland, where earth and grass and forests were known to be superior. Steps should soon be taken towards extending the settlement into the interior. Again Palm had been invited to join them, but refused for fear of offending the Professor who now pressed him to take up lodgings near his own and go daily to study the Law under his guidance.

He is reminded constantly: he must earn sufficient money for his own keep and also to put some away against the day he wishes to return to his father- land. This might not happen for some years.

Young Palm feels torn in all directions.

Studying the Law full-time means he would no longer be able to speak with...no, he must not, may not ever write or say her name. It would only be the cause of more trouble. Palm is deranged with this difficulty.

'It must remain secret, for all eternity.'

September, 1672.

During Mr Hackius' time there was mostly quiet routine. Last year he fell ill and lingered until his death a few months ago. Troubling events for him were limited to the destruction of preying beasts, particularly lions and leopards, attracted by our flocks and herds. Hyenas scrape up the dead in the churchyard. The councillors have now decreed the reward is to be raised to 77 gulden for each wild animal, two thirds of which is to be paid by the freemen.

I have come to value the intentions of the Council, plain honest men, who look very simply at the native question, show no mood to brook any wrong-doing; there is no desire to harm the Hottentots, they say, or interfering with their own rules, but should there be any attack on the new settlement there must come terrible punishment and revenge. Sheep-stealing and assaulting herdsmen is punished with flogging, branding and banishment for at least seven years to Robben island. For more grievous offences the strict governors use cruel punishments: beating, branding with red-hot knives, hard labour for years on the island, hanging in the castle and then dragging the dead through streets to be strung up on further gallows out by the Lion's rump.... this is where the birds come to feed.

If I were to become a councillor I would wish to moderate some of the cruel verdicts issued in this place. Somehow Good and Evil take on a different aspect here; my attempts to grasp what is right for life in the colony does not bring contentment. I often ask myself if we should have come at all.

By 'we' I mean all the men who have come from Europe to settle in the Cape and in the Far East, and for trying to change the ways dark-skinned strangers live their lives ....

In Law there is no distinction between black and white men. A baptized black man has all the rights of a European. Mohammedan slaves from the Indian islands and Asia remain slaves for some years, but usually become freemen. Children born here of the slaves are mostly black or half-breed, a fact which greatly disturbed the visiting commissioner Isbrand Goske last year. He made it known that all slaves were to be sent to church twice on Sundays, to assemble every evening for instruction and to learn and repeat prayers so they might become Christians and be baptized and married and eventually become free.

All children: black, white, mixed race, slaves, who live in the Cape, must attend the Company school, a small room in the Fort. I was offered work there when we first arrived, teaching children to read and write. I tried, but feeling inadequate I soon withdrew. Now, years later, a small school on the new settlement where the vines thrive, serves a similar purpose and has given me credibility as an occasional teacher on that other side of the mountain. But my great worry, the difficulty I have already mentioned, has made me come full circle: back to a small place near the Fort....all that riding around the Peak was simply using up too much of my day and my powers.

There has also been, for me, in the end, a choice between good and evil.

When one is asked to break the rules, well intentioned eternal rules, for the sake of intense feelings and fulfilment of <u>one</u> human being, over the supposed injury of another, where does one stand in the eyes of the <u>Law,</u> but above all, in the eyes of the <u>Lord</u>...who has inspired such rules?

How can I rest my conscience, find peace?

I lie awake in the night; my anguish allows me no rest. I see her, small and fragile, her sleek black hair loosely tied back, dark eyes gazing at me intently as she puts before me yet another lovingly cooked meal, offers me wine from a barrel in their modest homestead, sits beside me to keep me company when I have finished the task of the day, before I ride back, around the Duifes Piek to the Fort, to prepare for the next day at Court.

Every second she is in my thoughts. Were it not for my tutor, my studies, I would blow out my brains, before it is too late. My soul, my feelings... my body torment me.

I must think dispassionately: Her name is M. She was born here, daughter of a slave from the Far East. Her loveliness caught the eye of my employer, then already an ageing widower, lonesome and tired of solitary days and nights on his allotment, growing nothing but vines. Thus, soon married again, but now grown quite elderly, he continued to pray for a son with this young second wife, this woman of ravishing sweetness, with whom he had already shared a bed for some years, without the longed-for result.

She had taken me into her confidence: she was ten years older than I ...she loved him, gave the old man all she had to offer, but there was no quickening. Months, years passed...and she assumed she was unable to present him with an heir through no fault of hers....She told me how he had suffered this before, with his long departed first wife.

For me all this was like drowning. Her shy admiring glances, small gentle touches of hands, when she brought food, her quiet voice and thoughtful reading of my own needs had given us a special understanding... and now I must bear the consequences without complaint.

She first came to me when he, the grey-bearded one, had taken the road around the Peak back to town, to stop off at his sister's house for some days: there was unfinished business he said, and I was honoured to be left in charge of his property...in a manner of speaking. This miraculous occurrence, no, I must tell the truth, if only on this secret paper, these repeated enchanted encounters, had brought on the required swelling of her body. Now her old man looks on with benign pride, puts his arm around her, smiles, waiting for the day he will have a son. I pray it is a son. Boy-children look like their mothers.

I allow myself two short visits to the farm-school each month, where an acquaintance, Ernestus, teaches the baptised slave and Hottentot children without charge, the others, seven farm children of Dutch farmers, for one gulden a month. They learn to read and write, to sing psalms, say prayers. They also learn to count and cast up common coinage. They all know me and I sing with them and praise them for their progress. But increasingly I attend to the Law. It remains the only thing that helps me to push away the hurt, the worry about M., as far as possible, to a place where it *can, no, where it must no longer trouble me. It never will be far enough, but I must learn to be a man.*

1682. The town to the west of the castle has grown.

Now there are: Thyn Straat and Zee Straat, Heere Straat and Oliphant Straat and of course Burg Straat. Close to the lower side of the Lion's rump is the Company's new brick kiln, also a neat regular settlement of small houses, all at right angles starting near the shore and spreading up towards the Gardens, growing at a steady pace. Small rivulets flow from the mountain to help cultivate numerous private gardens and bring water to a reservoir near the site of the old Fort, by means of a wooden pipe to be laid down shortly. There is even a mill nearby for grinding corn. By the shore is the hospital, a brewery and a tannery and there appears to be the beginning of a new long path winding its way around the Lion's rump although there are Khoi families in their huts at the base of the softly undulating hill.

This is where Palm lives; his street so far only moderately long, with three houses on it. Now known as Mynheer Uhlfeld, with one or two grey hairs appearing, he tells himself: 'God willing, this new road will become *long* one day, one left fork to the gallows near the beach, the other fork leading down to the water front, and all this before I grow too old. In the meantime I enjoy this fine view towards the rocky top of 'Duifes Piek', that pointed portion of the mountain to the left of the valley.'

The professor has already set sail on a VOC ship, to return to Stralsund. Life 'at home' appears to have changed: from *his* letters Palm learns there has been another battle: the Elector of Brandenburg had at last re-captured the town from Sweden.

The numbers of dead are not known.

In a recent letter Palm reads: *Time has passed since I left you in charge of your own life...any thoughts about returning to Stralsund I suggest you put aside, this place is in a parlous state...everyone most restive and unsettled, you are better off in the Cape.../ trust you, my former and very dear pupil, have found satisfaction, remain in good health....*

'Already fifteen years! How speedily time has passed for me, here, still in the lap of my 'Grey Father'. Having re-read some of my professor's tragic letters and especially my own dangerous jottings (which have lain hidden, untouched in the back of my trunk, almost forgotten,) I am left deeply disturbed: It is dangerous to keep such things. I should, no I must, set fire to them. Even my tutor knew nothing about this. It is ten years since he sailed home.

There, I said it: Home! I sometimes wonder about that. It sounds I may be needed there more than I am here.

I sit about doing little, endlessly tempted to scribble, yet again.'

Palm leans back, his head against the white-washed brick and stone wall; he stares up at the mountain. His 'grey father'! He has planted a young palm tree: now ten years old it may soon be tall enough to give *some* shade. The setting sun has dropped behind the immense rocky surface of the mountain to his right, the shadows are lengthening.

He lights two candles, there is no breeze. He hopes they might give sufficient light for writing. He does not know he is being watched by a small Khoi child, peering through some shrubs in the dusk.

'I try to order my memories of the passing show of life in the Cape, penning yet another carefully worded letter to my dear old professor.....

.....First Isbrand Goske, then Johan Bax both governors, and yes, the acting Commander Hendrik Crudorp have been those, along with us kindred souls, who are still trying to lay the foundations of

this useful, stopping off place. And now....someone quite new, since 1679, recently installed as governor, already three years, how can this be? He is leaving his mark: all things Dutch are desirable, the institution, the language, the customs and the laws. His remarkable wit.... and common sense and patriotism, this is Simon van der Stel, a name people will remember: he is out to make all of the Cape resemble his home country, and why not..... we all like him! And his four sons with him, all hoping to become farmers, they are here too. His wife refuses to travel to this remote part of the world and remains in Amsterdam. Van der Stel is undeterred .But it has to be said: it no longer feels like a mere 'stopping-off place'.

Once our new Commander had inspected everything in and around the castle and then wished to visit areas lying further away towards the Hottentots-Holland Mountains. A riding party was arranged, I was invited ...this time I agreed: 'Good to get about, see what else there is,' I told myself.

Soon we were riding in finest Cape weather with an escort of soldiery and servants to visit an already well set-up farming area, after having spent the night at Kuilen, by a stream. Further along there was a pleasing valley, again with a stream of sweet water, the earth and grass wondrously rich and all those fine trees.... the commander decided to encamp surrounded and enchanted by the beauty of the land. He was deeply moved, we all were, by the splendour of the setting, so much that he decided to give it a name. After only a few moments Van der Stel announced: 'I would like this place to be called 'Stellenbosch', and also that he could see, in his mind, a body of freeholders who would come and attach themselves to this spot and that it would become a thriving settlement in a very short time.....

Van der Stel's vision is proving true: before the year was over there were eight families who moved as a group with their ploughs and cattle and permission to select any land they pleased in the valley of Stellenbosch. It was theirs for the taking.....

How tempting to consider accepting such an offer. Having spent the last ten years keeping records and studying every aspect of the law and its application in the Cape I too might be enticed into this project. I still ponder this prospect. I would own land, plant vines! But no, there are things that hold me back. Stralsund? When and why should I return? I have no-one there, only you, Professor...here I now also have one new good friend from German lands...

'Alas', sighs Palm, 'how can I ever return....I am unwell, truly unwell.' Bearded chin resting on his chest, he has nodded off. When he wakes the sun has gone down, he feels the chill as he sits in the dusk in his very small garden. He pulls a rug around his shoulders. This was the time of day which brought the saddest thoughts, the time when despair throttled all possibility of saying 'yes' to life. A distant dog was barking, gulls circled over him, pigeons settled on the fence of his garden. 'Company of a sort' he thinks. Living alone he had developed a habit of muttering quietly to himself, and to his cat:

'I have,*ja, ja,*with great care, studied my words written ten years ago, and *ja, ja,* they are true. There is this 'son', my son, I have seen him; he comes to the service with his mother. He will never know me. The supposed father is long dead; I will never forget the old man's delight: that long-wished-for boy-child brought into the world. But joy was short-lived: the old one suffered from a weak heart...God rest his soul. And may he forgive me! Ja, ja! I have been a law unto myself and my troubled conscience is only one of my punishments, brought on my own head. Still, at least *her* reputation remains unsullied. I will burn those papers tonight. She is still beautiful; she will find another husband.

Can *I* find forgiveness? *No, never...*'

Palm shuffles into his house, lights a candle and pours himself a jug of Barbetjie Geens,' specially licensed sugar beer. 'Bread and cheese, small green bananas, very sweet... I am not hungry...I force myself, this will give me strength'. Then he drags himself back to his garden, makes a small circle of stones, stuffs shredded and crumpled pages of his confession into the centre, and, holding a flickering candle to the papers...a bright flame shoots up. Within minutes there remains nothing but a neat pile of ashes. He feels relieved.

'I offer this up to you, Grey Father, I have turned disorder into order, and from something so dangerous and wonderful all that remains is a shadow, a trace...of purest love.

Ja, this is true and good.' He stares at Table Mountain. He is sorrowful.

'Immer Ja sagen', always say 'Yes' to life: my dear mother's wisdom.

1683. Lonesome, scruffy, neglected, dejected and unwell Palm sat among shrubs and exotic plants in his small back yard, hidden from sight by a fence around the house. Greenery and his striped cat were the only consolation along with his endless staring at jagged, eroding rocks of the mountain. Yesterday the cat had caught, fought and killed a 'boom-slang,' thought to be a harmless snake. Can one really be sure? Today there was the famous white 'cloth' of clouds, that frayed, mysterious substance, draped over the 'table-top' by unknown forces...

'Punishment' he muttered, 'a word, derived from the same root as 'pain'... pain is my penalty. I know about laws: I am not exempt. When even petty theft, to say nothing of adultery, can lead to the death penalty my own retribution is more than fair, albeit unpleasant: deadly tiredness: I can barely get out of bed for each new day. I drag myself (and my secret) to attend sessions at Court, attend executions, show a brave face, earn my keep, taking notes, endlessly scribbling records, not mingling.'

Lately he had taken to talking to himself, like a lonely, crazed, locked prisoner: 'Some say it was Christopher Columbus, who brought this sickness back from the New World...so, this is my new sin: I took up with Hettie, buxom, golden tresses, the prettiest in the group of hostesses at the 'Blaauwe Haan'...good name that, opened only a few years ago and instantly the liveliest place full of sailors and local bachelors like myself. Was that a sin? A trace of my Minna about her, I thought, my pretty first love in Stralsund harbour. Meeting strangers from ships, laughter, gossip, local and imported spirits, food...and women who look after guests in the time-honoured way, well, Hettie seemed wholesome enough and pleasingly modest and friendly. I fell for her, ja, ja...spent most evenings and a large sum of money there, for longer than was wise.

How deceived I was. Now I must remain as invisible and reclusive as possible, keep myself well covered to hide the unsightly chancres, the blight which appeared as from the stroke of a wide brush. At first there was only a rash and a fever,...then came the sore throat, and the headache, and now, thin and weak with a tremor and thinning hair and almost demented with worry that I may loose my teeth from taking mercury: such is the cure I have been advised by the trusted medicus from a VOC ship. It is said one can rid oneself of Syphilis by having intercourse with a healthy virgin. But the medicus suggested the 'Holy Wood' substance, which is obtained from the bark of the Guaiac Tree, unknown to us here.

It is costly: he has promised to obtain it for me.

Now I feel nothing but revulsion when I think about women, virgin or not. I wish to see no-one; only to remain safe in my small house, tended by a former slave, now freed and in my employ. A good man, from the Far East originally, he brings food and drink cooked by his wife, and keeps the place in order, asking no questions. I am thankful. He is quiet and withdrawn. We make a good pair. This 'infinite malady' makes one unable to love, to mourn or to smile.'

Palm paced restlessly from one side of his room to the other, stopped before the small blotchy mirror his mother had left him when she died, the one from Venice. He narrowed his eyes, looked sternly at himself, and continued the lecture: 'What I *must* do…and to excess: Jawohl! It is to reflect: why I am here? Why am I *still* here? Has the time come to return to Europe? I am aware of white men around me: how prideful and despising and unwilling they would be to have any dealings with anyone in this plight. Understandably: it is a matter of life and death. As before, when there was something to conceal, I struggle alone. I should not complain. There is no-one to love, to be close to.'

Overwhelmed with self-pity he drank himself into a stupor and slept soundly into the next day. Somehow he had managed, up to now, to forget his new trusted friend, Hans, but when he next wrote to his professor he told him the whole story:

….There is one man, an understanding new friend, my good Samaritan. Originally a ship's carpenter from Hamburg he is now a burgher of the Cape for twenty years; he likes to call on me. We speak our mother tongue…we are both forgetting it. There is consolation in hearing familiar sounds from time to time. Hans Grimp

is a widower. As there is an undeniable shortage of marriageable women in the Cape he hopes the next batch of Huguenots may bring new females. There is already a small contingent of them somewhere beyond the Cape valley and these men and women are said to be very good at growing vines.

We talk about the famous 'Huguenots'... often we open a bottle of Cape wine and read to each other in our own language: mostly history books you left here with me. They are a great consolation.

Palm and Hans gossiped and discussed the suffering of others:

'Those hardworking individuals, the farmers along the Liesbeek River, have you heard... a party of sixteen farmers or so, removed themselves and their stock to the new district of Stellenbosch—and now: a plague of 'goggas', a Khoi word for insects, denuding the crops and destroying everything. In November the commander had counted over one hundred grains of wheat on a single stalk, but then there was hardly one single healthy ear to be found...

'Hans coughed and spat on the ground, and Palm forgave him, as he was so alone.

'Also good news, hear this, Palm: a first school, soon to be established in Stellenbosch, can you believe it! Thirty of the new landowners have presented a petition: that they are now too far from the Fort to attend divine service on the Lord's Day, that their young would grow up as barbarians and therefore there must be found a suitable man to keep a school, to visit the sick and to lead prayers on Sundays. How do you like that? I will be away five days each week: we are to put up a home, attached to a large schoolroom, just for the teacher! There will be free timber and nails, several masons and carpenters. Too bad you are not well enough to come along, Palm. The teacher is Sybrand Mankadan, have you met him? The standard to be achieved by his students is to pass an examination before the Consistory, only then can they be publically admitted as members of the church....'

'Dominie Mankadan, no, I have not met him...he will have no time to be idle. He will put us to shame: not only teaching, but also visiting the sick, conducting divine service and acting as the district secretary, all for a salary of two and one-half gulden. But...he will have a free house, a garden and some small school fees.'

***

Palm's notes in his diary show increasing concerns about life in the Cape:

If I were not handicapped with my illness I would have jumped at such a post. What use am I now, just a 'scribbler' condemned to a silent life until my body is cured. I have time to reflect on the conditions of all black, brown, white and yellow-skinned men and women I come across. Their difficulties and differences become clearer each day.

After years of helping to develop this 'stopping-off point' at the other end of the earth there has come a gradual realisation: local tribesmen and women are not as fearsome, unruly and different as formerly believed.

One famous example is 'Eva', a Hottentot girl-child, born in 1643, the niece of 'Chief Harry', the strand-loper. My friend Hans actually met her years ago, in his early days at the Sunday services in the Fort. He said she was most appealing, elegantly dressed and animated. Her true name was Krotoa. From the age of ten she had grown up in Commander van Riebeeck's household, had become like a child from Europe in all ways except that of the colour of her skin. She learned to read, to act as a Christian, weaned as she was from the customs of her race. There were few occasions when her loyalties were uncertain, she was neither Khoi nor Dutch.

She once told van Riebeeck: 'I, Eva, have a Dutch heart' and he was delighted with this remark. She was without doubt the first Hottentot who conformed to European habits of living; her services as interpreter were invaluable during the earlier years of the settlement. Soon there were many girls like her, mostly children of the beach-rangers, who went into service, learned Dutch fluently and dressed very happily in European clothes.

In 1659 a Danish soldier and surgeon arrived here, a Pieter van Meerhof, who fell for Eva's charms, and married her. There was a small 'wedding Feast' in the Fort, the first one between a native woman and a white man; the current Commander hoped, as a result, 'the native tribes will become more and more attached to us'.

Soon after the wedding the married couple was posted to Robben Island, where Pieter had been offered the job as superintendant. Three children were born. After some years the couple began to assume they had been an embarrassment at the Fort, to have been sent away from the mainland for so long.

It is probably true that Krotoa was never truly trusted by the Dutch, nor by the Khoikhoi, even though she returned to her relations from time to time, adopting their customs and their dress.

After years of hardship and sorrow (her husband was murdered as head of an expedition to the East African coast) she gradually reverted to some of the Hottentot ways, excessive drink and dissolute idleness, gradually losing her mind. Was this the hurtful truth: that the Dutch had taken against her, that they had never admired the 'mixed' marriage of 'Klein Eva the Hottentot' as she was called and that being sent to live on Robben island had been an excellent way of hiding her away?

She was frequently found on the beach dancing and singing trance-like, in the way of her tribe, naked, lost, permanently drunk, sick and unhappy. Soon pregnant from Khoi prisoners on the island, aged only thirty-one she was despised and came to a sad end. She was buried in the Castle, her children were taken into care. The van Riebeeck family had set such a good example with Eva...but the story ended badly. Who was to blame?

***

Already twenty years ago there was at least one man in the Cape, the brother-in law of van Riebeeck, who, in his role as a 'Sick-Comforter' made a zealous start in teaching the Dutch language to the Khoi and slaves, as well as the principles of Christianity. There were only about fifty Khoi souls labouring in the settlement. I say Khoi in place of Hottentot as there seems some stigma attached to that longer name....

It was the sick-comforter's understanding that the Khoi manner of living was such that white men's attempts at improvement of their understanding was unrealistic. 'They think only about cattle, and the baptism of such people should be denied.' But Eva was baptised, just before the van Riebeecks left the Cape.

I ask myself: Where do I stand in this dilemma? My professor has shown me each culture is valuable, for human beings are not naturally bad...it is only fear of strangers that causes intolerance.

We, the whites, having come to this continent, are now building our future on land that belongs to others, but make little effort to understand, even less, to live in their way.

Are local people envious, angry, afraid? Do they wish to learn our ways? Why should they want to speak like us, wear clothes as we do, pray to our God? We learn so little about them, their magic and medicine, and strange trance-like states. This is the difficulty: more dialogue is needed. One lifetime may not be long enough, perhaps not even more than one. There will be angry divisions, passions. It is so much simpler to live with people who speak, think and look the same. And not to have so many questions......

As for life with free will and pleasure...it is as remote here for the Dutch and Germans and French as it is for the Khoi or Hottentots. But where do these thoughts lead me....., there appears to be a commotion, I shall walk to the beach where the shouting comes from. Yes, near the beach perhaps ...just for safety I carry my pistol hidden under my cloak. It is a wintry day...

SEVENTEEN

1684. August...a great feast on the beach: the Hottentots have found three dead whales, despite the chill and damp drizzle there is much merriment, they have managed to light a fire, they sing and dance. Now comes an order from the Commander to drive them away.... for the sake of the whale oil, which is to be secured.

There is an outcry: 'we are hungry...it is cold...'.

Then we hear a different order from the High Commissioner: nothing should be done to disturb the 'peace and friendly relations' which existed. 'No desire to anger the natives': Commander and High Commissioner are not in agreement. Now there is confusion, resentment, angry shouting from hungry Hottentots. They are still driven away.

Palm saw it all. He returned to his house. He felt for the hungry natives.

What should an upright man think...one who is not sure of the boundaries which exist between people? Should natives retire to reserves? Whales or similar problems will always re-appear. What is a perfect society, where is the perfect world? Whose whales are they anyway? He thought one should be able to give the correct answers to *such very big* questions.

Aristotle might advise... looking to the nature, the end and the purpose of such an event as the one today. Where and what is justice when the 'Company's interests' are always regarded as having preference over those of the natives. Can this ever become the perfect world, the perfect society?

The truth, the truth, the truth! It was a bitter pill to swallow.

Palm trudged back to his house. A Khoi youngster and a very much younger brother had attached themselves to him, following cautiously, a few paces behind.

Palm passed the Fort, then the Gardens, noted the excavations, the spot for that new 'proper' church...

When he'd walked around a small lake near the houses of the burghers he realised the boys were trailing behind, four brown eyes firmly fixed on his back. As ever, Palm's eyes were drawn to his beloved mountain. Filled with sorrow he sensed a troubling crisis ahead, an unfolding tragedy in this new place, unstoppable: an inner vision revealing the hopeless growth of mistrust, loathing, bloodshed and intense misery in years ahead. He became aware of a collapse of his resolve to make a life among these people, a tragic awareness of what surely lay ahead, along with a deep need to return to a place with cobbled roads, large dark churches with roaring, rumbling organs, where men and women spoke respectfully about and with each other, who knew their place in a firm structure of society,...a place where one heard one's own language and found stillness; all this had taken hold of poor Palm Uhlfeldt's mind.

Was it the syphilis, making him vulnerable, taking its toll? He saw events with new eyes. He was haunted by the VOC declaring itself the rightful 'possessor of the Cape' having paid tobacco, beads, brandy and bread worth 115 Rix dollars to Chief Schacher. And then there was that oration delivered during the founding of the new Fort: 'our conquests are extending further and further and all black and yellow people are being suppressed...with our stone walls we will frighten off our enemies, Europeans, Asians, Americans and wild Africans...'

These claims resonated, even ten years later.

For the past twenty years the belief, at least, had been put about that natives were not to be molested: there should be no interference in their domestic affairs. Only when there were offences against the Europeans they would become subject to the Dutch tribunals. Theft, of course, was not unusual, but robbery with violence was seldom committed except by Bushmen although *their* own chiefs were always ready to punish them. He considered four Hottentots who had been convicted for the murder of a Dutch servant and been executed by their own people, who beat all four Hottentots to death with clubs.

'There is now a friendly feeling between the Hottentots and us white men,' most white people claimed: 'their chiefs come to the fort to trade in safety and there is plenty of pasture for the use of all.......'

(...from a corner of his eye Palm noted the boys were still following, although the younger one could barely keep up, a pitiful scrap of a boy...)'one of the recent cases, flogging and imprisonment on Robben Island for theft, the culprit had already been released upon payment of two oxen and eight sheep.' Palm, now weary, was out of breath......

....'the other one, found guilty of assault, had also been released on payment...I think it was, yes, just eight fat sheep. Compared to punishments inflicted on Europeans for similar offences these were exceedingly mild...politics meant cultivating the virtue of all citizens, white and dark-skinned, to make them choose 'goodness' and fully realize their natures.'

Concepts such as these were not readily put into action, especially on a beach-front where hungry natives had found food lying freely before their very eyes.

'Might is right, and they feel the injustice... it creates an uncomfortable and threatening future'. With such ruminations he reached his house.

He looked behind him: the black children had vanished.

***

A clear, chilly day...Sunday service was over.

Had they been married men they would have been expected to spend the day quietly at home, according to strict rules of the Dutch Reformed Church. But Lutheran Germans like Palm and Hans, were getting out on horses borrowed from the Company Stables. Riding slowly along the highest path circling the Peak, towards the 'buitepos' for provision of timber, and having taken smaller paths to a tree-less look-out point, they gazed across the flat lands, saw distant mountains snow-topped: that rare treat visible from the southern side of the mountain. Palm usually avoided the smallholdings in this area: it was dangerous territory to him, with trying memories.

The friends enjoyed bracing winter air, admired the growth of plots with farms dotted all along the Liesbeek River and further down before them, they noted the planting of great numbers of oaks along new lands....

'Such beauty here, a true paradise, don't you think; at least a road to paradise, and so very different from Table valley, almost like a country scene in Germany. Shall we stop here, rest the horses... and ourselves for a while, before we return?

The men leaned their guns against a tree-stump, unpacked bread, two chunks of cheese, took a swig of Cape wine. For a while, chewing contentedly, they remained silent, watched spotted hen-like birds pecking around their feet. A strong, warm feeling of being comrades, on an adventure, awed by mysterious, grandiose beauty, united them.

'We must do this more often... blow away the cobwebs. Just look at this vast empty territory, imagine the wild beasts ...although it does not look like grazing land one sees black and white striped horse-like beasts sometimes. And the wild peach, often covered with black caterpillars? They become black and orange butterflies in the summer, have you seen these creatures? The green parts are further along, start much closer to the snowy mountains over there, near Stellenbosch.' The men stood, contemplating the hugeness and then,

all too soon, both rode back to the front of the mountain, where it was now grey, windy, chilly and wet...the ocean choppy and unfriendly. Once the horses were back in the stables they walked up to Palm's house... the wet dripping all over the 'stoep,' which, needless to say, was a good thing for his plants.

'Cape winters can be very trying; did you hear about those rocks falling from the mountain front? Things *look* so stable, but it is not so, and with strong winds and thatched roofs, our dramatic proximity is…unreliable, a permanent worry…apologies for the clay pots all over my floor catching the leaks, but do come in, the food my servant has left for me, 'potjie-kos', this iron-pot stew, full of good things, fish, potatoes. These Asians do have tasty food…do sit down here, we will hang the pot from the hook over the fire.'

Two bearded men rested by the smoky fireplace, stoked logs, tried to dry off the damp. Feeling elderly, as forty-year olds tend to do, unkempt, uncared-for bachelors, they now expected little more than necessities. In that near-dark haze, seated on chairs made of wood and strips of leather to support their weight, by flickering candle light, it was difficult to think of anything other than food and drink. 'But I thought of you, Palm, at the 'Blouwe Haan' last night. One so needs seeing life, hearing voices, laughter, you know how it is…'

Palm stirred the small black pot hanging over glowing logs and Hans chattered on about the crowd and the warmth and 'some new half-breed girls, quite pretty. Your Hettie has disappeared, I asked after her: it seems she left on a ship to Amsterdam, took all her things with her: you will not see *her* again, apparently she has some sickness, I understand.'

Palm studied his friend's face, considered telling everything…since this was the only friend he had. 'But then, would he wish to spend time with me… under such unhappy circumstances?'

'How-ev-er', continued Hans, now in expansive mood, 'I got talking with an elderly Dutchman, formerly a man in the woodcutting business: he was telling me about the English…I don't know where he got his story, would you care to hear it while you are cooking?'

'Why yes', says Palm, secretly relieved to have been let off once again.

'Well, there was some Englishman, skilled and fearless, who anchored his ship in Table Bay already in 1598...can you believe that? This man recorded, after riding about, rather as we did today: 'three fresh rivers and people who spoke with a *clocking* tongue, and who came along with large cattle *having upon their backe by the fore-shoulders a great lump of flesh like a camel's backe'*...Hans tried an unsuccessful imitation of an English accent...'so the English missed their chances, for ten years later an admiral of the Dutch fleet went ashore to barter for livestock and obtained thirty-eight sheep and two cows...*'the Khoikhoi made musicke and the admiral danced.*'

'Not the usual story we hear then, the one of Mynheer van Riebeeck's arrival? But there is more: In 1632, for reasons unclear, Dutch sailors poisoned relations with the Khoikhoi. What did they do? No-one knows. Then, some 12 years after that another ship was wrecked and 250 men from the VOC had to live on the shore of Table Bay for four whole months....which they did without harm until they were rescued. It appears Robben Island bountifully provided penguins, seal meat, cormorants and eggs in those days...and all this happened again, with another shipwreck in 1647.This time a group of sailors built a modest fort and stayed a full year before being picked up in 1648...then they went home, presenting their view that the Cape was a safe place to live, among people who were not particularly militant...provided their cattle and sheep were not taken from them...

But here, Palm, here is the crux of the matter: Jan van Riebeeck, a merchant at that time, was one of the passengers of this very ship! Did you know about this? No? Nor did I. Well, now...it all makes sense, coming back here to govern was *his* idea, but already born in earlier times.......'They stared at the fire for a while.

Then the men looked up: there was a scratching, scraping noise on the window. Whites of two wary eyes and two rows of teeth could be seen. 'Oubaas,' they heard,

'Oubaas, give me rice... 'ek is honger, give me rice.' A child, a black child, with rudimentary Dutch!

Palm opened the door to a small wretched figure; was it not that same boy-child from the beach, sent no doubt by his Khoi mother? The child held up an empty gourd; his nose was dripping, his teeth chattering.

'Kom in, jongetjie,' Palm smiled, bending forward to take the gourd from the child's small outstretched hand. He scooped dry rice from a sack against the wall, then handed it back, knowing this would now happen regularly since he'd never have the hardness of heart to send the child back empty-handed. The boy's eyes darted around, at the candles, the fire, the plates ready for dinner on the table. But then, muttering something incomprehensible, the cold, wet, half-naked creature slipped away, ran off into the night.

'Now he will return again and again, Palm; these people are suffering, especially now, in winter. Why did you do it?'

Palm had no answer for a while, then: 'do they come to you too, Hans Grimp?'

'Not any longer, my friend, I am a hard man: I tell beggars to find work...then they never come back.'

'You know, Hans,' Palm leaned back and stretched his legs: 'I would quite like to teach a boy like this one to read and write. To befriend him. Would he show willing? I could make something of him. His eyes showed such fear. What do you think? Could one reach his mind... and if I succeeded could I get him a *special* place in the school in the Fort? My servant understands the Khoi language; he could speak to the boy...and it would make a pleasing change from the endless legal matters I am involved in. It might take my mind off obligatory attendance at hangings and other punishments. There is so much cruelty here, on a daily basis.'

Both men sat staring at the burning logs.

'My own teacher, the Professor, tried to teach objectivity, to remain uninvolved. But the whole business of retribution makes me ill. I try to bear in mind their evil deeds, the suffering they have inflicted, but I must not look in the eyes of miscreants, for fear of feeling their terrors, even when bearing in mind their own cruelty and misdemeanours. Yes, looking into people's eyes…this is my weakness.'

'So, look away, fool, gaze at their ears instead, before you get a reputation for soft-heartedness! You may find yourself in serious trouble if you go against the tide: have you not heard of that John Cooke, son of a farmer in England, trained to be a solicitor? He saw poverty as a cause of crime and *he* ended up hung drawn and quartered himself….mind you, he also drafted an Act to abolish the monarchy in his country, *and* the House of Lords. He had it coming!'

Hans, a carpenter who had made his way in the Cape for over 25 years, was well-informed and made of sterner stuff than Palm.

'Such thinking will not serve you well in the new Petty Court. I hear soon there is to be a visit from Hendrik van Rheede; a man who expects much of his officials; he is answerable only to the Lords Seventeen in Amsterdam; you must make a good impression, strong and forward-looking…'

They sat thinking and said no more for a while.

Then: 'Palm, my friend: consider your position with care before you do anything. In the meantime, dear boy, *prosit…* one more glass of wine! We are allowed to drink to the future in this new world, yours and also mine, *our* new world.'

1688. *'It is wondrous, dear Professor, to see your hand- writing. It pleases me to tell you I am recovered from an illness, which lasted over a year. Now my health has returned. I trust you too are in good health.*

Last year a fleet of six ships, sent by the king of France to Siam, anchored in Table Bay. There were many sick on board and the admiral requested to lodge them in our hospital and to purchase fresh food. Our Governor, in his great wisdom, made one condition: all healthy men must return to the ship before sunset and that no arms were to be carried when ashore. The Cape militia was required to mount guard and Stellenbosch brought in an additional forty armed burghers, among them my dear new friend Hans, the carpenter. At his time we were also visited by a destructive disease. The fever which threatened many of us struck last winter, carried off hundreds...the natives suffered particularly, even Chief Schacher has died. Our Commander had to appoint a successor; he chose a nephew of the deceased chief. Then, toward the end of last year there was a plague of locusts, which however caused insufficient damage, for the crops were exceedingly good......

In Europe, after the annulment of the edict of Nantes, there came a tremendous impetus to the emigration of Protestants. Many of them entered the service of the East India Company in the Netherlands, by now a country filled with refugees. VOC directors had no intention of making the Cape a French colony but they did try to procure Huguenots emigrants who were considered suited to become good colonists. The Dutch settlers would, in no time at all, absorb this foreign element, they believed. Families and friends were kept together as far as possible and despatched on five ships, during 1687 and 1688.

The 'orphan chamber' of Rotterdam also added eight young women who consented to become industrious in farm work, and they were all married in the colony within a few months of their arrival.

More men than women came out. Commander van der Stel never ceased to complain about this.

***

'From April to August we had 'Voorschoten', 'Oosterland', 'China' and Zuid Beveland' cast anchor in Table Bay. Do you remember our arrival, Professor, when I stayed behind to unload the ship? This seems a lifetime ago...Now I am one of those who go to the wooden jetty to welcome newcomers.

The passengers on the 'China' endured a disastrous journey lasting seven months: twenty French refugees died during the journey and the crew as well of the passengers were sick. All of these Huguenots have landed here without any goods or money. A quantity of salt meat, peas and biscuits is provided for a few months (also planks for the woodwork of temporary houses), and whatever else they need can be obtained on credit from the Company stores.

Individuals already in the colony contribute cattle, grain or money into a benefit fund, much praised by Van Der Stel: 'very creditable of the old colonists,' he is purported to have said. I am glad to say I was one of them! Our contribution has been sent to the Reverend Simond in Stellenbosch, for distribution. Burgher councillors have also furnished six ox wagons free of charge to convey the immigrants to Stellenbosch and a little further along to the Drakenstein. Care is taken they should mingle with Dutch colonists who are arriving at the same time, although they have expressed a strong desire not to be separated. The Company promises a supply of slaves as soon as possible, but these are in short supply...'

1689. Evermore Huguenots arrive, in great numbers, young and old. Monies from charitable funds will be distributed in April of next year. Commissioners take into consideration the needs of all new settlers. Commander van der Stel is friendly to all although he would prefer immigrants from the Netherlands.

There is trouble ahead; the Dutch and the French do not see eye to eye, above all they dislike having to share a church. The Council must remind them of their oath of allegiance, that they should be satisfied with remaining a branch congregation of the church of Stellenbosch. A spirit of hostility has arisen. The Huguenots do not wish to become Dutch, or to intermarry with the Dutch, and Dutch colonists are reported to say they would rather give bread to a Hottentot or to a dog than to a Frenchman. Evil will triumph if good men do nothing. None of this bodes well.

***

Lately Palm's life has changed in an unexpected manner: he welcomes each new day with delight and surprise.

'I have set myself a task: each day I spend time with young 'Manda', that slippery Khoi boy, who has developed a habit of following me, hiding from me, then re-appearing, teasing me, but who has now, strangely, become part of my daily routine. I call him 'Manda' because he is like the Salamander, who hides, skitters across rocks and boulders, then re-appears, allegedly a messenger from the spirits, who gets into trouble but seems to be able to endure great heat. Manda trusts me. His mother knows and frowns her child comes to my house, that he learns to write and speak Dutch... and to read.

A strange creature is my little Manda, no more than eight years...small with legs like sticks, but very quick. His mother, a garrulous, scolding woman, who speaks with a clicking tongue cannot be trusted. She drinks heavily and orders the boy to bring food to their hut, whenever he finds any. She is vague about the winters he has lived. There are at least three other children, but no father.

Is it my fate to become a father-substitute?

I've had him measured by a seamstress: Manda now wears European garments when he is with me. This has led to raised eyebrows among the Dutch (glimpsed by me), but as they are so furtive I have learned to look the other way. Why should Manda not have some advantage? He likes to parade his European garments when I take him to church on Sundays, but removes them when he slips back to his 'real' life... to his siblings and his crazed, mostly drunken mother. Just the shoes, he will not wear those: he becomes like someone paralysed, looks at his feet and will not put them to use. I must be patient. I have already learned to trick the boy into all manner of habits, including the use of a fork. Others surmise it is some game we play, but it is very real to me: I enjoy his trusting eyes and he is quick and readily brought to laughter and enjoyment when I cannot click my tongue like he does. I must see to it he attends the school in the Fort and becomes, one day, a leader of his clan, helping to cement the fragile relationship between white people and his own people. I have suggested, when he is older, to call himself Master Manda, that is, 'Sala Manda.' He has come to enjoy our little joke.'

This had become Palm's contentment... it was what kept him in the Cape. His duty had long been to conduct prosecutions in criminal cases. The rule that prisoners who did not admit guilt must be tortured, (they could not be executed unless they did), Palm found unendurable...while punishments like flogging, the use of thumbscrews, stocks, leg-fetters and the rack...keel-hauling and carrying shells on Robben Island, cutting off of thumbs, tongues or ears...often for very minor offences, such as drawing a knife from a scabbard...or running away...well, it made his flesh crawl, his heart beat very fast. Increasingly he distanced himself; he was losing the will to live. Early one morning, staring from his window at the bay before him, he reminded himself: 'I must return to Stralsund.'

How soon could he get away? The only concern was his small friend, who would suffer... if and when he was abandoned.

'Who will continue the task I have set myself with my little Salamander?'

In the fullness of time the 'grey father' would surely permit his return to Stralsund... 'where I belong, where I will remember, with strong feelings, this magical country on the opposite side of the globe...the birds with long blue tail feathers resting their yellow feet on flowers with hairy petals, silvery leaves glittering in the sun, and fierce beasts roaming. I will remember the vast green turtles and whales washed up on the beaches.

Alas, my childlike wish for certainty in this land can no longer be gratified.'

The threat of some truth, of hostility ahead, pervaded each day, Palm could not quite put his finger on it. He had reached the Slough of Despond. He was in a hopeless depression.

Consolation would come from remembering his small, trusting Manda, who, when he last saw him had said:' I am so happy to be your friend.'s

Surely one day he would become a man commanding respect. He would fear no-one, particularly not white men...although, for now, he was afraid of simply everyone, especially his older brother who, hostile and brutish, seemed to be up to no good.

PART FIVE
APOTHEOSIS

EIGHTEEN

Near Alt-Käbelich. March 1690.

'A messenger, dear Papa, galloping very fast... yes, the usual one from Stralsund, I recognise the colour of his coat. I will prepare refreshment.'

Maria leaned over her father, tidied his slipping rug. The white-haired professor was dozing in his armchair, endlessly cold feet kept warm by a white sheepskin and a large grey cat. A book, as usual, had slipped to the tiled floor, he had nodded off; nights afforded little peace from pain in his joints, so he caught up on missing sleep whenever he could. With a hopeful voice he replied: 'Daughter, pray he brings good news.'

Maria stroked his gnarled hands, busied herself by the open fire, found cups and plates. The two of them lived quietly, at a slow pace: his ancient mother had passed away shortly after his return from the Cape, 'now already,' what is it, ten, no, thirteen years ago', he barely remembered. All days were the same. Tenants, trusted men and women, allowed their landlord's life to remain tolerably comfortable, that is, when there were no battles or unknown horsemen invading the peace. The Swedish occupation, still a thorn in the flesh, continued in some parts of German lands, despite occasional skirmishes and revolts.

The dog barked when a messenger appeared in the large entrance hall. He carried a large sealed envelope: instantly recognisable as the next instalment of letters from Palm. Despatched into the kitchen for refreshment the weary postman left both father and daughter smiling, revived and animated by this break in their monotonous routines. With his bushy white eyebrows raised high, the professor broke open the seal on the envelope, drew out a letter, then, savouring each word, he enunciated with great care and pleasure:

At sea, somewhere near Tenerife.'...'upon my word, Maria, he must be back, for this was written on board ship, some time ago! Come closer, daughter, hear this:

My dear Professor, I pass the time with greater confidence than on our last journey, now so many years ago. I was told the second journey is invariably better from every point of view, and indeed it has proved to be so.

I prepare myself for the immense joy of seeing you again and also of meeting Fräulein Maria, about whom you spoke so often in the past.....' Father and daughter exchanged fond smiles.

Whatever lies ahead for me is unclear: I am saddened and confused since I left in such haste from the bustling 'Kaap Stad'. There had been an incident which caused unpleasantness and pain. I will send this on arrival in Stralsund (at least another sixty days hence). I must ask for advice from the Swedish Governor, with regard to a place of work. Only when settled will I allow myself to send this greeting, in the hope you may permit me to call on you and spend a little time.

Your devoted Palm Uhlenfeldt.

(I have finally changed my name to the above, and will perhaps take it even further, by replacing the U with Ü, or a Y or even an I)...

'Quick, daughter, bring paper and pen, we must ask him to stay with us as soon as he can, for as long as he pleases, as soon as possible.... what can be troubling him, what has happened? The letter sounds so unlike the Palm I know!

I will send instructions how to find us and to be with us...will that suit as far as our hospitality is concerned; do we need anything? Ah yes, certainly some casks of wine, to be brought from town...but is there anything else?' The Professor, frail and with a furrowed brow, studies his daughters face: 'No time must be wasted, Maria, Palm is a good man: I want him to know he is always welcome here; let us prepare for his visit. What can I do to help?' Shaking his head he put his fingers to his lips, deep in thought.

Maria remained silent and reserved.

'Frei-fräulein', a titled spinster, was the daughter's correct appellation. She was not accustomed to strangers. Before and since her father's return from Africa visitors could be counted on the fingers of one hand. Until that time, brought up entirely by the professor's widowed mother, this shy creature had become in turn, an obedient child, a flawless housekeeper, an un-questioning spinster and later a devoted carer of her ageing 'mother' and father. Since her 'mother's' death she preferred to cook, bake, sew and mend, even though there could be any number of servants in the home. She had learnt to instruct loyal dependants, to advise tenants,...she made decisions about livestock and harvests, and appeared barely conscious that the years were passing, that she had begun her thirtieth year.

She had a tendency to frown. Sometimes, looking out from her window, across the low-lying fields to the woods, and even further, her eyes filled with tears. She never quite knew why.

Years ago, on his return, the professor had explained, with painstaking honesty, the troubling circumstances of her birth, the truth about her real mother, but above all: that *he* truly was her father. Maria, at first incredulous, had broken down. That distant writer of letters had always been her brother! Soon, in a modest and accepting way, she allowed her spirits to be restored. Controlling disturbing thoughts she learned to come to terms, to accept and even count her blessings.

‘I love my father, and will make great efforts to entertain his favourite former pupil. Shall I see him as an adoptive *brother,*’ she asked, ‘since he has taken up so many years of your life, dear Papa? I will face his presence squarely, this Palm, who like me, has been deprived of a real family for so long, although he did have those early years,’ she remembered what her father had told her: ‘with a mother and father and even a brother…and he did believe *they* were truly his family then.’

Yet the prospect of welcoming the much discussed Palm filled her with uncertainty. Unused to visitors her fondness was reserved for her elderly father, some of the locals, the dress-maker, the parson, and mostly the animals kept in their home and in the stables. It pleased her to talk to those, recognising their slightest reactions, also to the dogs, and cats and even the geese, hens, goats, cows and pigs. Perhaps not so much the goats, ‘they have strange unseeing eyes’, she claimed.

***

Since her father’s return from the Cape, twelve years earlier, there was a lute, hanging from a peg on the wall; she had become so very fond of this instrument.

It was a gift brought from one of his rare trips to Stralsund: the most bonding token bestowed on her during their tenuous early relationship. There was design in his thoughtful giving: visits from music masters were arranged…they soon became the only rare visitors, calling from time to time. For the past ten years, the professor had been greatly in need of company, to keep in touch with the outside world …and he longed to hear music. Acutely aware of a daughter who had been nowhere, met almost no-one, expected nothing and who made no demands, he now read to her, filled her mind, tried to expand her horizons, despite her advancing years.

‘My greatest happiness, as you well know, Papa, lies in tuning my instrument and practising simple dances and songs for you and my teacher. Even our dog and the cat sits quietly when I play.

What will your Palm think if and when he calls on us?'

She could not quite picture how this much spoken-of Palm might feel about *his* own unusual life. 'How could he call himself fortunate? Does he still attend hangings?'

***

This year Spring was late in Pomerania. Until the end of April lakes remained frozen, and the fields were white with snow or frost. During daytime, with only few hours of sunlight, the roads thawed a little, but in the dark night there was no mercy and whatever hopes had sprung were crushed again and again.

When the messenger brought the letter the air had been damp, a fog clinging to the bare landscape. Somehow there was hope at last, ...the longed-for suggestion of renewal, even, here and there, the tiniest hint of colour other that just grey and white and brown. And now there came that welcome dripping sound, outside the window, even some birds, flying north, wings flapping.

***

Maria took a deep breath, pulled back the curtains, and selected a garment rarely worn, dark-blue, very plain. Blue was the colour for 'healing the spirit,' was what the village dress-maker had suggested on her last visit. 'Perhaps, she may be right', thought Maria, as she walked home considering this. 'I am plain, and so is this dress, and all my clothes, and my old shoes with thick heels and square toes. Everything Palm will see is dreary. What will he think of me?' When she got home she brushed a dark flood of brown hair to the back of her head, fastened it securely into a bun, stared at her face in a large spotty mirror, then, trying to smile, she hastily looked away, embarrassed by what she'd just seen. The frowning Frei-fräulein hurried away to

join her father downstairs and remarked drily: 'Any time now your Palm will arrive'. Eyebrows up the professor looked at his daughter in surprise: she seemed to have made some attempt with her appearance.
He needed no reminding…he could barely wait.

***

'And this will be your room, Palm Uhlenfeldt,'…Maria had accompanied the guest upstairs, shown him to a bedroom on a dark passage way. 'You have a fine view of our forest, the ones you rode through coming from the coast.'

'Thank you Fräulein Ruetz,' he replied politely, gazing dutifully across the courtyard, the garden, the ploughed fields and the muddy track vanishing into the trees. The land was flat and he had journeyed a whole day. Then, turning a little, Palm looked over his shoulder and their eyes met.

'She seems fearful,' he thought, she 'looks down as soon as I speak, but her eyes are pleasing and kind, just like her father's.'

'Here you are then, Master Palm, standing before me… no longer in Africa,' she observed, faltering, 'and now…well, I mean, it feels no different from reading your letters! Your presence and your words have become reality. Please forgive me, don't mind me.' Tongue-tied she tried once more: 'we could converse downstairs, when you have made yourself at home. Papa can barely wait to hear your news.'

'Not at all how I imagined her', Palm thought, 'so very thin, so tall, as tall as I am…but I do see the resemblance with my dear professor. But *he* has aged, his nose sharper, cheeks sunken, long snowy whiskers, and worst of all those milky searching eyes: an unbearable change, his body gnarled, and bent. I must pretend not to notice' and then, turning to her: 'thank-you, Fräulein Maria…may I call you that? I will not delay you any longer.'

For some sorrowful moments he observed, from his window, the setting sun behind the forests.'My thoughts need fresh air', he thought.

'What has she already been told about me?'

***

'To your most excellent health, dear Professor, and to you, Fräulein Maria,' Palm raised a glass to his host while his left hand stroked the head of the dog who had decided to befriend him...'with my warmest thanks for this meal, in your beautiful home.' He was not all that fond of dogs. But this was different: surrounded by timbered walls decorated with antlers and old framed portraits of earnest men and women, candles on silver candlesticks flickering before them, also fine rugs on the stone floor, not unlike the ones he'd seen in Amsterdam, yes, he was in a festive mood.

Very soon the traveller had given an account of his journey back to Europe, and his plans to settle in Stralsund, also his hope to find work related to the application of the law in Northern Europe.

He did not spell this out.

Maria took great care of their guest. After eating they moved closer to the fire while the hostess, discreetly supervising the duties of a maid, returned to sit by her father. At last an occasion to entertain in the manner to which, one might say, a Frei-Fräulein was born...with her flushed cheeks, although her lips had hardly touched the wine, she'd smiled and talked more tonight than, well, since she could recall. Palm and her father, still so attuned to one another, drew her in, encouraged her views, asked questions,...and Maria basked in their warmth.

She was also aware Palm had not yet revealed what had brought him 'home' from his lucrative post in the Cape. Maria and the Professor did not press him, fearing some kind of unpleasant news.

'Tonight I am not myself', she thought to herself: I have released some other person living hidden inside me. Plain as I am I feel I have become part of a rare painting by some famed artist, or of a rich tapestry; here in the warmth, with red wine, glistening cut glass, silver cutlery, even our special plates, above all, laughter, and this lively exchange of reminiscences'.

Meanwhile Palm's eyes had come to rest on a lute hanging from a hook on the wall.

'No-one has spoken of a lutenist in this house', he called out, his voice and eyebrows raised and his eyes sparkling. Maria, emboldened by the wine, instantly rose from the table and carried the instrument over to their guest, who reached for it with reverence.

'I adore lutes,' he whispered, 'and how it reminds me of Amsterdam. Do play something, Fräulein Maria, it *must* be you who plays, I beg you, for I know my professor has no talent for such things...and I've forgotten the little I ever knew.'

So she touched the strings, the pegs, tuning with deep concentration. She leaned over each one, biting her lower lip, and forgetting her audience she gently fingered and plucked a soothing, languid Siciliano.

Palm listened to an angel, for so she suddenly seemed, coaxing forth this elegant dance with almost accurate accompanying figures.

He was in seventh heaven.

And the professor sat back, arms folded over his stomach, benign, content. He had closed his eyes. 'What more could a man wish for?'

***

Only on the following morning Palm told them his tale:

'For years I became increasingly conscious of an attitude in the Cape: a falsity, a pretext, a sham, between the various peoples who inhabit the new colony. There was that feeling of 'us' and 'them', the mightier lording it over the less able...yes, yes, you may well say it is the same the world over, has always been thus.

Constraints and criticism were placed on those who had no education, who could or would not conform in ways expected by strangers, the persons who had brought themselves and their language and beliefs with them… from so far afield.

I try to explain these challenges. One becomes so aware of them on the other side of the globe, where black-skinned men and women are closer to nature. To the eyes of those who came from Europe the locals seemed like children, often worse, like animals. There was, and remained, growing mistrust, even fear. It came from both sides.

Many lifetimes will pass before such differences can be overcome. This is how I and others understood it. Were we mistaken?

The locals, understandably, saw all us white men as invaders.

'But we are colonisers,' was the reply: 'we behave fairly, we wish to help.'

The facts remained…well, professor, you know as well as I do. Brandy, beads and tobacco…such things are still offered in return for land.

'One day a small boy from the Khoi tribe began to follow me. I soon discovered he came from a large family; a mother and many siblings, but there seemed to be no father. The boy attached himself to me, became like a shadow, following and begging for food. I was touched by his simple pleading and his comical and endearing nature… soon he came to my house each day to receive what he began to accept as his due.

I fed him gladly but also tried to teach him words in the Dutch language, and then, gradually, to write and read. He was quick to learn, and innocently amusing. Rising in me were tender feelings, paternal and caring: the child seemed so vulnerable, so trusting. I took him to the tailor, kitted him out in clothes similar to the local Dutch children. I took him with me to church on Sundays and taught him to sing the songs and to sit quietly listening to the Dominee. I called him 'Manda', from the word 'Salamanda', because he moved so deftly, in such a slippery fashion.....'

Maria, interrupted: 'but what age was this boy, Palm..?' 'Perhaps eight, nine years, no-one seemed to know. Not even his mother. I think she encouraged him, welcomed the additional food he took home to her each evening. There was an elder brother who looked sourly on his sibling's good fortune; he was a lay-about, un-teachable...falling into the category of 'hunter-gatherer' but more likely, 'thief'. It was my belief he initially set his younger brother on the path of wringing my heart and bringing me into this condition of so wanting to better the life of this one small boy....'

Palm paused, looked at his professor, then at Maria, both of them listening intently to his tale. They looked puzzled, where would this end, what could be the trouble?

'Manda was almost ready to go to the school for Cape children, a primitive daily gathering, still housed in one of the rooms of the castle. His older brother, who for a while had been one of those pupils, was asked to leave for disruptive behaviour; I was told of his fury, and later about his threats of revenge.

A few days on, after midnight, soundly asleep for several hours, I was awakened by a feeling of great heat and, choked by smoke welling up around my bed, I saw the entire roof of my house in flames, and through falling bits of burning straw, above and all around me I stumbled toward the door which was firmly bolted....

...so, numbed with shock, smoke in my throat and eyes, I tried to escape shouting loudly, 'fire' and 'help', my path made difficult in the dark by numbers of large stones piled up in my way, and so, losing my balance I fell to the ground, cracking open my forehead, blood pouring over my eyes,...still, I did get away; helpful neighbours came running from their houses but there was nothing any of us could do but beat out flames, watchful the fire did not spread any further. There we stood, staring at the smoking embers, above us my gloomy, implacable 'Grey Father' looking on...while all I owned was burnt to a cinder.

In the morning, having surveyed the scene, I walked the short path to Manda and his family in their reed hut. But they had rolled up their mats, pulled up the reeds, and disappeared. No-one knew where or when they'd gone... Pulling up reeds was a sure sign they would not return...and possibly of their guilt.

At that moment something died in me. How little one understands oneself when such things happen! With a blind compulsion I needed to leave the Cape. I looked up at my 'Grey Father' and wondered why I had been so punished.'

The professor shook his head. Soothing, patiently, he reached across and took Palm's hand. Maria looked on. She too was filled with pity.

'We thank you Palm for telling us all this. We thank God you were spared. Your fate might have been similar to that of your step-brother, so many years ago. At last we understand why you returned to Stralsund.

But now, do also tell us about the 'small things' in your life: *your* hopes and your fears, so we may surmise your future happiness and how we can help. Besides, Maria has asked me to request you call her by her first name only...as if she were your sister.'

The guest's eyes were brimming over. 'Why, yes, and thank-you dear Maria, it is truly consoling to be under the roof of such kind friends'.

When, later, Palm returned to his bedroom, he closed his eyes and imagined the weathered grey sandstone of Table Mountain, the white clouds, the blue bay; but also reminded himself of the fearful re-enforcement of laws he had been involved with.

He attempted to analyse all he had learnt.

'Never look behind you', say wise men, 'the past is the past'.

Palm raised his shoulders, pulled his lips tightly together. He sighed.

***

<u>Stralsund.</u> March 1694.

'Come quickly, Palm, I fear father is dying.'

Palm had read the message; there were tears in his eyes and his hands were shaking.

'Think, think clearly; first, a horse, second: my servant must take apologies to the Town Clerk, and the Law Court...and, yes, to the Hangman...those changes, improvements...dear God, I might only get to Maria by tomorrow evening.'

With a quivering hand Palm wrote apologies marked *URGENT* to all concerned, then commandeered his man-servant to take care of the rest. He would set out at dawn to cover close on one hundred miles, changing horses, crossing the river, to arrive before sunset. He now knew the quickest route. For the past four years he had travelled to stay with the professor at regular intervals: Maria and her father had become his family.

***

On this terrible day, dreading the loss of his 'third' father, half frozen to death himself, he was let in by Maria. Her eyes were red from weeping.

The old man, still breathing, lay on a bed made up near the fireplace. When he heard Palm's voice his eyelids fluttered, and for a brief moment he appeared to look straight at the longed-for caller, then, trying to raise his hand, he opened his lips to speak. They leaned over him, but the words did not come, there was only gasping and a harrowing struggle for breath.

Palm clasped his old teacher's hand, spoke softly, reassuringly: 'I am here, professor, you will feel better soon, Maria and I will take care of you together. They leaned forward, strained to hear him whisper: 'Palm, my son, take..' was all they heard. Then a .silence, as if he were thinking of an appropriate consolation: but a rattling upheaval in his chest stopped any further breathing.' Maria knelt down, put her ear to her father's chest, and listened to his heart. She understood when a body breaks down; she had tended sick and dying animals on the estate. With a sigh, she bowed her head and said:

'He has left us, Palm. I heard the owls for the two past nights. Then I knew.' She rose to her feet, unsteady, her face white, but seemed able to recover her composure.

She turned to face the ashen-faced guest:

'Sit Palm, here, by the fire. I will bring you something warm. Father was waiting to see you before he allowed his soul to go. He knew you would arrive in time. It was miraculous you arrived when you did'... as she spoke her lips began to tremble and tears poured down her cheeks.

Palm had never seen anyone weep in this way. While taking care of everything, while speaking, her tears continued to flow.

He stood up and tried to put his arm around her shoulders. But she shook her head and gently pushed him aside.

'Dear, kind Palm' she managed...her voice strangled, 'I will bring you something hot. And the Pastor, we must send for him to arrange the service and burial'.

'How how strong she is,' thought Palm. 'Unstoppable. She thinks clearly even while her tears stream. She is unlike anyone I have met, not like any other women I have known.'

***

Before darkness enveloped the forest, the lakes and the farm buildings, white owls near the barn had begun their renewed cries. Called in to help in this frightening time of death and sorrow, the tenants, who at first turned away in fear from the ghostly maligned birds, now wiped away accumulated dust from the stored coffin, carried it from the outbuilding to position it reverently on trestles in the main room. Only a few hours after his death the professor lay bedded in the fine oak coffin he himself had measured and helped to construct.

During the night, Palm, now upstairs in his former teacher's house, turned about in bed struggling with heavy bedclothes. He tried to block his ears from the screeching calls of owls swooping after their prey. Owls are wise, he reminded himself. Torn between fear, exhaustion and pity, he also heard clearly the heart-rending sobs from Maria's bedroom. She was crying out, whimpering, and Palm feared for her: her pain was his pain. He got out of bed and hearing no response to his knock on her door he decided, trembling, to enter, all the while speaking softly.

Palm bent over her to stroke her brow, bathed in sweat as it was.

It came as a surprise to him: the powerful Maria had become pitiful, helpless, and weak, mourning the loss of her only remaining relative.

Palm sat down on the edge of her bed.

'Maria', he whispered. Then, pleading, when there was no response: 'do you hear me? First, drink this water, your father would be distressed to see your suffering; his soul has moved to that eternal life we all strive for...he loves you dearly and he continues to do so. There now, calm yourself, Maria, here...try this, that's better', Palm stroked a limp arm, an icy hand, 'I am here with you and you will make a new life, find a way which would make him proud of you, let him go now, your distress serves no-one, let me pull you up a little, so you can drink... there, I will fetch that cloth from your wash bowl, I will moisten it and soothe your forehead, cool it, gently, softly...'

Maria's convulsions and spasms were subsiding, she was trying to look up at him, but her dazed eyes seemed to be looking inwards to some other world he could not reach.

'Strange, your head is hot but your hands are like ice: you shiver. I will lie by your side and pass my warmth to you, Maria, here, let me steady you, reassure you, all will be well, poor, dear Maria, if only you close your eyes, let go of your fear, breathe deeply, there now...is this not better....' and Palm, cautiously recumbent by her side, close to her slender body, sensed her heaving, anguished breathing against his, her sobbing gradually ebbing away. In its place she sighed and then, turning, she clung to him like someone drowning. Barely conscious she melted into the warm presence of his comforting body, and soon they became as close as a man and a woman can ever be, whimpering softly in the dark, while, in gradual, inevitable stages, both silenced, surprised bodies evolved into something archaic, powerful, rhythmic...and unstoppable.

In that most complex of all silences their fate, as well as that of many yet unborn, was determined.

***

The following dark morning brought a large gathering of villagers, workers and tenants. Distant bells tolled for what seemed like an eternity. The Pastor and several village families huddled together outside the barn; they had come to support their lonely Frei-Fräulein on this dark, cold, trying, terrible day.

Palm was treated as a member of the family. Coach-and-horses stood in readiness and the day passed like a shadowy nightmare: Palm, by Maria's side, behaved with dignified composure; only when the coffin was lowered did he feel a searing pain of loss, and he trembled with her. Maria's silent tears streamed again and again.

'What do I say to her when we find ourselves alone?' Palm was troubled. He had hardly slept, dreading a confrontation about the night before.

After the funeral, returned to the house, the maid brought steaming potato soup with warm bread, butter and cheese.

Maria took a deep breath, turned to stare briefly at Palm, stated she was not hungry, only very, very tired, and asked when he planned to return to Stralsund.

He studied *her* face: 'You seem to wish to be alone, Maria. I respect your need'. He looked for some sort of sign. He felt uneasy.

'I can leave tomorrow morning. You will be alone. Is that what your father would have wished? Did you discuss your own future with him? I feel he must have sensed he was leaving us since he had already made his coffin. He was not so very old, only about twenty years older than myself...well yes, I never saw him as an *old* man, perhaps just a little, since I returned from the Cape.

Maria, how will it be for you, alone in this vast old house?'

She looked at her lute, stroked the affectionate dog, put her hands together as if in prayer. During a very long silence there seemed to be much thinking, but few answers.

At first Maria avoided looking at her guest.

‘I had a strange dream last night’ she stated finally, as if she were dreaming even now, but’... hesitating, ‘I am tired, my limbs ache and I long to sleep. Can we talk tomorrow Palm, before you go?’

Palm nodded, watched her apparent sleep-walking up the stairs to her room. He sensed an unresolved problem, a threatening cloud, hovering over them both. He tried to push the cloud away.

Resting he listened to the hideous, howling, cold Pomeranian wind, straight from the Baltic Sea.

Once again he prepared for his departure. His thoughts, his body seemed to need the fresh air from the Baltic.

***

Nineteen

Stralsund, August, 1694.

Dear Maria, Your letter brought me such pleasure! I am relieved to hear from you and delight in every scrap of news. Please understand I feel a great responsibility towards you because of the years of care and protection your father offered me. I worry you prefer to remain so alone. But indeed, I would very much enjoy seeing you again. I will try to arrive before sunset on the last Saturday of this month. I want you to know I have now made an outline of the earliest studies in writing and spelling proposed for the neglected children in your area. Might we visit a few of the farms to explain what we have in mind?

This is my good news: I have managed to acquire a lute from the music master at the Dominican school. I practise each morning.

With respect and affection, I remain your 'adoptive' brother,

Palm Ihlenfeldt.

Dear 'brother' Palm,

Your letter concerning the 'school' with the proposed dates of a visit has arrived safely. You are welcome to come when it best pleases you. I will expect you on the day you mention. There is sufficient paper in the house to write several books, for our young beginners. We will need slate and slate pens, all such things are in plentiful supply here. Should I invite the Pastor so he may hear about our plans ?

I note the changed the spelling of your name.

With respect and admiration I remain, your 'sister' in spirit,
Maria.

***

'Maria has taken to my idea,' thinks Palm, 'at least and at last there is a bridge between us, quite apart from the lute instruction she so graciously offers. Although I have an instrument of my own my progress is extremely slow. Maria appears to have gained in confidence since she lives alone.

It seems men can never understand women: I feared she would crumble without her father in the house, but she is entirely composed and shows no overpowering feelings of loneliness or sorrow. Does she wait for me to mention *that* night, or are we both waiting for the other to reveal our thoughts? As *her* father used to say: *it will all be the same in a hundred years...*'

On an unusually hot day at the end of July, Palm, who had been riding since dawn, kept closing his eyes. He was tired. When they opened he saw a great vision across the land: with the sun hovering by the horizon, he found, emerging from the woodland a mysterious distant lady, standing still, with some beast, waiting for him: A 'Fata Morgana' he thought. His professor had once mentioned such strange visions.

In the end it was not a mystery: it was Maria, and the sheep-dog waiting by her side. Palm approached. The welcome was cordial.

'I bring a surprise,' he told her. I hope it might please you, Maria.' Palm leaped from his horse, drew out, fumbling, carefully, slowly, from the depths of his coat pocket, 'ah, yes...here it is,' a necklace, fashioned from exquisite, translucent amber.

'A pedlar who came to my lodgings sold me this precious object.'

Fleetingly Maria touched his hand as he placed the chain over her head onto her blue dress. He looked in her eyes, so often vulnerable, apologetic, but for once she acknowledged the truth: her eyes lit with gratitude and surprise. Even the dog seemed delighted, stood on his hind legs, tail wagging, as he tried to lick Palm's hands. They walked together, across the paved yard, past the Linden tree, to the house with Palm leading his horse and from time to time, patting the dog.

'One learns and learns. And Maria has become a different woman,' were Palm's thoughts.

'Do you remember, Palm, when you came in the winter, how drab the flat landscape looked? Look at the fruit trees now, and here, these for-get-me-not's and even the sunflowers, all flowering. I will pick some so we can have this happiness indoors with us...and we must call on the Pastor tomorrow, also my dressmaker, while we are in Alt-Käbelich; my clothes don't quite fit, I will ask her to let my dresses out, since I only have three of them...we will take the cart and horses, Palm, after we have done some practice on the lute, now do tell me, how does your instrument sound, does it play as pleasingly as mine?'

'I will play for you, Maria, a Dance by one Valentin Haussmann.'

'Such strange names these composers have, don't you think? I have a new Gavotte composed by Praetorius'.

'Delightful, delightful!' Palm's face turned to smile at her.

'She seems to have unstoppably more to say than on all our previous encounters,' thought Palm.

Together they inspected the barn, encouraged and praised the carpenter, who, standing back, proudly showed the new low tables and benches. 'Mmm, that pleasing scent of freshly sawn wood, and those piles of sawdust and trestles still on the forecourt.....'

Slate was being cut into squares, light enough for small hands to handle. Eight, possibly nine youngsters were now listed and eager to begin their classes for three days each week, all from tenants close by, but also children of labourers who worked on the lands surrounding the main house.

The couple sat late into the night discussing the coming months. They would practise 'teaching': Maria was to start with ***A***....while Palm pretended to be a boy aged seven, who had never held a slate pen or slate before. He noted her talent for patient application: the same skills she showed when she passed on the latest fingering for a new piece of music; she was a natural teacher, just like her father.

Both Maria and Palm now had two existences: one for themselves and one for the eyes of the other. They worked hard at keeping their own confusions to themselves.

When it was time to sleep, Palm was led, not to his former room, but to the professor's bedroom, at the darkest and most distant end of the corridor. Holding up a flickering candle Maria announced:

'This will be your room for as long as it pleases you, it offers more space. And you may make use of the books father kept with so much pleasure throughout his life. You may also sit at his desk...he would have liked you to. I hope you will be comfortable; I have decided to sleep downstairs now, (you look surprised, Palm), to be closer to the dogs. It is better that way.'

Giving no signs of particular thoughts and reasons regarding her move downstairs Palm saw it as declaration of the wish to keep her distance.

After two days it was time to return to Stralsund, leaving at dawn. Maria expressed the hope he would return after some months, to see how she was getting on.

Having exchanged assurance of fondness in a fraternal way their lives reverted to what was customary. By late August Palm heard from Maria: she had made great strides with her pupils, the classes were a success. 'If it pleases you, do take time off, and, if at all possible, inspect and advise on further progress.' 'A few days in the country', as she put it, 'will be a fine thing, although that long ride to the outskirts of Alt-Käbelich must be wearing for you'.

'I will be able to help with apple-picking, or inspire some simple historical instruction, to widen the intellectual level of

Maria's teaching,' he re- assured himself. Deep down he knew only too well he wished to be with her. But neither of them seemed to want to hear their small inner voices, those which tell the *true* story of ones life.

***

August: Dark clouds were announcing a thunderstorm, they had been gathering all day, the air was heavy.

Palm saw, heard and rejoiced in the customary welcome, first the dog, then that of the servant maid, also the gardener, cap in hand, and even the purring grey cat, soon languidly weaving around his legs...but the house was quite still. He looked around.

Where was the Frei-Fräulein?

'She will come shortly,' he was told. Standing by the entrance he heard footsteps advancing slowly towards the upstairs landing, as if she were carrying something both precious and cumbersome. He observed her grand entrance, swathed in a large shawl, draped loosely over her body. He saw his gift, the amber necklace around her neck and, holding the banister, she now smiled down at him.

'Palm, welcome, welcome', she called out, then, approaching in regal fashion, she offered him a chair while pointing to a jug of apple-juice on the table: 'do you care for the remains of last year's pressed juice?'

'How very fine you look, Maria, although I see shadows from sleeplessness under your eyes. Does the teaching suit you? You have acquired an air of grand authority...and yes, the apple-juice is still outstanding.' Palm felt she was putting on a show for his benefit, although he saw well enough that she was carrying a child, *his* child, for sure.

'These are the last drops of last year's crop...it has become cider with quite a kick to it....like all good things which take time to mature'.

***

For one more day Maria smiled mysteriously, keeping her own burning thoughts and knowledge to herself.

The old, trusted dressmaker had, just the other day, come straight out with it: 'we see you are with child, dear Frei-Fräulein, well advanced... even to the stage when it moves and kicks mightily: your stomach is higher, larger', and 'just feel that!' And so, in placing Maria's hand on an expanse of stretched belly the experienced old woman created the first open connection and true acceptance between a new mother and the innocent life inside her.

'Who is the father, Fräulein Ruetz, do confess,' she smiled encouragingly,' who is your secret husband?'

'I beg you, do not tell a soul,' Maria beseeched the old woman, 'you are my friend, you are sworn to secrecy! Then, after explaining everything Maria added: 'I need you to adjust my garments to allow for a further four months of expansion'.

Others had convinced themselves Maria had become large because she consoled herself with much food, now that she was living alone.

'How did all this happen', Maria pretended to ask herself, knowing full well, buried in that dark cloud of distress and despair, '*one thing followed another*,' only five months ago, on the very night when her father had closed his eyes forever. The joy, but also the shame of it!

'There were times when I thought I had nothing to live for, that I might perish from boredom, from lack of completeness, and now, and now...here it is: the one final solution: I can't allow myself to think about it, nor to hold back any longer. I must, I will inform Palm.'

This thought kept her awake at night. Dark shadows under *her* eyes told their tale on the following morning.

***

Palm was also finding it difficult to sleep. He heard owls hoot, just as he had when he was a boy. What were these creatures doing here?

Only days ago he'd again been to the sinister three-story building in Stralsund, the house with hardly any windows: the home of the hangman. There he'd called on various captives, in rooms furnished according to the ranks of the miscreants, a place for keeping them, or applying torture to make them confess, before they were taken to Gallows Hill, or to the market place for public humiliation and punishment. That is where the owls should be, not here.

While brooding about his grim and ghastly calling, his contact with evil-doers, with executioners and hangmen, legitimised to do the dirty work, Palm tried to develop stoical detachment, seeking to find good in it. 'Daily I am with those who strive to clean up society, whose minds create laws to enforce good, or to punish and eradicate evil. Was there not some belief that hands of hangmen have healing, magical power?' He knew all this but no, he no longer felt he had the strength. And now, the son of a traitor, despised by an entire country, Palm wondered how he might look into the eyes of this, his as yet unborn child? How could he distance himself from all that? Had he inherited his father's guilt? How could he, Palm, present himself to the world, to a child,... but above all to a woman who lived in blameless innocence? She knew nothing about that father of his, nor what he, Palm, faced each day. Which woman would wish to have a child from a man such as himself?

Palm sometimes thought of the beautiful creature he once knew in Cape Town, and *their* child he'd vowed he would never speak to. He had kept that vow. And what about his resolve to go to Denmark to plead for his mother, presumably still locked up in a prison, not too far from Stralsund?

'*I* must first learn to love, just as she has. Love is by no means simple.'

All one has ever learnt, done, endured, seems to be an apprenticeship for the ultimate test, the one of bonding with another.

***

Two exhausted people greeted each other soon after sunrise:

'I ride back early, Maria. Looking at you I would say you had little rest in the night. It was the same for me. I have been thinking ....'

'..and so have I, Palm,' Maria interrupted, taking a deep breath: 'people begin to whisper, even about us! You surely accept that a child, our child, is preparing itself to come into the world?' Boldly she took his hand, placed it on her stomach and looked him straight in the eye:

'My time draws near, Palm. Will *you* accept responsibility for this new life and stay with us here in the country? It is but a return to your own earliest years, to simplicity and family and life on the land. You knew it well as a young boy.' Palm had closed his eyes. For some moments he felt he was perhaps, after- all, only a visitor in a strange world.

'My father looked upon you as a son,' she continued undeterred, 'and I, we,... we all need you here, Palm. Life could be good. Besides, our teaching must not stop now, there is much work ahead, even for you.'

'Of course you are right, Maria, and yes, this child belongs to us both. We will christen it with your best cider! Life *will* be good'! Palm, gazing in shy wonderment at Maria's swollen body, was listening to and marvelling at the words they had just spoken.

'I may be able to come away by November. I will resign. Will you advise the Pastor we are to be married?' He heard his own voice; it resonated in his skull. Although his head hung low the usual apologetic cough had not come. Shamed by his former restraint he now felt shocked by the simple logic of it all: 'Yes, this is what life is about: caring for those one loves.' At last, he'd understood.

Looking up, he saw a buzzard circling boldly, high in a cloudless sky. Then, for some tender moments Palm studied Maria's face. He embraced her awkwardly, and leaping up on his snorting horse, ready to take his leave, it seemed to him his beloved teacher was looking down on them both.

'Are you content, professor?' thought Palm, eyes shut, without moving. The horse reared up and they were off, in the direction of the woods.

Maria felt faint. Gazing out across the fields, through the dust from the horses' hooves, she waved fondly as Palm turned to look back at her.

'I have everything I ever wished for', she admitted to herself, but especially to her absent father. She too seemed to be flying across the surface of the earth, despite the unborn kicking under her shawl.

There was so much to do.

The only Facts we have:

A son, Christian, was born eight days before the wedding, on the 6th November, 1694. Palm Ilenfeldt and Maria Ruetz were married on the 14th November 1694, according to Church records in Alt Käbelich, Mecklenburg.

A daughter, Elisabeth, wasting no time, followed in 1695.

Palm became a successful farmer who was able to pay his taxes in 1703 with: *3 horses, 8 cows, 5 pigs, 19 sheep, 4 goats, 3 bee-hives.*

This was documented in the mayoral office of Stargard, Mecklenburg.

Palm Ilenfeldt died in 1733, in Alt-Käbelich.

The coat of arms, almost 1000 years old, is in the State Archives of Mecklenburg Vorpommern, in Schwerin.

***

The handwritten text on the next page is a copy of a genuine letter, requesting a new lease of land, written and signed by Palm Ilenfeldt.

It is to be seen in a museum in Mecklenburg.

It is dated the 17th October, 1705.

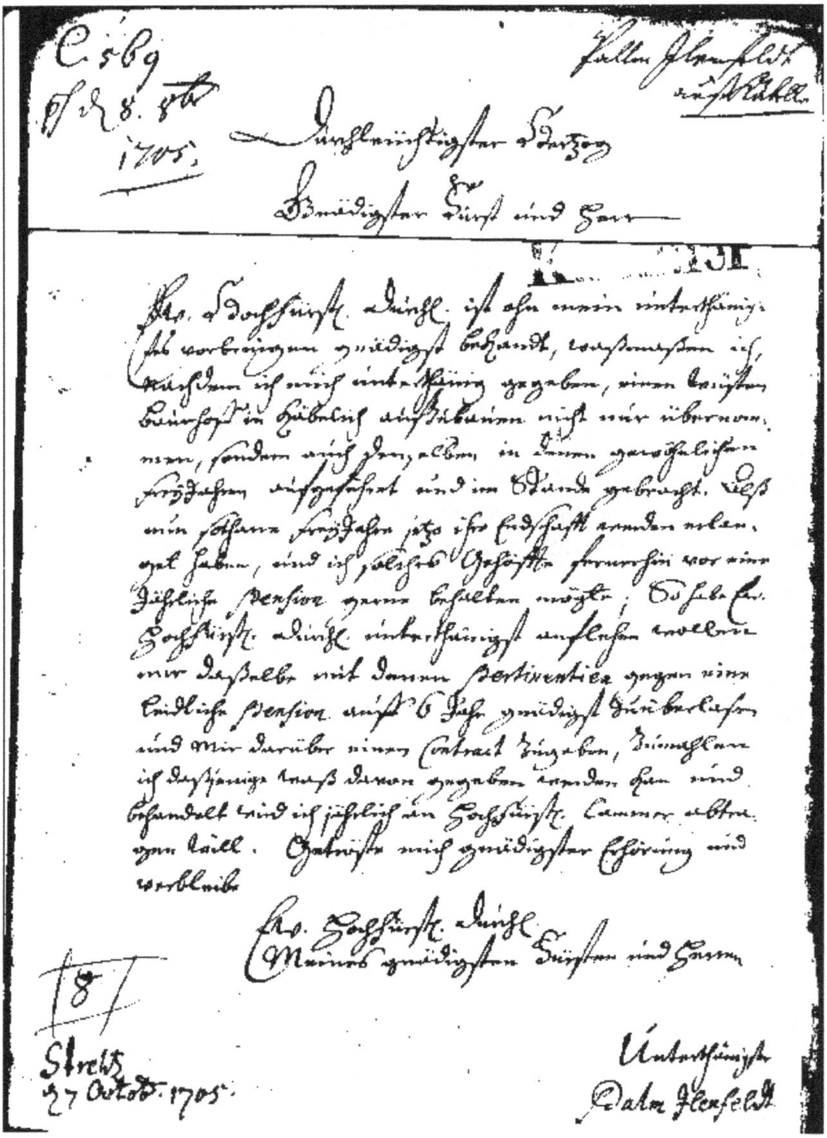

C. 569
Pr. d. 8. 9br
1705.

Dahm Ilenfeldt
[illegible]

Durchlauchtigster Hertzog
Gnädigster Fürst und Herr

Ew. Hochfürstl. Durchl. ist ohn mein unterthänig-
stes vorbringen gnädigst bekandt, welgestalten ich
nachdem ich mich unterthänig gegeben, einen wüsten
Bauerhof in Lübbelin aufzubauen nicht nur übernom-
men, sondern auch denselben in einen gerechtlichen
Zustande aufgeführet und im Stande gebracht. Weil
nun solchen Zustand jetzo ihr Erbschaft worden [illegible]
gut haben, und ich solche Gehöfte fernerhin vor eine
jährliche Pension gerne behalten möchte; So habe Ew.
Hochfürstl. Durchl. unterthänigst anflehen wollen
mir dasselbe mit denen Pertinentien gegen eine
leidliche Pension auf 6 Jahr gnädigst zu überlassen
und mir darüber einen Contract zu geben, dennoch
ich dasjenige was darin gegeben worden schon und
behandelt wird ich jährlich an Hochfürstl. Cammer abtra-
gen will. Getröste mich gnädigster Erhörung und
verbleibe

Ew. Hochfürstl. Durchl.
Meines gnädigsten Fürsten und Herrn

[8]

Strelitz
27 Octob. 1705.

Unterthänigster
Dahm Ilenfeldt

On the Danish island of Bornholm. 2006.

'Stop! Come back, look what I've found!'

Stumbling over a broken-up inscribed stone inside the ruins of Hammershus Castle on Bornholm, I deciphered, in one electrifying instant, what appears to be my maiden-name, 'Ihlenfeldt'. On closer examination the inscription read more like 'Ulefeldt' but, goodness, what a shiver down my spine... knowing that spelling was a variable skill in those days. According to the cruise map we've stopped about 80 km from the German coast, the place where my family tree begins with Palm's dates on the previous page.

My mind went into overdrive: whose name was this? Might the Ihlenfeldts have hailed from Denmark, even Sweden? The pronunciation of vowels **U, I** and **Y** sound similar in these areas...spelling was a variable thing, as only the elect learned to read and write. The name is relatively rare. Had this family come from more Nordic parts? But then there was also that knight, Ulric van Ylvelde, documented in 1304, in the Low Lands.

Much googling, reading and research revealed the story of Leonora Christina, Countess of Schleswig Holstein and her traitorous husband Corfitz Ulfeldt, both once locked up in this very castle. A seed was sown; an unstoppable fantasy reaching out across land and sea of Baltic regions including my own family records beginning in the late 1600's.

A 'Bildungs-Roman' was the result. It has become a gentle mixture of elusive fact and wild fantasy, to stimulate those who may never have heard of 'Pomerania,' 'Mecklenburg,' nor of Stralsund, that town full of mysteries by the Baltic Sea.

This history, fantasy, day-dream, is dedicated to *all* my grandsons, but especially to my grandson Huw, who is brave enough to learn German.

Acknowledgement

Firstly, SAGA Holidays in 2006, for walking us around Bornholm Island. It was there and then I became bewitched by the idea.
One year later Annette and Palle Wolfsberg in Denmark helped with historical details of Leonora Christina and husband Corfitz Ulfeldt.
Further inspiration was found in 'Typisch Pommern', a compilation of knowledge and anecdotes about Pomerania put together by Klaus Granzow, 1982.

Rose Tremain's 'Music and Silence' provided the orchestra in the King's cellar, while most of the nautical information was assembled from 'Across the Atlantic': accounts by numerous authors published in Massachusetts in 1973. South African events were inspired by Dan Sleigh's acclaimed book 'Islands' and greatly reinforced by two stout volumes of 'History of South Africa' by G. Mc Call Theal, LL.D. published in 1897.

Many dates and our venerable coat of arms were sent by cousins Christian Ihlenfeldt in Brisbane, and Helmut Ihlenfeldt in Hamburg. The coat of arms can be seen carved on a wooden epitaph, formerly in a church in Sadelkow, now in the Museum of Neubrandenburg. There are later, modernised versions. Last but not least, a special thank-you to my patient partner Alan, who insisted on greater structure and order of events, after ploughing through the first draft.

The drawings by H. Rothgaengel and W. Thiele are copied from 'Hermann Löns und seine Heide' (Berlin, 1924).

www.ingramcontent.com/pod-product-compliance
Lightning Source LLC
Chambersburg PA
CBHW021006260626
47169CB00006B/1965
9781910266137